THE LONG ROAD BACK

By James Dick

Book 1 of the Coastal Carolina Series

Cover photography by Jim Feaster of Rodanthe, NC

See his work at planetrodanthe dot com

This book is dedicated to my maternal family and the heritage they gave me from their Outer Banks roots. God bless them all and the wonderful land on the Outer Banks shore. They and their land provided my motivation to write this fictional history.

PROLOGUE

The Civil War years and the following Reconstruction in the South was a difficult time for all Southerners and the people of rural Currituck County and the Outer Banks of North Carolina were no different. Food shortages caused from confiscation by both Southern and Northern forces had left them barely enough to eat. Add to that the Reconstruction by the victors in the war, quite different from the approach Abraham Lincoln would have taken. In many ways it brutalized small businesses and farms and forced many into a subsistence state of life with each family fending for itself. Strong and determined and being of good English stock and a God-fearing people, they learned to work together with one another to survive.

Soldiers coming home from losing battle were demoralized and uncertain how to recapture what they had lost. Some gave up, yet others like young Joshua Eldridge, a soldier who was wounded and spent months of brutal treatment in the notorious Point Lookout prisoner of war camp in Maryland, had a will to live. This is his fictional story based in a true setting, a story that was very real to many of the men, many boys actually, and one which tells the story of the fight for survival of these tough Tar Heels from the coastal region. They just wanted to forget and build a new life in the place they called home.

ONE

He was cold, wet, hungry and in despair. His uniform issue gray topcoat was tattered and threadbare, allowing the drizzling rain, sleet and wind to reach into his bones and make him shudder. He couldn't remember when he last had a real meal or what it was, he just knew he was hungry, but he was so hungry that it didn't even hurt anymore.

The others gathered with him were no better off, some were near death, others trying to put themselves in a state of oblivion to avoid reality. They were all gathered together closely against a wooden log wall, trying to ward off the biting wind with their group body heat. While they didn't speak of it, they knew they would die here unless things changed soon.

It was February of 1865 and Joshua Eldridge was one of thousands of Confederate soldiers held captive at the Point Lookout prisoner of war camp on the southeastern tip of Southern Maryland. It was bounded on the north by the Patuxent River, the south by the Potomac and the two came together there as they entered the Chesapeake Bay. Joshua and his compatriots would already be dead were it not for sympathetic local residents sneaking food to them by bribing guards or creating holes in the wooden walls. Most of the locals had closer ties to those supporting the Confederacy than the Union and the camp Provost Marshal, Major Brady, tried to avoid getting their dander up. Among the prisoners were a number of Marylanders who were openly supportive of the Confederacy. These included a number of women and even one baby who was born in the atrocious conditions.

Brady would on occasion avoid stopping a mercy mission by the locals by looking the other way or even fail to patch a break in the wall that was found. He hated his assignment and knew that all of his permanent party staff did as well, plus their pay was low and they sent most of it home to families strapped by wartime economy measures. Most of the boys on both sides were of modest means who really didn't know what they had gotten themselves into. The bribes supplemented their paltry military pay and made the difference in mere survival and having a few extra things to make soldiering more bearable. They all by this time just wanted it to be over so they could go home.

 The freedmen (freed slaves) pulling guard duty on the walls were a different matter. The Major knew that they would use any opportunity they could find to beat and even kill prisoners, a natural response in wartime based upon their earlier experience. After the last four years, there was very little compassion in anyone's heart for their opponents on either side. They all just wanted to survive at any cost until it ended.

The matter of beatings and shootings was a concerning one since Major Brady knew the war would soon end and there could be a board of inquiry concerning the condition of prisoners. Nearly four thousand had died since the camp started receiving prisoners in 1863. It was designed to hold ten thousand, at times it held nearly double that and was short on food and water by a similar proportion. He requested reassignment but it was turned down, leaving him no option but carrying out his duties. The only saving grace about his situation was that he also knew of the horrible treatment that Union soldiers received in Southern prisoner camps like the notorious Andersonville. The outrage Northerners would express at the end of the war because of that fact would likely muffle any concern about Point Lookout. If he could just make it for a couple of more months in this horrible job, he knew it would become a thing of the past.

While many of his fellow prisoners had giving up all hope, Corporal Eldridge had heard the rumors about the war ending. He knew after the Siege of Petersburg, during which he was captured, that the South couldn't keep up the fight much longer. Now nearly a year later, the only things that kept him going were his longing to get back to his home in Currituck County, North Carolina and his friendship with Joe Alphonse, a fellow prisoner from Virginia who served with him at Petersburg. Alphonse was captured after Josh and when he showed up as a prisoner, the two encouraged each other to stay alive.

Josh's father, John Eldridge, a kind and hard-working man who adopted him after his birth parents died in a boating accident, was a pig farmer and fisherman. While

Josh really didn't like farming, right now the smell of pigs would even be a pleasant change from the sick smell of death at Point Lookout. His mother, Emma, was very stoic and quiet woman, but she was a devoted Methodist who instilled her faith in Joshua and there were times when he knew it was all he had.

To escape his present predicament, he often let his mind wander back first to childhood, but then to November 1861 when he bid farewell to his adopted parents at Currituck Court House. From there, he hitched a ride with other recruits by buckboard to Elizabeth City. It was in that larger town that his nearly four years of war and sacrifice began a few days later.

John arrived at his first duty station of Roanoke Island by steamer on November 11, 1861, two days before his eighteenth birthday. He was wide-eyed with excitement but also concerned since he knew nothing of being a soldier and wondered how he would be prepared for whatever duties he was assigned. He would find out very fast.

His unit was nicknamed Shaw's Guard and was Company B of the Eighth North Carolina Regiment, made up entirely of men from Currituck County. Due to the critical need for men right away in defense of their state, his training took place right on the front lines on Roanoke Island. It was known that the region would be under siege soon and Union soldiers already largely controlled the shores of the Outer Banks. The Union goal was to block off shipping of Carolina goods as another step toward cutting off funding for the Southern war effort.

Drill and military combat training, what there was of it, and physical fitness were interspersed with hard labor on the island as they desperately worked to be ready for the coming assault. The men fortified the fortress, an earthen facility, cut trees for lines of fire and pulled guard watch, looking for Union spy vessels reconnoitering the Pamlico Sound, seeking weaknesses to exploit. Some of young Eldridge's compatriots were as young as fifteen, some as old as the early thirties, yet they all were expected to do what they were told with no exception. Food was spartan but sufficient and the only enjoyment they got each day was sitting around a campfire singing at night and swapping tales.

Time was of the essence and the unit commander knew that Union forces would soon be testing their resolve, both on the island and on the inner banks to their west. Cutting off the Albemarle and the Pamlico would also help to shut off the burgeoning port of Norfolk and the Hampton Road to the north from Southern access to deep water and resupply from sea. Fortress Monroe at Old Point Comfort had already been secured by the Yankees and most of the Norfolk waterfront was as well. This meant that the process of sealing off the Confederate capital city of Richmond was proceeding well. Complete capitulation by the Currituck and other

Carolina troops would close off the southeast quadrant to escape from Richmond in the future.

Josh and his men were joined by a unit sergeant to prepare them for what was coming. The Union had control of Hatteras Island despite an earlier skirmish at Chicamacomico which showed promise of turning the tide. Less than two months earlier, on October 1, 1861, Confederate sailors from the Mosquito Fleet on board three steamers, the Curlew, Raleigh and Junaluska spotted a Union tugboat, the Fanny, sailing north from Hatteras Inlet. They followed her from a distance and spotted the Union troop encampment, named Camp Live Oak, at Chicamacomico, not far above Rodanthe. They opened fire on her, she quickly surrendered, and they took the craft and the supplies back to Roanoke Island. This emboldened the Confederates to quickly plan an attack a few days later.

On October 4, 1861 Southern troops from the Eighth North Carolina and the Third Georgia embarked on ships from Roanoke Island headed for Chicamacomico. The skirmish, short-lived, would be known as the Chicamacomico Races. As the Georgia troops neared shore, the water was so shallow that the troops had to disembark nearly a mile off shore. The ship leveled advance fire on the shore but rather than burrow in to fight, the Union soldiers, from the 20th Indiana, began to run south. While the Georgian contingent slowly came to shore, the Carolinians sailed south, hoping to catch the running soldiers as their energy waned. They ran into the same problem as the Georgians and by the time they reached shore the Union soldiers had escaped to the south. They then joined in the race, but little did they know that Union reinforcements were on the way north and another surprise awaited them in the open Atlantic.

As they tired of the chase, they started taking heavy shelling from the Monticello, a Union gunboat with larger guns sitting near shore in the Atlantic. They ran and waded back to their vessel to escape destruction. Dodging shells, they quickly sailed toward Roanoke Island since they were low on gunpowder and were no match for the larger, more powerful Union guns.

By the time the discouraged soldiers arrived back on Roanoke Island, the Union secured their control of all of Hatteras Island, including both inlets. Any effort to head out to sea from the inland waters by Southern vessels was now halted for the remainder of the war. Their only hope left was to keep the Northern combatants from using the inland waterways to advance inland and north and the outcome would depend on what would soon take place at Roanoke Island. As December ended, they knew the inevitable battle wouldn't be long coming, for a cold winter for the soldiers at Hatteras made Roanoke Island seem like a picnic by comparison.

So, at the ripe old age of barely eighteen, Josh continued building fortifications for an impending battle, learned a limited amount of military custom including drill, fitness and lifestyle while getting only the minimum of combat readiness training due to lack of good equipment and sufficient ammunition. He was just one of many, all brave young men, fighting for their homeland who had no idea what to expect. Soon, they would be called upon to defend Roanoke Island and the adjacent waters which protected that mainland from incursion. Josh would find himself right in the middle of the fray.

In early January 1862, Union General Burnside gathered a fleet of sixty ships and a large contingent of men near Hatteras to head westward into the Pamlico Sound. Hatteras had been under Union control since the past August and served as a gathering point for blocking Confederate movement out into the open Atlantic. Now it was time to gain control of the inland seas, the sounds, to seal off North Carolina from warring at sea or transporting supplies. Burnside's efforts were hampered by weather issues, with several ships being grounded in sand in the treacherous inlet and an important munitions ship, the New York, was a total loss. Also lost was a transport ship, the Pocahontas with a cargo of over one hundred prize horses for use in the coming battle. All but twenty-three were lost at sea in a strong nor'easter, victims of the Graveyard of the Atlantic which the Hatteras waters were already being called by many.

Despite his setback, Burnside's men labored on, knowing that the Southerners would not have nearly as many men or munitions and his first stop was Stumpy Point, some thirty miles distant across the Pamlico Sound on the mainland shore. There his men received a short break after being confined to ship for a significant period and final plans for the assault of Roanoke Island were planned.

Meanwhile, young Private Eldridge and the other men of Company B of the North Carolina Eighth continued improving their earthen fortress while alternating watch on the Croatan Sound for an invasion force. They knew the Union vessels required too much draft to sail up the Roanoke Sound east of the island. While they wouldn't be surprised, they knew that they were a big underdog with a poorly trained force and not enough weapons to match the Yanks. Yet they did have cannon to fire lethal volleys at the incoming ships if they could draw them in close while they were still unaware of their location.

Knowing they had to slow the assault, the Confederates on Roanoke Island began to construct barriers to keep vessels from coming to shore. Using an imaginary line from Fort Bartow on Roanoke Island to Fort Forrest on the mainland adjacent to Manns Harbor, they drove planks and sank ships in the water to thwart the Union vessels passing to the north. Their assault would have to come ashore in swampy, boggy land which would slow their march and maneuver. This would create a traffic jam for Burnside's ships and their thirteen thousand soldiers to offload and they would be in open water. The plan was to keep the Union forces off of the higher ground and roadways and in the swamps for they counted on them being almost impassable.

When the attack came, the Southerners were wrong on their assessment of what the swamps could do, for they hadn't counted on the overwhelming firepower that was levelled at the entire Confederate controlled areas. All the Southerners could do was fire their cannons but they didn't have the freedom of motion to watch their accuracy due to the blistering volume of incoming artillery. In the end, despite their valiant defense, the Yankee forces came right up the middle and the Confederate troops surrendered in full.

Casualties were light on both sides, no more than sixty dead and a few dozen injured but twenty-five hundred soldiers of the gray, over eighty percent of their original forces, were taken prisoner. As a result, Josh Eldridge and his compatriots were held in the compound, unsure of their future as they awaited a vessel to take them where they knew not. They sat silently under guard while the Union troops broke into song and cheers to acknowledge their victory and taunt their enemy.

In less than a full day, they learned of their fate while being loaded on a prisoner transport vessel. Much to their surprise, instead of being taken to a Union prisoner of war camp they were transported to Elizabeth City under a flag of truce and released. The Union didn't have the resources to use a ship for the long transport north and they also wanted several of their own returned who were being held in the town. Besides, they knew that most of these young men, boys really, didn't have their heart for blood. They joined the Confederacy more in support of their home state and having tasted a defeat due to poor training, lack of weapons and ammunition as well as food rations, many were likely to desert. That proved true for a number of soldiers who walked out of their temporary barracks awaiting reassignment, but not Josh and most of his group. They didn't want to disgrace their family names.

Private Eldridge and most of the others were initially expected to be assigned to the defense of Plymouth, an agricultural port which was to be used to run the Yankee blockade but, before they could be moved, Plymouth fell. It was then decided the Eighth North Carolina would be used to protect the state's interior from attack from the Albemarle, ready to move toward Plymouth if the situation allowed. Over the next eighteen months, they primarily were involved in skirmishes with small raiding parties, testing them, but they knew they were better off than the Georgia boys who had been moved north or west to do battle with large Union contingents.

Josh's fate was sealed in the Spring of 1864 when the Battle of Plymouth, an attempt to retake the port by the Confederacy, was successful, yet still not able to ship much needed supplies. The Union blockade of the Albemarle kept the Southerners from coming out into the open water, so its utility was minimal. The now Corporal Eldridge was also injured that day, taking a direct hit in the thigh which sent him back to Elizabeth City to convalesce. He was glad to be out of the fray for at least a time, but he knew that his trials would not be over until the war was done.

By early June he was getting better and the field doctor said he'd be released back to his unit by July. He asked for and was given a long weekend pass to visit his parents, who had received his letter and invited him home. A local supply merchant who traveled monthly over to Currituck, offered to take him over and bring him back on his return trip. The hospital authorities approved it and John was excited about seeing his adopted parents and home again.

As he smiled in his dream state thinking of going home, he was awakened by a rifle stock hitting him hard in the shoulder. Coming back to consciousness in pain, the freedman with the rifle told him to get up and move those sacks of potatoes that were being delivered.

"And Reb, don't think you can steal any, because I'm watching you," the sneering guard said, adding, "If you do what you're told, maybe we'll give you a couple of peels for dinner."

He walked away laughing while Josh and his physically weakened compatriots groaned under the weight of the sixty-pound sacks they carried to the staff mess tent. All he knew was he had to survive somehow and get back home to Carolina. He finished his task, again made himself unnoticed against the aging windbreak of a building, and dozed back off to sleep.

TWO

In late March, the prisoners noted that changes were taking place in the Union force. The soldiers were beginning to act cheerful, although treatment of prisoners continued largely as it had been. The hard labor was less frequent, however, and they were actually even getting a piece of bread and real soup for dinner. It didn't fill them up, but it did make Josh Eldridge and the others have hope. He and his only friend, Joe Alphonse, even began to talk about how they could help each other get home, but then the reality of their continuing plight brought them back to the present. So, he continued to doze off into dreamland whenever he could.

Corporal Eldridge dreamed about the visit with his parents, learning that they had given up on pig farming when soldiers from both North and South confiscated all of their stock. He dreamed about his sadness on returning to Elizabeth City to learn that, within weeks of his pass he was considered fully fit for duty. Accordingly, he was shipped north to the dreaded Petersburg battlefield which was coming under constant siege. The dream covered Josh's capture there, the physical beating the victors gave him and learning he was being shipped to Point Lookout. It was an agonizing dream cycle, for the word was out that no one returned once they were shipped to Point Lookout. He shuddered when he awoke from the vivid reminder.

One morning about two weeks later, the prisoners were assembled in formation and informed that Robert E. Lee had surrendered at Appomattox and the war was over. Unfortunately for the prisoners, until the official release paperwork came from Washington, they would remain where they were. They knew that as long as they were under armed guard, the freedmen guards would continue to abuse their authority when they could. So, Joshua resigned himself to be thankful for at least the soup and bread and clean water for the first time since he got there and he accepted the beatings by rifle butt without a word to avoid a worse altercation.

On April 29, 1865, Joshua Eldridge and a large group of prisoners were returned issued war worn Confederate caps which were taken up when they were sent to the POW camp. They were told they would be released in small groups with a short time gap in between and were to walk up the St. Mary's City road. Somewhere along the way a convoy would pick up small groups at a time. Each convoy would consist of a few horse-drawn wagons with beds capable of carrying eight to ten soldiers. Overflows would continue walking and with hundreds of prisoners spread out along the road, more would be walking than riding. The caps would be used for identification purposes, that and the small form they were given identifying them as former prisoners of war who had taken the oath of allegiance to the United States. As each group was assembled, they were given the oath; none refused as they realized that their fight was done.

Josh and his compatriots were given blue pants and a shirt to replace their ragged appearance, yet no boots were given and most had been shoeless for months. When his group was shown the gate, they merely showed a small smile on their lips and never looked back. There release time was nearly one in the afternoon meaning they would be out in the cold if the expected convoy failed to show. They had no idea how few wagons were really operating, but by late afternoon, they were becoming discouraged. After all, it was going to get chilly at night and their feet were bare on the rocky road, cut and bleeding as time went on. Only one wagon passed his group, empty and heading north, with two soldiers on board snickering at them and leaving them in the dust.

Taking a short rest break on the side of the road, Joe Alphonse, his compatriot from Richmond, sat down beside Josh. They said nothing to one another for a long time, each wondering how they would find shelter and a way out of this dreaded land.

Suddenly Joe spoke, asking, "Do you think this is a trick, Josh? Something doesn't seem right."

"I don't know, Joe," he replied. "Something was certainly strange as we walked away, I noticed a steamer come to the dock near the camp and I swear I saw soldiers in Confederate uniforms being taken into camp. They weren't free, they were prisoners.

"We better keep our guard up and be ready to run for cover if something comes up, Joe. Let's stick together."

The marching crowd was now broken down into groups of two or three since all were wary of being sitting ducks in a group formation. Most had decided they had to fend for themselves and that was best done in small numbers. They came through St. Mary's, the location that had been the state capital and was home to the first Free Staters who arrived from England in Colonial times. The locals looked at them and one even said that they shouldn't go to Washington as they passed. About another mile and half up the road with the shades of night falling, they saw a light up ahead coming from a small house at the edge of the woods. Walking toward it, a voice spoke in the distance.

"I see you, whoever you are," came a deep warning from someone unseen. "Are you Yankees or Southerners. I want to know because I hate Yankees, and you better tell me the truth."

Joshua knew he'd better answer and said, "We're Southern, just released from Point Lookout and we've been walking all afternoon. We just need a place with some shelter for the night and will be on our way."

The door opened and a grizzled old man walked out with his shotgun at the ready. They held out their release papers as he walked warily to them, gun at the ready the entire way. He took the papers, looked at them carefully including their Johnny Reb caps, then broke out into a big grin as he handed the papers back.

"Well, come on in, boys," Robert Shaw said. "I don't have much, but I have some corn bread and beans with coffee that you're welcome to and I can let you sleep on blankets on the rug, if you'd like. I know you boys have been through a lot."

They thanked him and took him up on his offer, scarfing up what he offered and feeling as if they just completed a banquet after where they had been. They chatted for a few minutes then the old man gave them blankets and helped set them up for the night. They were asleep within five minutes.

When they awoke, the sun was coming up and they smelled the aroma of coffee. Shaw wished them good morning, then told them to get up and pull up a chair as he was baking some biscuits. He also had a special treat, hickory smoked bacon, which he was holding for a special day. Having visitors other than Yankees was something he considered to be just such a day.

As they ate their breakfast and enjoyed the luxury of coffee, Shaw asked them where they were headed.

Joshua responded, "We're trying to find the convoy that we were promised will be taking freed prisoners south toward home. Do you know anything about that, Sir?"

Old Robert Shaw rubbed the stubble on his chin and said, "Well, there is no convoy, at least not now. What I've heard is that they let you out blindly in the direction of Washington and then, when you get tired and feeling hopeless, they pick you up and put you on a construction or repair project. Oh, they'll eventually let you go, but not before they get all the work out of you they can. At least those boys get fed."

He also mentioned a rumor which really got Josh's mind thinking, saying, "Even though the war is over, new prisoners are still arriving. I guess they needed you guys gone to make room. The postmaster in St. Mary's City says it's the last troops that defended Lee during his escape from Richmond and they hold them in great contempt. They've been bringing them up by ship from the docks on the James River in Newport News."

Eldridge decided to just put that in his memory in case it might be useful later. He wondered if it was because of the change in government leadership in Washington with the assassination of Lincoln. Even the prisoners knew about that from overhearing the chatter among the guards. They also heard the stories about how Lincoln wanted to reunite the restored nation but that with him gone the emphasis was changed. It would only be later that he would learn the meaning of reconstruction and hear the term carpetbagger.

Now Shaw changed the topic and started giving them an idea of where to go when they left. He knew they were basically walking blind. He wanted to at least give them an option for getting home as soon as possible.

"Let me suggest, fellows, "he continued, "that instead of walking toward Washington, change direction once you get past the head of the river. About two miles along you'll come up on a road that goes south, there should be a sign posted for Piney Point. Go left onto that road and walk about five miles. Along the way you'll see the St. Mary's River from the other side and look for a small farm with a faded painted fence and a sign for Clausen, the family living there. John Clausen is a farmer turned fisherman who lost a son in the war fighting for the Confederacy. He's a Virginian by birth but came up here when he inherited this land. He felt it was safer than staying in Virginia on the south side of the Potomac River. He is angry over his son's death and will help you find your way back home. And if and when you get to the other side of the Potomac, support will be easier to find. Most of us Marylanders are on your side but everyone is afraid with so many soldiers still in place."

He found the back of an old cigar box and drew a map and gave it to Joshua who looked at it carefully and memorized it, then handed it back. He didn't want anyone else causing problems and even though they were free, he knew they weren't safe.

They quickly picked up after themselves, got ready and said their goodbyes. Mr. Shaw even gave them each a hug and told them good luck. They thought they even detected a small tear in his eye; the old loner had appreciated their company. They headed out with two biscuits and some bacon for each of them and followed the river north to its end, then rounded the water and headed back south. Both men were thinking to themselves that they have walked about fourteen miles so far and another five miles and they'd be good for the day.

As if on cue, at almost exactly the five mile point they saw the Clausen name on a post. The old man's directions and distance estimate were right on the mark. As they approached the property, an older man waved at them. Only Joshua saw the wave, he signaled to Joe and the two walked toward him. It did look like a farm but there were no animals except some chickens scratching in the yard and a cow under a tree. Fishing nets were drying on a fence and they saw a boat over toward the water's edge. It was a beautiful piece of property.

Fisherman Clausen stood on the porch of his small frame home waving them in, yet holding a shotgun at his side. He didn't raise it, so Joshua and Joe figured he was just taking precautions and who could blame him.

As they got closer, Mr. Clausen asked them if they had their "freedom papers," the document they had been given on release the prior day. Clausen examined the papers, then put a smile on his face and relaxed his grip and invited them into his home.

A big, ruddy man with deep blue eyes that twinkled, he said to the two of them, "Boys, you look worn out. Now you couldn't have made the trip in one day, so you must have spent a night outside. There have been reports of soldiers on the Leonardtown road coming from Point Lookout. You must be hungry."

Joe nudged Joshua to do the talking and he said, "Well, we started yesterday after being released from Point Lookout, Sir, but ended up stopping on the road and an elderly man who was kind took us in for the night. He gave us the first edible food in quite a few months."

Clausen interrupted Joshua and said, "Well, that must have been Old Man Shaw. He's sent me quite a few boys like you in the past. He's a real loner but he has a good heart and I'm glad you found him. Now come on in and I'll get Mrs. Clausen to rustle up some food and we'll figure out the best way to get you on your way home."

Once in the house, John Clausen pulled out a picture of a young man in Confederate uniform. He explained it was his son, since the family was originally from Virginia. They supported the Confederacy and the boy joined the rebels and was killed in Richmond, only a month ago.

"I despise the Yankees but try to keep a low profile as I can accomplish so much more quietly than being too open," he told the tired soldiers. "I would have hoped that someone would have done the same for my boy. Now you boys go out and sit under the boast house roof on the pier while the missus fixes some food. You can relax for the rest of the day and then we'll figure out a transportation plan."

Mrs. Clausen, a pretty but weathered and slightly built woman came out and welcomed them and told them she'd have some food for them within the hour. So, they headed out on the pier and dangled their feet over the side, looking to the south where the expanse of water opened wide.

Clausen was smiling as he came to join them. He had a big package and a brown bag. He opened the bag and handed them a bottle of corn whiskey, thinking after all these months they might enjoy a swig.

"Be careful with that stuff, boys," he said with a grin. "It will help you relax but on and empty stomach and having been alcohol free for months, it can go right to your head. Just take a couple of sips and be done."

Then he opened the package and pulled out two new pair of military boots. He told them to try them on and they were pretty good fits, maybe just a little too big.

"Not bad," he said. "We can stuff some paper in to keep them from slipping and at least you won't be barefoot. I got these from a friend who is a government supplier. He sold them at wholesale since the market is drying up now that the war is over."

Clausen pointed down river where the two former POWs were looking, explaining the wide expanse was the Potomac. He explained he would try and take them to the Virginia side under sail, but it would require the right time which might take a slight delay. To head out into the river without proper conditions would result in a wasted attempt.

"In normal times, you boys could have walked to Leonardtown and caught a ride," he said. "But now it is full of scoundrels and fights are breaking out against the former POWs while the Union troops look the other way. They use them for cheap labor before releasing them, likely delaying their real freedom for at least a month or more."

Josh responded, "I'm not going to stick around here to work for those thugs a day longer than I must. Your help in avoiding that, and the boots you have given us, will never be forgotten."

Before dinner, Mr. Clausen showed them the boat they would be using. It was a dug-out canoe fitted with a single sail. Josh was impressed and wanted to know more.

"Did you build it yourself or where did you get it," was his question.

"Well, a logging friend who lives up at Tall Timbers, hollowed out three big logs and I put it together," was the answer. "It was a slow process but it works great for oyster tonging and even catching rockfish. I can also use a throw net when the bait fish are running and I keep them and some eels in the big water tub in the covered area on the pier. Want to see."

Clausen explained that digging oysters was primarily done in the cold months but the rockfish would be plentiful in about another month. He sold his oysters to the shucking operation just beyond Tall Timbers and some rock, but he and his wife subsisted substantially off of the water's bounty.

Just then, the dinner bell by the back door rang and Clausen told them the bell meant food was ready. He gave them the shush sign as he stashed the corn whiskey bottle in a corner table in the boat house and told them his wife was opposed to whiskey. They then walked toward the house, and upon entering, the two soldiers were overtaken by the aroma of a home cooked meal. It actually made them shed a tear.

Mrs. Clausen smiled at them, told them to wash up using the well hand pump on the porch with the hand towels and soap she placed nearby. Real soap was another luxury and when they returned, they were presentable.

Mrs. Clausen was bringing out a grand seafood meal consisting of fish, crab cakes and oysters, with corn, green beans and hush puppies. She was an expert at canning and they had a small icebox in the cool cellar where a block of ice kept the seafood edible. She told them to enjoy but eat slowly since they could easily make themselves sick. Then husband and wife joined them and Clausen said grace.

Taking their time as suggested and savoring every delicious morsel, Josh and Joe couldn't believe their good fortune and Joshua said, "How can we repay you, Mr. Clausen, we have no money or anything to give you?"

"What you can give me is a promise you will go home as fast as you can and get your lives back to normal," Clausen said with a tear of remembrance for his son. "I certainly would have expected others to do the same for my boy. But let's talk about better times and tell us a little about yourselves."

Josh explained he came from Currituck County, North Carolina, south of Norfolk across the state line. He said that his father had been a hog farmer but gave it up when his stock was taken by the military. He was now a fisherman, living a subsistence life, trading fish for other items while also tending a small garden and a cow just like Clausen. He also had good woodworking skills.

Joe Alphonse spoke more than he had since leaving Point Lookout. He explained that he left the family farm north of Richmond to go to war and had no idea if the farm would be left. He vowed, however, to rebuild and renew his life and that of his family if it took him the rest of his life.

Joe's last comment told his whole attitude when he said, "I don't care if I ever see another rifle or shotgun and I never want to kill another human as long as I live."

Clausen rubbed his chin, then said, "Well, boys, you aren't much different from us. When the farm animals were taken, except the one cow and a few chickens, I went back to fishing. That the Lord made this area so abundant in seafood is what allows us to live. We just do what it takes to survive and pray the future will be better."

They slowly ate and talked, all of them loving the camaraderie and when the boys could eat no more, they insisted on doing the dishes. When they told Mrs. Clausen that fresh soap on their hands felt so good, she let them do the work. She knew they were grateful and she and her husband went out to sit on the porch.

Later, while the sun was still above the trees, the two Southerners joined them and, surprisingly, Joe asked Mrs. Clausen to check their work.

"Ma'am, my mom was always a stickler in the kitchen and she taught me well," he said. "Would you do us the honor of approving our work."

She nodded her head with a smile and got up, while John Clausen told Joshua to stay put.

"I think your friend misses his mom, Son, so let him live a small special moment," he said. "You fellows don't know how appreciative she is for getting the break."

Mrs. Clausen and Joe returned momentarily and she was effusive in praise for what they had done, telling them that they outdid her own kitchen performance. They all sat down together on the porch to watch the beautiful sunset, then Josh and Joe both stifled a yawn, a signal to Mr. Clausen that they were ready for sleep. He showed them to their son's room and the large double bed they would share. He knew after what they had been through it would do them well.

The two men cleaned up, said their prayers of thanks for the first time since Petersburg and were asleep within moments. When Clausen came up to check, he chuckled when he heard the snoring and nodded his head yes, for he knew they had a long road ahead to make their way back home. What he didn't know was that the dreams they were having this night were not about war.

THREE

Joshua sat up suddenly and realized the sun was up. On the other side of the bed, Joe Alphonse was snoring loudly. Neither of the two released prisoners had slept in a real bed in years, not to mention soundly and with no sudden wake-up.

Mr. Clausen heard them moving around upstairs and came up to see how they were, knocked on the door and said, "It looks like you fellows slept well and that's good. Now clean up and get ready and the Missus will have breakfast ready soon."

They hustled when they heard that and were bounding down the stairs soon to the wafting aroma of fresh coffee and bacon. Mrs. Clausen smiled as she signaled them to the table and she brought out coffee with real cream, sugar and biscuits, then returned to finish cooking.

"Go ahead and have a biscuit with your coffee, boys," Mr. Clausen said as he joined them. "We've got fresh fried eggs, bacon and grits coming up in a minute and while we wait I want to tell you what I've planned."

"Please do, Mr. Clausen, we're all ears," Josh replied with Joe nodding in agreement.

"The wind is blowing out of the west and that might present a problem with the tide. I can put up the sail and with the tide coming in early in the afternoon, I don't know if we can make it across before dark. I don't mind staying on the other shore overnight if need be but I don't want you boys starting out over there at night. I could use some help here today if we can't go and then we can just pray for better winds tomorrow. If they swing around to the east we can make it over fast even if the tide is wrong."

The weather refused to cooperate over the next few hours, so they settled in to help him with whatever he needed, glad to have something to do without a man with a gun standing over them. That wonderful breakfast gave them energy and they were even provided with a fresh change of clothes. Mrs. Clausen wanted them to at least be fresh to start their journey and an extra set of clothes would be something they hadn't seen in years. She said it made her reminiscent of the days when her son would come home to visit.

Since both young men had experience with rural life, the chores were a breeze and Mr. Clausen enjoyed having someone to keep him company. Josh mended fishing nets, something he did for his uncle as a boy while Joe worked in the small barn, milking a cow, collecting eggs and repairing a few holes in the wall and fixing broken boards on the front fence. Later both Josh and Joe cleared a clogged ditch for drainage and the day passed quickly.

Happy but tired at the end of the day, they enjoyed more seafood as their reward and sat out on the pier to watch the sun drop below the horizon. Mr. Clausen said it looked like their prayers would be answered the next day with a front moving in over night and a likely switch in wind direction.

After another good night's sleep and another first-class breakfast, they were ready to cross the river. Mr. Clausen went to put the boat in the water while the two soldiers told their hostess goodbye.

"Thank you, ma'am, for your hospitality," said Joe, taking the lead. 'We'll both remember this and wish you folks well. If you ever make it to Richmond, come look for the Alphonse farm, we are north of town near Ashland."

This time Josh was the quiet one, actually showing a little sentiment for such good treatment and Mrs. Clausen picked up on it, giving him a warm goodbye hug, then Joe.

"God bless you, boys," she said. "Go with God and have a wonderful life," then she turned and walked back into the kitchen.

When they arrived on the pier the boat was in the water, Clausen having lowered the reinforced heavy canvas hammock with four strands of heavy rope holding the boat. He used a hand pully which gently placed it in the water. Once in the water, he pulled the boat close to the pier and climbed aboard and untied the line from the canoe while holding the line taut. As soon as the two passengers were aboard, he threw the line up on the dock.

Now floating free, he used a large paddle to turn it into the river and slowly raised the sail which filled with the wind and they were off. With the tide and wind both pushing them, they made the trek across to Virginia at Coles Point in about forty-five minutes.

They came to a sheltered anchorage near Coles Point, walked the boat the final ten feet to the shore and tied it off to a large pine. John Clausen led them up the embankment to a small frame house set in a clearing. He waved at the man outside who was working on a fishing pole with some pretty heavy-duty line. This was his friend, Sam Montague.

"Hey, Sam," said John. "How have you been? It's been a while."

Clausen introduced the young men to Montague and he invited them all inside for a cup of coffee. His wife, a pretty younger woman named Sally smiled and went to get cups and the pot of coffee. She was known for keeping a fresh pot brewing for surprise company.

"Well, John," Sam began. "Are these a couple more of our boys from Point Lookout?"

When all three nodded yes, Sam continued, "Well, welcome boys and I'm sorry for what you've been through. Let's enjoy our coffee and I'll give you my lowdown on how best to get you home. And where is home?"

Josh Eldridge spoke up, "I'm from North Carolina, Sir, Currituck County and Joe here is from north of Richmond. Mr. Clausen said you might know the best way for us to proceed."

Sam Montague rubbed his chin, then told them it would be easy for Joe to get home but a longer stretch for Josh. There was a freight wagon that went by on the way to Port Royal every few days and that would be the best option for Joe. As for Josh, that would be a longer route since the docks there were destroyed and the only thing going through there were wagon trains taking supplies to Richmond. If they went on to North Carolina, it was usually to Raleigh, a long way from Currituck.

"We can set Joe up on the freight wagon day after tomorrow and once he gets to Port Royal, he can catch the wagon trains south. As for you, Josh, our best bet is to get you on a small schooner on the Rappahannock next week out of Carter's Creek. They have a supply run down to Old Point Comfort once a week. The freight wagon that will take Joe to Port Royal will pick up supplies and come back this way at that time. We can take Joe in the buckboard down to Montross Road to put him on board and make arrangements for next week."

The hackles went up on Josh's hair at the mention of Old Point Comfort. He remembered the just ended war and the part that Yankee citadel in the middle of Southern territory had played in their defeat, yet he knew it was time to forget and move on.

So, the boys agreed to work for Sam in return for his help. It was a good arrangement, they had a place to stay, food to eat and a plan to get home and in return they would do odd jobs that anyone needed along the way.

John Clausen stayed for a mid-day meal and then said it was time for him to get back to the other side. Before leaving he asked Sam if he knew what happened to his old family property near Montross.

"Well, it's a good thing you were where you are, John," he said, 'because the Yanks burned it to the ground on a raid for spoils. Happened about a month ago. They just did it for meanness."

Clausen just shook his head and turned to say goodbye to his young soldier friends. They exchanged handshakes which turned into big manly hugs and he was off. He was singing Maryland, My Maryland as he walked down the pathway to the anchorage. Without comment, Josh rushed down the lane after him.

"Don't you need a push-off from the mud, Mr. Clausen," he said. "I'll push you out into the open water."

Clausen clapped him on the back and smiled. The two men began to push the canoe made easier by Josh's help, then Clausen climbed on board and, once clear, sailed away with a wave.

Two days later, Sam Montague loaded his cargo of two barrels of dried and salted eel on the buckboard and Josh and Joe Alphonse climbed aboard. An hour later when they reached the Montross Road pick up point for Joe, they transferred the barrels for sale in Port Royal and Sam got the okay for Joe to hop on board. He then arranged for the teamster driver to pick up Josh Eldridge on his return trip. The man lived right outside Carter's Creek (now Irvington).

It was a bitter sweet moment for Josh and Joe as they said goodbye. They each realized that for the last six months they had been a lifeline for one another. Now that purpose was done and it was time to move on with their lives.

On the way back to Coles Point, Sam asked Josh, "Have you ever been net fishing? I could use some help tomorrow. I'm going to need some bait for the upcoming rockfish season and eels work great, plus an excess when smoked and salted make great substitute for jerky. People developed a taste in the lean war years and now find they like them."

"I'd love it, Mr. Montague," was his response. "I helped my uncle a bunch as a kid and when I get home it will probably be my work as well. Judging from what happened on leave before captured when, all of Dad's pigs were confiscated, I'm sure there will be no pig farm."

They shared how both of their lives had changed over the last four years as well as their hopes and dreams for the future. Upon return to the home, they checked the nets for tears or holes, laid them out in a fashion so they would be easy to put on board for the next day's run. Then the two of them went to work rehanging and repairing a barn door in need of work.

"You know, Josh," Montague opined, "Down where you come from showed promise as a sportsman's delight before the war and I would imagine that hunting guides will be in demand. If you can fish, can guide hunters and even big city fishermen on outings, you can probably make a decent living."

Josh Eldridge smiled, picturing himself in hip waders leading a group of New York hot shots through the marsh grass looking for ducks. He knew, though, that Sam Montague was right, for the natural beauty of both Currituck and the Outer Banks would someday be someplace special. After all, there were already some wealthy planters down the Albemarle who summered there. One day it will be much more popular than that and, at a minimum, the comment gave Josh something to think about.

The next day the two men expertly put out the nets, anchored in the middle and at each end and would come the next morning to bring them in. When they returned, they not only found eels, but several rockfish, surprisingly large, entangled in the nets, probably knowing the eels were there. Sam Montague was so pleased that they decided the best of the rock would be served for a great dinner. He was also pleased with how competent Josh was in his work. He really liked the young man who had a great attitude about life. Young Joe also was nice, but he was so reserved it was hard to get to know him.

"Your boat is bigger with more working space than Mr. Clausen's, Mr. Montague," John commented. "What is the difference and what is it called.?"

"Spoken like a true waterman, Josh," Montague laughed. "My boat is called the bugeye and it is a step up from the sailing canoe. You are right about it being bigger with more working space, but you'll also notice it is higher on both sides as it comes forward and is much more finished off. All I know is it is an in-between step before something bigger, stronger and faster comes along, but that sooner or later will come along."

That night over dinner, they talked about Josh's travel plans. Sam told him that when Ed O'Reilly, the teamster, returned and Josh left, the young man might need to work a trip or two with Ed to cover his schooner fare. Thinking that Josh might be disappointed, he was surprised to see this good-looking young man with manners also smiling instead.

"That's no problem, Mr. Montague," Josh responded. "I know it will be a lengthy process but a little work along the way is a good change of pace and finding rides instead of having to walk like a soldier will be a wonderful relief."

In his last day with the Montagues, he learned all he could about the Chesapeake boats and vowed he'd build one of his own one day. He also learned all about the use of eels, how to salt and smoke them and their many uses. He remembered as a boy catching them and either throwing them away or using them for bait but after having a small piece of the smoked meat over dinner, he learned something of value.

Finally, it was time to go and Sam Montague said goodbye by giving him a lift down to Montross Road. He bid his adieu to Mrs. Montague and they were off.

Soon they heard singing through the trees down the road and Sam said it was the Irishman, O'Reilly, singing and whistling Yankee Doodle Dandy as he came into sight.

"Any time you want to come back up and learn more about our Chesapeake boats, Josh, you're welcome," was Sam's farewell. The younger and older man gave each other a manly hug and he was gone, headed north while Josh and Ed O'Reilly headed east toward Carter's Creek and the Rappahannock River.

O'Reilly was a ruddy Irishman with smiling eyes and a neatly clipped beard which matched his dark red hair. He told Josh that he came to America in the early 1850s, worked as a stevedore in Norfolk but came to Westmoreland County before the war started. He limped from a knife wound which came during his younger days and it kept him from serving in the war. He ran supply runs as a contract teamster for the Confederacy but when the Union took over the area, he wisely offered his services. He sympathized with the south but knew from the beginning that it would be a lost cause.

"You Southern boys are usually gutsier, Josh," he explained, "but you didn't have enough men or weapons to win a lengthy struggle. The Army should have made a run on Washington just after the first Manassas battle and it may have been different, for the Yanks weren't ready."

The two men talked as if they had known each for years and Ed asked Josh if he could help with a couple of supply runs and in return, he would pay for Josh's passenger fare to Hampton Roads.

"That would be fantastic, Mr. O'Reilly," Josh replied. "And I think the physical work and seeing a little of the Virginia countryside would be good. When I was at Petersburg, trust me, there was nothing pretty to look at."

Late in the day they made it to Carter's Creek and immediately headed to the dock area. The schooner would be arriving in the morning and leave late in the day; O'Reilly wanted to have his supplies unloaded in the warehouse so that he could come by in the morning for payment.

He pulled the wagon up to the loading door and the unloading started. Most of the materials looked like war surplus that would probably be offered up at a discount but there were also a number of large and heavy crates marked DO NOT OPEN. It made up about half of the load and it took all their strength to get them off. While Josh was busy, O'Reilly opened and looked inside a crate, then immediately closed it. Josh noticed but kept it to himself.

Once completed, he took the remaining goods to the general store, which served as the delivery point and post office for the town. They dropped off a sack of mail as well as several packages for delivery to local residents. Several crates of canned vegetable from last year's crops would be sold at the store.

O'Reilly told Josh he could stay with him and that tomorrow he'd show him the sights. The following day they'd make another trip to Port Royal.

"After that's done, Josh," he said, "you'll be free to travel unless you want to stick around for a while. You're welcome to stay as long as you want and I appreciate the help."

Josh was surprised when they arrived at a neat little white clapboard house in town and he found out this was O'Reilly's home. They walked inside and there was even a bigger surprise. The living room definitely had the touch of a woman's handiwork, but there was no one else there.

Josh obviously had surprise on his face and Ed O'Reilly explained his situation, saying, "This home was my Maura's, Josh. She died of the fever almost a year ago and I've kept it just the way she liked it. It keeps her alive in my heart."

Josh gulped, "I'm so sorry, Mr. O'Reilly. I've never been in love but I know from my dad that he'd be lost without Ma."

Ed explained that he didn't know if he could ever love another woman and that's one of the reasons he works so hard. It keeps him busy.

"Look, Josh," O'Reilly said. "I am fortunate that I have this great contract for work that pays me well and keeps me moving around. I was blessed, however, even during the war when young fellows like you were being killed, maimed or living in prison. So, my hat is off to you. Now let's run into the Schooner Tavern for a bite to eat and a beer. It will be the perfect ending to a productive day."

Seated at a corner table, O'Reilly told Josh a secret that he had told no one else. He wanted Josh to remember to be careful of who he trusted in the tumultuous times that were unfolding in the South.

"I know you wanted to know about those heavy crates and why they were marked to remain closed," the old Irishman said, "They are spoils of war, Josh, beautiful heirloom and antique items taken from homes they ransacked here in Virginia. I opened a crate because I just had a gut feeling that it was something like that."

Josh looked wide-eyed as he said, "So, what are you going to do? Will you report it.?"

O'Reilly told Josh he just put it in the recesses of his memory, that those things were the spoils of war and there is nothing anyone can do, especially if you live in the South. He also told Josh that on the next run to Port Royal that he just needed to stay quiet. Being an ex-Confederate soldier, they could just shoot him on the spot and no one would question it. The old man said he didn't think it would have been like this had Lincoln lived, but the new leaders of the North were out for blood, not reconciliation.

Josh ended up helping O'Reilly for over a month, making six runs instead of just one. He got to know the man and what drove him and developed deep respect for his honesty and energy. He also enjoyed meeting the people of the Northern Neck and seeing the beautiful spring of Virginia with no war. It was beautiful country and they were fortunate that not too much was destroyed, but he felt sorry for his new friend in Maryland, John Clausen, who lost his family home in Montross.

O'Reilly was quite fond of the young former soldier and told him if things didn't work out in North Carolina, he could always come work for him. He was optimistic about his business and wanted to expand it to several wagons and a man like Josh would be a wonderful addition. Josh was flattered but knew he must go home, He did make sure, however, that he had O'Reilly's mailing address, something he recorded for both John Clausen and Sam Montague. Keeping contact with others who might be of assistance was always a good idea.

His last day in Carter's Creek before leaving for Hampton Roads was a Sunday and Josh was surprised when O'Reilly asked him if he wanted to go to church.

Josh looked inquisitive but asked, "Where do you go to church, Mr. O'Reilly? I haven't seen any around here."

"Well,' the Irishman responded, "there sure aren't any Catholic churches in these parts but after my experiences as a boy with a brutal nun I never went back. I guess I deserved it, though, for sassing her. As it turns out, I really do like to go to a Methodist Church over near White Stone. I do feel that sometimes I need to talk to God since we don't do such a great job on our own. I like the formality of the kneeling rail where I can get down and talk to Him quietly"

Josh said he would love to go, having been brought up as a Methodist with a grandfather who was a circuit riding preacher. So, they got ready, got the buckboard and headed out.

"I'll warn you, Josh," Ed O'Reilly said, "we'll have to leave the wagon at the log bridge about a mile from the church and hoof it the rest of the way. They still don't have a decent walk or road over there."

So, arriving at the single log footbridge, they walked the remainder of the way to the small clapboard church that would seat about fifty. It was nearly full when they walked in and they took a seat at the rear, but a kindly man came over and welcomed them. Both men enjoyed the sermon about the tribulations of the Apostle Paul on his travels and how man is expected to deal with suffering while maintaining faith in God. As they shook the minister's hand on the way out of the church, they were glad they came.

"I'm glad we went, Josh," O'Reilly said after they climbed on the buckboard and faithful Suzy steadily walked them home. "Let's stop at the pub since they serve cold cuts and cheeses included with the price of a tankard. They aren't supposed to serve alcohol on Sunday but they do it anyway."

John smiled and after completing their meal, he was glad he had been to church. Excepting his one visit home during the war and a short sermon in the trenches at Petersburg by a Presbyterian chaplain, his only religious practice had been infrequent prayers for his release. The service in White Stone reminded him how much he needed God every day.

That night, sitting out in front of O'Reilly's little house, the old man surprised him with the earnings for his work, eight splendid silver dollars. A silver dollar could get you a long way back then and by today's paper standard eight silver dollars would be worth thousands. He couldn't believe it and he told O'Reilly so.

"Well, Son, you've earned it and I'm a pretty good saver. My home is paid for and my business is going well and besides, if you ever change your mind and need a place to work, I know that you would then come here."

He hugged his new friend, then turned in, for the schooner was scheduled to sail at seven in the morning. For only the second time in many months, he said his prayers before going to sleep. He slept soundly, dreaming about things back home as he saw his ma and dad smiling together with him as they sat down for a meal. His mind was helping the anticipation build for that long-awaited family reunion.

FOUR

When Josh arose early the next morning, O'Reilly was snoring like a log, so he left him a thank you note and tiptoed out into the darkness. The sky was beginning to lighten to the east and he wanted to arrive early and make sure there was no chance of missing the schooner. As he walked up the dock, the schooner was sitting and waiting. She had come in from Baltimore the night before. The run to Old Point Comfort would be a quick one, only about fifty nautical miles and although she was a steam-powered ship with sail, sails were used if the wind was good, saving coal for use when needed. Under sail it was about a five-hour trip, steam would take longer.

A bursar was at the top of the gangway, looked warily at Josh but took his money and told him there would be food in the small dining area adjacent to the galley in about thirty minutes. Josh was thrilled, he had no idea that food came with his one-dollar passage and he was hungry. He spent the next ten minutes just looking at Carter's Creek as the day lightened, noticing what a quaint and pretty little place it was. He reminded himself that if things were really bad at home, he had the offer to work for O'Reilly and that was a comforting thought.

A few minutes later a very distinguished man dressed immaculately walked up beside the rail and introduced himself.

"Hello, young man," he began. "My name is Earl Winslow and I'm just curious. Are you headed home after the war? Obviously, by heading south, may I assume you were a Confederate soldier? Pardon me for being nosy but I have a personal interest in how you boys are faring."

Josh was astonished at his interest but smiled and said, "Well, yes Sir, Mr. Winslow. My name is Joshua Eldridge and I'm working my way back to Currituck County, North Carolina. I spent the last six months of the war at Point Lookout and when released worked my way here by the grace of God. If I get to Old Point Comfort, I'll just try and work my way to the other side of the big harbor and walk home."

Winslow told him he was a retired Union Army Colonel, now working for the War Department as survivor agent trying to assist young men in the South transition back to a normal life following war.

"You boys are important to us, Eldridge," he continued, "You just did what you had to do and you are some of the best in the South and we want to try to help all of you get back on your feet. It's beneficial to the whole country, but unfortunately, some in Washington don't see it that way. I was given this job just before Mr. Lincoln died but now many are just using us for lip service. I hope I can do more than that. How about joining me for some breakfast and continue our talk? I'm famished and I know you must be, too."

Josh enjoyed the Colonel's company and he appreciated his offer of help. He also told him getting from Old Point Comfort directly to Norfolk wouldn't be easy since the Point was Army territory and Norfolk was Navy and the two sometimes don't work together well. He did, however, have an idea that might be helpful.

He said, "There's a small port town west of Fortress Monroe about ten miles or so on the same side of the harbor called Newport News Point. There is a small boat harbor there and they run barges to and from Norfolk. They dock at the shipyard there and other barges run down the Dismal Swamp Canal to Elizabeth City where they pick up lumber needed for the shipbuilding trade. They sometimes have trouble getting help to load and unload and I bet they'd give you a lift if you were willing.

"By the way, that area around Newport News Point will someday be some kind of big-name port operation. Rumor has it that the railroad folks are starting to look at it for the future. Put that in the back of your head for future reference."

Josh appreciated the information. He knew that the industrial age was gaining steam and that these beautiful and empty bay and riverfront towns wouldn't be small for very long. They finished their meal and decided to spend the trip on deck, watching the beautiful land as they sailed by.

They were full from the nice breakfast and looking skyward, they could see the sails were full. They were running at a good clip. The greenery on the shore and the clear blue sky overhead above the beautiful bay was a gorgeous sight to behold. The sun was warm but the air cool on the water and it was invigorating. A number of quaint fishing villages were passed and sailboats dotted the inshore water. They were running south about two miles out.

Soon they came by the mouth of a large river, the York and Colonel Winslow pointed toward Yorktown on the south side of the river. Josh nodded, knowing from his school history the significance of the surrender that took place there by Cornwallis less than one hundred years earlier. Another hour and they would be passing west of where the Marquis de Lafayette used his fleet to keep the British at bay, thereby trapping the Redcoats between the river and the Continental Army. It marked the end of the Revolutionary War and the real beginning of a free land.

Young Eldridge wondered how a nation founded on such hope and promise could have thrown itself into an internal war in such a short period of time. He did realize, however, that money and power have a way of creating horrible things and from what he saw there was plenty of blame to go around on both sides. All he knew was he didn't care about slavery since his family owned no slaves and he remembered working side by side with them as a boy to help his family survive. He wanted nothing to do with war and hate and was determined to strive to live a peaceful and helpful life as the Good Lord intended. He learned the hard way that war and constant conflict were not things to be desired.

As the bay widened and the land to the west became more populated, he was beginning to see the breadth of the Hampton Roads, making out Norfolk across the harbor. It wasn't long before their course turned west and he could see Fortress Monroe and her moat and the Old Point Comfort docks just ahead to starboard. He also knew that while it would take him some time to get home, he was now no more than sixty miles as the crow flies from where he wanted to go.

They docked shortly after noon, Colonel Winslow asked him to wait on a bench under the trees and when he came back he'd try to hook Josh up with a way to Newport News Point. He returned in half an hour and told the ex-soldier that a smaller supply sailing vessel would be departing from the docks at about three for Newport News Point.

Colonel Winslow cautioned, "I'll warn you, Josh, the sailors over there can be rough. If you know the Outer Banks and that part of the water, you've seen them in action, I'm sure. Go look for a man named Drummond at the dock and he'll direct you. Give him my name since he knows me. And take this card with my name and contact. I want to hear from you when you get settled."

Eldridge thanked him profusely and headed to the dock, finding Mr. Drummond easily since everyone knew him. He introduced himself and told him who sent him.

The grizzled old salt looked Josh up and down and said, "Well, if you know the Colonel that's good enough for me. He's good people, but why do you want to go to Newport News Point?"

Josh told him where he was coming from and where he wanted to go. Drummond's eyes lit up when he found out the boy had survived Point Lookout in one piece and told him he should wait until tomorrow and go over on the early morning run.

"You can sleep in the warehouse here, Son," Drummond explained. "If you get over there late in the day you'll be stuck until tomorrow anyway. The only barge traffic these days leaves in the early morning and comes back. It's a once a day service. There should be something directly from here to Norfolk but the Navy and the Army are squabbling over who has authority."

So, that settled it, Drummond gave him a cot and a dry place to sleep with blankets. And there was even a hand water pump where he could get some water to freshen up. Josh spent the afternoon walking along the docks, looking at the scenic view of Fortress Monroe and the Hampton Roads and he found a little eating establishment where he got food and a beer. It had been a long day and that beer tasted good. He then turned in early and quickly fell asleep, being awakened by

Drummond before six in the morning. The old man with the limp even brought him two warm biscuits for breakfast.

"You've been kind," Josh said. "How can I repay you for that?"

Drummond winked and said, "Just get yourself home. You've seen enough for a lifetime; it's time to make your mark on the world. And if you ever sail up this way from Currituck, drop by. I can always find work for a nice young man who needs it."

As the sun came up, Josh hopped on board the old sailing schooner, the Margie B, which would take a load of supplies to Newport News Point, then return with goods to be delivered at Old Point Comfort. The skipper, Captain McMaster, was a tall, thin man with a long scar on the left side of his face. It made him look menacing but he had a big smile on his face. He loved what he was doing as he directed his two deck hands in finishing the stowing of the goods for delivery. McMaster looked quickly at Josh's papers, returned them within moments and simply said they would sail in ten minutes. They would travel just far enough offshore to have depth clearance for passage.

With a steady wind out of the east, they made the trip in less than an hour on a morning that was bright and clear. Josh enjoyed the scenery of the bustling harbor, unlike any he ever saw and looked at the northern shore which showed promise of being a fine residential area one day.

Nearing Newport News Point, he looked with interest at the sprawling Union Army camp before the Point, shuddering to realize that the occupation was extensive in this area and how it must impact the locals, many of whom were still grieving over their lost soldier boys.

Suddenly, Josh could see the jetties with the narrow waterway between which was the harbor entrance. Captain McMaster brought the vessel about and put slack in the sails as they entered the harbor and literally coasted slowly to the dock as the sails were lowered. As Josh prepared to depart the vessel and seek follow on passage, Captain McMaster signaled through the window for him to come to the wheelhouse. He walked over, knocked and entered.

"So, you were at Point Lookout, young man," he began. "I hear that was pretty rough. And I'm sorry you had to come this way instead of directly to Norfolk, but I guess old Drummond told you about the Army-Navy squabble. That will clear itself up soon, but since Mr. Lincoln died, everyone has been trying to gain power in the vacuum which was left. As soon as they solve their issues, I'll thankfully be back running tugs instead of this old schooner, but sailing is still a joy.

"By the way, I was a tug captain sneaking out of Isle of Wight to run supplies right under Yankee noses for the Confederacy until she was sunk near the Monitor-Merrimack battle. I was captured, but when the Yanks learned of my knowledge of this harbor, they agreed to release me if I ran supplies for them. Realizing that both sides of the harbor would be under full union control very soon, I accepted the offer. I knew even then that things weren't going to turn out well for the South. We just didn't have the resources to win a long war. Running boats in this harbor is all I know and I didn't feel I had any choice."

Josh told him about his own action and POW time and where he was headed. Captain McMaster advised him that he would put in a good word at the dock and if he'd help load things aboard the Norfolk barge when it arrived, the skipper going to Norfolk later in the day would transport him in payment.

"If you get a chance, soldier," McMaster advised. "Ask the skipper about the possibility of working your way to Elizabeth City on a tug. The Norfolk dock, at the Gosford Shipyard, routinely has barges headed down the Dismal Swamp Canal to pick up lumber for return to the shipyard. They pick up a load of raw timber at a dock on the canal, carry it to Elizabeth City for trimming and bring finished work back to Norfolk. They are always looking for a good man. Mention my name to him as it might help, he's a good guy."

Josh thanked him, realizing that he was just as kind as O'Reilly up in Carter's Creek had been and he knew he needed money. He was again willing to work for awhile for he knew it would help his family and besides, from

Elizabeth City, he would be only fourteen miles from home.

Later, as the incoming tug from Norfolk pushed her barge toward the dock, deckhands on the barge and tug threw the lines over to the dockhands as the tug was inching into position. Docking of tug and barge was smooth, showing the skills of a good skipper.

Once in place, the skipper, a short, stocky man in his forties, looked for laborers and Josh stepped up smartly. He outdid all comers in terms of loading volume and following instructions and the skipper was pleased to bring him aboard. Loading done, Josh watched every action taken by the experienced deckhands, putting them to memory for future use.

Once ready to depart, the skipper showed his skill as he nudged the barge out to turn while keeping it in correct alignment. He slowly aligned barge and tug with the centerline between the harbor jetties and pushed his cargo forward. Then they quickly steamed out into to open Hampton Road and made a slight turn to port, now heading directly for the Elizabeth River and Norfolk on the southern shore or Hampton Roads.

Josh felt liberated and alive. While he knew he wasn't heading home yet, he knew soon he would be in Norfolk, a place where his father had taken him a number of times. The heritage of his family in America began in Virginia just below Norfolk several hundred years earlier when they arrived from England to farm for the Crown.

Josh was beginning to feel like he was almost home and he liked the feeling.

Josh also didn't know it yet, but he was on the verge of gaining a mentor, an older man who would help him, give him guidance and encourage him. The support would be a hand up, not a handout, and would play a major role in determining much of the future of his life.

FIVE

When the tug and barge docked at the shipyard, Josh quickly asked the skipper if he could help with the unloading. Captain Shorty Weston was pleasantly surprised and put him to work, pleased to have a man who was highly motivated, not just going through the motions for a buck. It was a time in a port where transients were far too many and it was hard to run a tugboat operation without hard working men. He watched with amazement as Josh did the work of three men, paying attention to the unloading protocol while also looking for whatever else needed to be done. When the work was done and it was time to take the Miss Margaret back to her overnight dock, he called Josh to the wheelhouse.

Josh walked into the small wheelhouse while Shorty Weston looked at him inquisitively. He explained who he was, how he got here and where he was trying to go. He volunteered to do anything he could to get help in getting to Elizabeth City. The tough little skipper, after hearing the story of Point Lookout and seeing his work ethic, told him he would help him but there were a few caveats.

"If you'll work a couple of weeks for me, Josh, I'll see that you get a ride on a tug going to Elizabeth City. Just be patient while I work it out and I'm also going to pay you well. You'll see, when I pay you at the end of the week. I'll make sure you have a warm, dry bed and food while you're working with me. What do you say?"

Josh agreed and Shorty told him that it was a light day for him since he was on the return trip only but the next day would be full and they'd start out early. They would leave the barge at the dock for overnight loading and move the tug to the Norfolk side of the river where he lived.

"I'll put you up at the Seaman's Home for tonight, Josh," he said, "It's a clean and safe place that offers a good dinner and will pack you a carryout breakfast and I'll pick you up in the morning at six on the way to the boat."

The facility was on Shorty's route for walking home, so he dropped Josh off on his way. They shook hands and both men felt good about the day. Josh could make some money and learn about commercial water operations and Shorty would, at least temporarily, gain a quality employee.

The next morning right on schedule, Shorty walked up to the Seaman's Home and Josh was ready and waiting. They walked to the boat, the two other deck hands were there, and Shorty told Josh to ride with him in the wheelhouse.

"I want you to understand the operation of the engine and start up procedures," Shorty explained. "You can handle the tug deck and oversee the two barge hands who frankly are a pair of lunkhead who really don't want to work. You learned more yesterday by paying attention to load protocol than they have in months and you can help me keep them straight."

Josh said he'd do his best and they were off to the shipyard in Portsmouth. They both laughed as they talked about how strange it was that the old Gosport Shipyard, after being captured by the Union was named the Norfolk Naval Shipyard even though in Portsmouth. Shorty said it was so that it had the same name as the growing Naval Base.

Upon arrival at the shipyard docks, Josh watched and even directed adjustments where he saw lack of proper loading protocol. When completed and properly secured, Josh hopped on the tug and Shorty increased power, slowly pushed the barge away from the dock and made the turn up the Elizabeth River toward Hampton Roads. As they entered the open Hampton Roads, Shorty brought up the war and he showed his soft side.

He began, "I'm sorry, Son, for what you've been through. My own much younger brother was held there for a while and we never heard anything more about him. He must have died. This damn war has ruined many young men and families as well and for what? Nobody has a good answer. Since most of this area and the Norfolk shipyard fell quickly under Union control, it was easy for me to just be a tugboat captain and keep my mouth shut. I don't know if I should be ashamed of that, but I never knew anyone with slaves and I've lived in these parts all my life except for a few years in the merchant marines. It was in my younger years and it's where I became enamored with harbors.

"I am surprised that they let you out because they are still taking prisoners up there, boarding them on the pier right around the point on the peninsula up ahead where we came from yesterday."

Josh responded, "I saw a ship bringing in prisoners as I was freed and a man in Maryland said they were coming from Virginia. Do you know any more about it?"

Shorty's brow furrowed and he said, "Well, I'll show you myself after our stop at Newport News Point. We have supplies also to go to that dock around the point and up the James River where they can take larger vessels. And there is a schooner that has been taking on men in gray under guard and transporting them to Maryland. The story goes that they are the last defenses behind Lee holding back those coming after him between Richmond and Appomattox. It seems there were those in the War Department that didn't want Lee released and his men free; they wanted him dead. Now that Lincoln is gone, it is said they are taking it out on them."

Later, after their unloading and taking on cargo for Norfolk at Newport News Point, Shorty steered the tug, the Miss Margaret, with barge out front around the point to the one long pier that could take larger vessels. There was a platform on one side where barges could dock, awaiting loading, with ships on the other. About a dozen soldiers still in gray were being boarded and they were clearly under guard.

As a cart of baggage, crates and goods to go to Norfolk was delivered, Josh and two others loaded the barge and when done, Shorty signaled Josh to come back on board the tug.

"Well, Josh, "the older man replied, now you see what the Union is doing to those they claim they want to bring back in the fold. Keep it to yourself, Son, because they'll shoot you just for the fun of it if you try to create problems. I fear our new problems are just starting."

Josh continued to teach himself about the tug operation on the way back to Norfolk. He checked the steam engine and the stowage of coal, the gauges for monitoring operation and watched closely as Shorty maintained course despite a strong incoming tide. There was a natural tendency of the barge to try to slip off slightly to either port or starboard. There is no way the blunt bow and tied lines could do it alone. The skilled skipper was the added dimension needed, and Weston was the best. Meanwhile, Josh stoked coal as needed and the vessel just purred along.

As they headed down the Elizabeth River, a few old Confederate docks that had been empty for nearly three years were now berthing partially sunk vessels flying the Stars and Stripes. There were also two scuttled ships which still flew the tattered Stars and Bars from a mast just above the waterline. They passed by the downtown area, passing continuing past the eastern branch of the river and entering the southern branch.

"They left those ships in that condition just to remind us," Shorty invoked, "that they rule the roost. They also probably don't want those docks working since the owner was an outspoken supporter of Virginia's secession. They'll probably disappear once his bankruptcy ends his ownership. I just hope the animosity settles and we can truly go back to our decent lives again. None of us want any more war."

As the Miss Margaret nudged into the receiving dock on the starboard side at the Norfolk Naval Shipyard, dock hands came out to secure both tug and barge to the lines thrown to them by Josh and the two other crewmen. The others were stationed underway on the barge in case anything had to be suddenly secured.

Shorty told Josh to take charge of the other two men and direct the unloading. It was important to make sure goods were cleared in a balanced order to avoid bigger problems. Two wagons arrived and the unloading was done in record time.

Once completed the tug crew returned to stations after releasing the ties to the tug and leaving the barge in place. It would remain in place until the morning when all would return to reload for the next day's trip. The tug then turned to port as it left the parallel dock and headed north on the river, then heading starboard on the eastern branch of the Elizabeth River. They traveled a short distance before docking at the tug pier from which they departed in the morning, just across from what would soon become the Colonna Shipyards.

Shorty explained that the tug captains take turns being responsible for security of the vessels overnight and the Miss Margaret was on schedule this day. Shorty would bring Josh food and he pointed out the fold out cabinet that was actually outfitted with a feather mattress. He also showed him where the shotgun was, complete with shells packed with rock salt.

"I don't want you killing anyone, Josh," Shorty said, half laughing, "but if anyone starts nosing around the tug docks, give them a warning and if they don't respond fire one warning shot. If you need another shoot them, just not in the face. That rock salt burns like hell."

Shorty further explained that if an ex-Confederate soldier actually shot someone with a lethal round, there would be hell to pay. With the rock salt, when a federal harbor cop shows up, the round used would allay fears. They would probably hold Josh until Shorty could be roused, but it would be okay.

The bunk was the most comfortable bed Josh had slept in for years, excepting Claussen's featherbed in Maryland. The cabin door could be bolted from the inside or locked from the outside and with the windows open by the helm, anything moving nearby could be heard. The docks naturally creaked when people were present.

After Shorty brought food to Josh, he departed for the night and Josh ate before deciding to turn in. It was cool in the cabin and wrapped in a blanket, Josh fell asleep to the gentle lapping of the water on the hull. He dreamed about being back home, going fishing and enjoying the beauty of the sound and the deep blue sky. He awakened suddenly but, for a moment, didn't know why or where he was until he heard footsteps slowly coming down the dock. They seemed to stop at each tugboat as if looking for something then continued.

Josh quietly arose, put two rounds into the barrels and left the breach open and peered out through the darkness from the darkened helm window. Josh saw a man, unrecognizable in dark clothing, approach the tug, stop and then stealthily come on board. Josh held the shotgun at the ready and tiptoed to the doorway and waited. The man disembarked from the tug and now moved toward the next tug, pulling something out of his pocket and trying to pick the lock. Josh knew it was now time to do something.

He quietly stepped out of the wheelhouse raised the shotgun into firing position and said with a firm voice, "Stop where you are, raise your hands and slowly turn around. State your name and business and then just stand still."

The man appeared to be beginning to turn when instead he took off full speed and jumped onto the dock, trying to make a getaway. Josh opened fire, one shot into the arm and reloaded quickly, firing a second round of rock salt into the culprit's buttocks. He yelled in pain but Josh knew it was just the sting from the rock salt. He would recover. Within a minute, two federal uniformed officers came running toward the tug and told Josh to drop the weapon and get down on his knees.

Josh did as he was told and responded from his knees with hands held high, "Don't shoot, officers, I work for Captain Weston, the skipper and I was sleeping on board as a guard. The shotgun was only loaded with rock salt, not lethal force. The man was snooping around the tugs and was trying to break a lock on another tug."

Officer Muldoon stayed with Josh while Officer Felton went to get Shorty. They obviously knew him and wanted to corroborate the story. Within twenty minutes, Felton came back not only with Shorty dressed in a night shirt, but also the perpetrator, who was rubbing his backside.

"Okay, officers," Shorty said, "this man is Josh and he's my crewman. He was just doing his job and this perp is a guy who has bothered with the boats for weeks. He's always trying to steal things, too stupid to figure out that there's nothing here he could carry away. He's probably hungry and looking for anything of value."

The officers tipped their hats and quickly departed with the guilty party and Shorty walked over to Josh and shook his hand. He complimented his marksmanship, went in the wheelhouse and pulled out a bottle of whiskey and both men had a belt before returning to where they came from. The rest of the night was quiet and sleep came easy.

In the morning, they got underway and the tug went back to the shipyard docks where the day's shipment was on the dock, awaiting loading. As directed by Shorty, Josh took over directing the work and quickly had things in order and balanced for the trip to Newport News Point. The shipment contained foodstuffs for the Union troops still camped near the Point and construction materials and machinery from the shipyard for delivery to Old Point Comfort. It would be a long day as they would make the two stops on the north shore and then return via Newport News to Norfolk. It was the first indication that a thaw in the animosity between Union Army and Naval authorities was underway.

It was a crisp and clear day in mid-July, unseasonably cool as they entered the open water of Hampton Roads. It was actually chilly in the middle of the summer. The day went well, Shorty was very pleased with Josh's work and he told him he had a surprise. Finishing up work for the day, Josh was not going to be required to sleep on the boat. Another tug captain was taking responsibility for securing the boats at dock and Josh was going home with Shorty for a home cooked dinner.

"I've never told you much about myself, Josh," Shorty said, "but tonight you're going home with me for dinner. I know you probably thought of me as an old guy with a girl in every port but no, I have a wife I love very much and she is a great cook. So, tonight you're going to get some homemade goulash made by my wife, Natasha, born in Hungary but a naturalized American citizen. I met her in Liverpool when I was a ship's officer on a merchantman and her father ran a ships' stores shop at the port. She worked for him and I saw one smile on her face and I was a goner. I paid her way to America six months later and we've been together ever since. We got married by a justice of the peace two days after she arrived."

Josh was impressed when he saw Shorty's place and his wife was a pretty, but very modest woman about fifteen years her husband's junior, making her about seven years older than Josh. Before dinner, Shorty brought out a special bottle of wine and the three of them shared a leisurely glass before dinner.

Soon, Natasha excused herself, then returned with a large pot full of a delicious smelling thick soup full of spiced meat, then followed by a large container of homemade spätzle, rich Eastern European egg noodles. The perfect hostess, Natasha served each of the men, putting a thick layer of spätzle in a large bowl and then smothered in goulash.

Natasha smiled as she served Josh, saying, "I hope you like my goulash, Josh. You are the first worker Shorty has ever brought home and that is quite the compliment to you. Eat hearty and I'll bring some hard rolls and fresh coffee."

Shorty turned red, saying, "Don't think because you're the first one here that you get special treatment at work," but then he broke into laughter. He was actually a taskmaster but he also had a soft spot for any young man who wanted to work.

The work schedule changed the next day. Shorty's tug was pulled off the line for some maintenance and he would be working on the dock as stevedore leader for loading the other tugs as needed. Josh went wherever Shorty went and performed any task asked. At the end of the day, he was tired and sore but now staying at Shorty's home, he was a regular at the dinner table and was treated almost like family. He also enjoyed taking a walk in the evening around the Norfolk neighborhood, even attending church on the Sunday before the tug was returned to service. While at church, he saw a beautiful young lady singing in the choir and he couldn't take his eyes off her. He thought to himself that is the kind of girl he'd like to take home to meet his mother someday.

The manual labor was building his strength and with all the good food, he was looking better than he had since going off to war. He wondered if his family had it nearly so well. He wanted to head home quickly, but Shorty was so nice to him he felt obligated not to be impatient as he trusted the older man explicitly.

It was a Monday morning when the tug was returned to service and they pushed off from the tugboat dock and headed toward the shipyard to the south for their first trip.

"Where are the other deck hands, Skipper?"

"They weren't cutting it, Josh, so I fired them. We'll pick up a couple at the shipyard. There are always young men looking for work, unfortunately most of them don't have initiative and pick up on things like you."

Josh thought about the compliment and he was momentarily dazed, then threw the tie line to the dock hand as they pulled in right behind the barge which, surprisingly, had no shipment on dock to load.

Shorty went into the shipping office and came out with some papers and two dockhands. He told Josh to get the barge hooked up and ready for the push. The new deck hands, like the old ones, would stay on the barge.

Josh was further surprised when they left the dock with an empty barge and Shorty continued south instead of heading toward Hampton Roads.

"Guess what, Josh," Shorty said. "We're heading for the Dismal Swamp Canal and our first load of timber for Elizabeth City. The tug has been transferred to this route and if all goes well, I will want to talk more with you about that. In any case, when you leave to go home, I want to be the one to get you as close as we can to leave you with only a short walk. I'm working on an even bigger deal with the shipyard but I won't know for a few days if it will come through. If it does, it will make my life much better and it might be good for you as well, but let's leave it at that for now."

Josh didn't take in all of what Shorty could mean but he did know he was getting another step closer to him. He responded, "I thought it was kind of weird when we didn't load up at the dock. I'm excited."

They continued down the southern branch of the river until making a turn on Deep Creek, which would take them to the Dismal Swamp Canal. He explained the situation to Josh.

"I have a few issues with the Dismal Swamp route, Josh. It's still under control of the Union Army and it has a few maintenance problems. It's a shorter route to Elizabeth City but sometimes it has bank slides. We have to go down this way because the cut lumber pickup is there, but returning by the Albemarle and Chesapeake Canal, while longer, avoids complications. We'll see how it goes in the future. Let's just hope that the Army guards don't want to hassle you. Are your papers in order, Josh?"

"Don't worry, Skipper," said Josh. "I keep them in a waterproof packet right here," as he tapped his deep pocket.

At the Deep Creek lock they were quickly waved through; the next stop would be the loading dock adjacent to the entry to Lake Drummond. As they pulled up to the dock, there was a work gang of former slaves who carted the logs, mostly live oak and red cedar. They tied up at the dock and Shorty walked over to the guard house and presented his shipment papers.

The corporal on guard inquired, "Who's that with you, Shorty on the tug? I've never seen him before."

"He's been with me for a while on the Norfolk-Newport News-Old Point Comfort run," was Shorty's comment. "He's on his way home and is working for me to make some money on the way."

The guard looked over and yelled, "Hey, Boy, come over here," to which the former slaves laughed.

Josh stayed calm with a smile on his face and approached, pulling the papers out of his pocket. The guard looked at them and made a snide remark about Point Lookout, keeping his eyes on Josh. Josh just remained silent with the fixed smile until the papers were returned. He then went over to the loading dock and supervised placement and balance and tied the logs securely in place before releasing the crew.

As Shorty fired up the engine and Josh jumped on board with the tie line, Shorty said, "That guard was trying to get you riled up but you handled it as cool as a cucumber. I was sure when he said something about

Point Lookout you'd respond but that perpetual smile played havoc with the soldier's mind."

Josh figured he probably never saw any war duty. He looked like a greenhorn or maybe he spent the war right on this mosquito-laden canal. He explained that he had been through enough to handle anything, particularly when being stupid would just cause problems. A fair fight, however, would have been something different and he would have loved the opportunity.

Another hour and one half passed and they reached Great Mills and entered the headwaters of the Pasquotank River. Josh knew where he was now and felt right at home. Not too much time went by before they entered the main river and shortly he saw Elizabeth City and they headed for the dock near the lumber yard. Once docked, Shorty contacted the mill manager who said they would be unloading shortly. He was asked to keep a man on site until completed and since Josh was the only one he could trust, it was Josh who remained.

"It shouldn't take but about an hour, Josh," Shorty told his trusted mate, "and when I return we'll move the tug to overnight dockage and go for some dinner and a place to sleep. There's a place here the Navy opened for seamen with overnight accommodations and I want to make sure it's suitable. See you in a bit."

As he walked off, the lumber mill superintendent came to Josh and asked him to verify the load by type and volume. Josh did a second count to what was already provided and oversaw the unloading, keeping in mind the balance of the tug. Unloading went without issue, he signed for the volume and Shorty was coming back.

"We're in luck, Josh," Shorty said on arrival. "They have rooms available with dinner thrown in. It's pot roast night with vegetables and fresh apple pie. And the best part for you is since you're on duty with me it costs you nothing. The only thing you'll need money for is a beer or two at Clancy's. Let me give you an advance to cover whatever it is you want to do tonight. Be careful, though, there are lots of sailors and some unsavory types hanging around here and someone will con you if you aren't careful."

Josh just laughed, thinking that Shorty was acting just like his father, but the age difference was about right and he was a good soul. After a couple of beers at the tavern and dinner back at the boarding house, both men were sleepy, so they turned in. The last thing Josh remembered was the loud laughter in the streets as the transients in town were painting her red.

On the trip back with a processed load of lumber the next day, Josh was once again hassled by the guard at the checkpoint where they unloaded. It was very unusual to check a tug twice on the same trip, but the soldier obviously wanted to see if he could get Josh upset. As he and Shorty disembarked from the tug, the soldier yelled at Josh.

"Hey, Johnny Reb, come here," was his taunt and he repeated it even louder, completely ignored by Josh except he continued to walk in his direction with his papers.

As Josh stopped close by the soldier got ugly, "How dare you ignore the summons of a United States Army sentry, I could shoot you for that and no one would care."

"Excuse me, soldier," said Josh, "but I'm not Johnny Reb. As a matter of fact, I swore an oath of allegiance to the United States before departure from Point Lookout and my citizenship was reinstated. Maybe you need to look at your own protocols a little closer because as a citizen, my rights have been reinstated."

The soldier had a scowl on his face but as Shorty drew closer and another soldier was now paying attention, he thought better of it. He told Josh he didn't need the papers and walked back to the guard station.

As Josh and Shorty walked toward the tug to continue the trip back to Norfolk, they both silently chuckled. Shorty was very proud of how young Eldridge handled the situation and he knew he had a good man with him. Now he just had to figure out a way to keep him on while also being able to see his family. When they got back to Norfolk, they made sure all was well with the lumber and accounted for, the tug was tied up and they went back to Shorty's place.

After dinner, Josh bid them good night and went to bed. He was tired and his absence gave Shorty the chance to talk over a plan he had hatched with his wife Natasha.

"I've got a dilemma, Natasha, and it involves Josh," he began. "I like that young man. He learns quick, follows instructions and he's worth more than any I've seen since getting into the tug business. There is something else. In about two years, the Miss Margaret will be mine free and clear and it would be good to have someone as a junior partner in the business. But I know he is anxious to get home and see family and spend some time with them. Can you think of anything that might work?"

Natasha smiled and simply said, "Well, Shorty Weston, you're a smart man, so why don't you do what you wanted to do last year. Didn't you say that the Corps of Engineers was talking about hauling the rough trees on their own to the lumber yard. If they did that, you could pick up the one-way supply route down the new canal and Currituck, then pick up the finished lumber for the trip back home. And if you did that, I'm sure you could work out something for Josh. After all, since the lumber moves for about three weeks and then there's a lull, you could give him time off then. It could be kind of like your merchant marine work was along the coast, three or four weeks on and then several off. You know the shipyard shipping office loves you, they always brag about your work. I think they'll give you anything you want."

"Oh, and by the way, I like Josh, too, he's such a higher quality than the transients you've had before. All you would have to do is have Josh oversee the customers offload at waterfront stops southbound and in Elizabeth City. He would just do what you have him doing now plus I'll bet you could get him fully qualified to maintain the boat and even be a back-up skipper if you wanted to. You've got the experience and knowledge and he's eager to learn. You've got nothing to lose and a lot for both of you to gain. I know you love what you do but you are under a lot or stress. It would be good to get rid of some of it."

Shorty took her by the hand and began dancing a jig around the kitchen. That was the perfect solution, for on the profitable runs there are weeks off at a time and Josh can stay during those period in Currituck. Besides, after the hassle on the canal, they could even start using the longer run and avoid all that, which also takes them right within two miles of where Josh lived. Currituck Court House was a potential customer, as was Coinjock to the south.

Josh awakened to the sound of feet moving and laughing in the living room, but he smiled knowing that Shorty and his wife were having some fun. Little did he know what they were cooking up, but something was going on down there. He needed his sleep, however, and did what he did when he wanted to go to sleep. He remembered his good times. Tomorrow would offer a great turn in his life that would hasten his happiness and well-being.

SIX

At four thirty the next morning, Shorty Weston dressed a little spiffier than usual and walked to the dock, fired up the Miss Margaret and headed over to the shipyard. He was lucky that a dock hand was already at work to help him cast off. He was sailing solo, something he normally wouldn't do. Shorty threw all caution to the wind that morning since he was in a hurry to see the shipping manager. He knew the man was a workaholic and was always at work hours before others. His shipping schedule had to be ready by six to meet operational requirements. So, Shorty entered the administrative building before dawn. He entered the office building at the shipyard and knocked on his door.

David Watson, shipping manager, was a studious hardworking man who was hard to please, but Shorty was a man who always got the job done. When Watson saw who was at the door, he smiled and let Shorty in. He went back to his desk, told his visitor to help himself to a cup of coffee and have a seat.

"I'm surprised to see you here at this hour, Captain," he said. "You are about two hours ahead of your normal time and even then, you don't have a run this morning so it must be important."

It's not an emergency, Mr. Watson, but I wanted to follow up on something we talked about sometime ago. I have a request to make."

Watson knew what it was about and put him right at ease. He said that he would award Shorty the delivery route through Currituck and continue the return trip with lumber. He said Shorty could grow the route as more business means more for them all. The only stumbling block was the slowness of the Corps making arrangements for moving the rough timber. They don't want us on the failing canal but they have been sitting on their hands.

"I'll tell you what, Skipper," Watson said. "I'll get the shipyard commander to talk to the Corps of Engineers commander and put some heat on. In the meantime, can you run the route for another week or so? I think after that we'll see something break. Oh, and by the way, I heard a rumor about one of the canal guards giving your ex-Confederate boy a hard time. I hear the shipyard commander knows about that, too, and he's hot. He's itching to talk to the Corps anyway. I know how dependable you are and appreciate it. Just keep the faith for a little bit and we'll get her done."

As Shorty was in his meeting with David Watson, Josh was waking up. He washed up, got dressed and headed for the kitchen at six. He expected to find Shorty there but was surprised to find Natasha instead. She was humming a tune while frying bacon and was startled when Josh said hello.

"Oh, hi, Josh," she said recovering quickly. "I guess I was humming so loudly that I didn't hear you coming in. Shorty had to go on a quick errand but will be back. He said for you two to have breakfast here and then go to the docks. You won't be steaming today. Shorty said something about an issue at the Dismal Swamp locks and they'll have the canal open again tomorrow. Have a seat and I'll pour you a cup of coffee. I won't start the eggs until the dancing devil returns."

She told Josh about their dancing but didn't explain why and said Shorty had a surprise for him. As he drank his coffee, he thought about what it could mean. He knew not to ask anymore of Natasha, for when she didn't offer she had her reasons. So, he just sat there pondering. Fifteen minutes turned into an hour and a half and he was really wondering what was going on when in walked a smiling Shorty. He grabbed a cup of coffee, kissed Natasha good morning and sat down at the table with Josh.

"I guess Natasha told you about the lock problem on the canal. I went to the shipyard early to see management with an idea we've been discussing for some time. It involves you, so let me tell you what is on my mind; hopefully you'll like it."

"I'm all ears, Skipper" was the former soldier's comment and he then just sat forward in his chair, sipping his coffee, eager to hear what his new boss had to say.

Shorty explained his earlier trip was to discuss his request to change assignment routes for the tug. He was asking to move to the Elizabeth City route full time and had been lobbying for it for months. He had some positive results and he wanted Josh involved.

"I want to propose that you come to work for me, Josh," he began, "and there's a way to do it which will allow you to both spend time with your family and also earn a living to help your family financially as well. You see, and I've never told you this, I will own the tug free and clear in two years and I requested and gained approval to work the Elizabeth City route exclusively. Note that I said Elizabeth City route and not Dismal Swamp. Now, after what happened on the Dismal Swamp passage we just completed, I want to change my route to the longer Albemarle and Chesapeake Canal waterway. It's safer, bigger and there won't be any military problems there. Are you with me so far?"

Josh just nodded with rapt attention and asked his skipper to continue.

"The shipyard is being awarded a stores contract from the Corps of Engineers to deliver commercial supplies to small business on the Albemarle and Chesapeake route to Elizabeth City. I'm going to get that contract plus continue the finished timber run back to Norfolk, only following the new route. No more hassles on the Dismal Swamp.

"The workload will be sufficient to run multiple runs a week, possibly three, estimating three weeks on and two weeks off. You would be away from home for three weeks, then spend two consecutive weeks home at a stretch, sometimes longer. I'm working on a pay plan but I want it to be salaried so that you have some certainty. I'll add an incentive for when we exceed our targets, meaning more money in a bonus for both of us. You could think of yourself as the tug assistant and supervise the deck hands, plus fill in as I need. Plus, and this is something special, your overnight accommodations and two meals a day are covered by the contract for the weeks you are working. I'll meet with Mr. Watson to finalize things tomorrow. If I can work it out fairly, are you interested?"

Josh smiled and nodded, saying, "You've already been good to me, Skipper, of course I'll work for you. I'll be able to make some money for family plus have some certainty in my life. Two weeks at a time at home will work just fine. I can really get things up and running for Ma and Dad again."

That settled for the time being, Weston told Josh to take the day off and come back tonight for dinner, he had some business to attend to at the shipyard and then, in the morning, they would make the old Elizabeth City run after his meeting again with Watson.

Josh decided he'd just walk around in Norfolk and get to know the town. He really wasn't used to spending time in a city and he wanted to see what it had to offer. All he remembered was coming to town with his dad, but not lengthy stays. So, breakfast over, he and Shorty went their separate ways.

Josh went window shopping, enjoyed watching men go to work, women scurrying about shopping for needed things, with the hustle and bustle seen everywhere. Horse and buggy rigs were out and about with a streetsweeper making rounds behind the animals with a push cart and shovel. He found a little coffee shop attached to a bakery and walked in, immediately noticing the pretty young woman behind the counter who smiled at him shyly. He recognized her. She was that beautiful girl he saw in the choir when he went to church on that earlier Sunday.

"Excuse me, Miss," he said nervously. "Could I get a cup of hot black coffee, please? And how about one of those sweet buns?"

The young lady went and filled his order, took his payment and then said, "Are you new around here, Sir? I don't think I've seen you in here before."

Josh told her that he worked on a tug and just came here after the war. She looked troubled and told him her brother had been killed at Petersburg in the second siege. Josh gave her a sympathetic response, mentioning his time on the line in Petersburg and his prisoner status, but then had to move on since a line was forming behind him. It was prime coffee hour in the downtown district.

As he sat down with the large mug of hot coffee and the freshly made sweet roll baked next door, he looked around the shop. It was like none other he had ever seen, quite nice with quality furniture and a spit-shined floor. He was in no hurry and just enjoyed the peace and quiet. Suddenly he was interrupted as the young lady at the counter came up and asked if she could join him for a moment.

"Why, of course you can," Josh responded cheerfully. "It's nice to have some company, especially someone as pretty as you. I'm Josh, Josh Eldridge."

He couldn't believe that he blurted out how pretty she was and she turned red but demurely thanked him with a smile. She was on her break after being at work for nearly four hours and she wanted to know about his experience. She could relate him to her brother, only this man was alive.

Her break was for fifteen minutes and they talked for the entire time. It was as if they had known each other for years, it just seemed natural. Before going back to work she asked if he would be around for long. He explained he would be in and out, that Norfolk was his home port although he was gone a lot. He did say, though, that he'd like to talk with her again and promised to come back. He got her name, Annie Pickett and as he stood up to bid her goodbye, she actually put her hand on his and said she would look forward to seeing him again. Then she was off.

Josh spent most of the day roaming around town getting to know downtown Norfolk. He visited a book store, had a sausage sandwich at a small corner place and found a small park where he could sit and ponder. It was near the river and he watched the squirrels while being accompanied by the sound of ships giving warnings to small craft in their way.

Again walking, he picked up a newspaper and read about the state of reconstruction and the changing and growing country, then found a single bench along the river where the bustling ships were sailing by in both directions. Watching the beautiful sailing craft, he knew their days were numbered for commercial business as the steam engine would lead to much more change in travel on the rivers and seas. He was at peace and enjoying himself and was so pleased with the events that had taken place recently in his life. Then he thought of that pretty young woman he just met, Annie. He hoped he would see her again.

As late afternoon approached on a warm but not unpleasant late summer day, he decided it was time to go back to Shorty's home. He knew that Natasha was a stickler for having no stragglers at the dinner table and he wasn't about to offend her.

As he rose to leave, a familiar voice spoke from behind him saying, "What are you doing here, Josh?"

It was Annie and she was walking right to him with a big smile on her face, quickly reciprocated by Josh. He hardly knew this girl but there was something about her that warmed his soul. She was medium height with a nice figure, but not voluptuous, but her smile, light brown hair and blue eyes just got to him in a big way.

He stood in a gentlemanly fashion, then she told him she would sit with him for a few moments as she was ahead of schedule.

Josh inquired, "Is this on your way home, Annie? I just spent my free day wandering around Norfolk. My dad used to spend time up here as a young man and I thought I'd check things out."

"This is a bit out of my way for going home, Josh," she said, "but I always like to come by here on my way home to get a good look at the bustling river in the late afternoon. It's always fascinated me. I live about a mile from here off Church Street. How about you?"

Josh explained that he was boarding when in Norfolk with the Weston's. They offered him a place since it was close to the dock on the eastern branch. He thought he had seen Church Street but he wasn't sure. He was watching Annie and noticed she looked surprised by something he said.

"I know Captain Weston's wife, Natasha, quite well," she replied. "She gave me piano lessons when I was younger and I still see her from time to time when she comes downtown. She is a wonderful person and while I've only met her husband once, he seems very sincere.

"And guess what? You are staying not too far from me. I hope you didn't think I was being too forward when I touched your hand this morning or now as I ask would you like to walk me home? It's just I sense something about you that makes me want to know you better."

Josh couldn't believe it. This pretty young woman that he was taking a fancy to lived fairly close to where he was staying and she just asked him to walk her home. He thought there must be something fateful about that. He threw caution to the wind and hoped Natasha would forgive him as he told Annie he'd love to walk her home.

As they walked along, they just opened up with each other like long lost friends. Annie told him about losing her parents to a runaway carting accident and how she and her grandmother were so close. Josh, in turn, told her about Currituck, the new opportunity he was being given and how it would finally put his life on a firm footing, or so it seemed. She smiled broadly when he said he saw her in the choir that Sunday, thought she was beautiful and immediately recognized her at the coffee shop.

When they reached Annie's house, they stopped and she looked all around, then quickly touched his hand and leaned over and kissed him on the cheek.

She quickly turned and went through the picket fence gate and before entering her grandmother's house, looked back with a smile and said, "I want to see you again, Josh. Say hello to Natasha," and she was gone.

Josh was in a semi-daze, thinking about his day, but he quickly came down from the stars. He knew Miss Natasha's rules about timeliness for dinner and he knew he violated them, but he rushed there as fast as he could. He also was anxious to find out what she would say about Annie.

As he walked up the street toward Shorty's house he saw Shorty hurrying home from the other direction. Good, he thought, this way at least he wouldn't be alone in his tardiness. As they walked in, both men noted on the big grandfather clock that they were home fifteen minutes late and they quickly went to wash up before standing by their chairs, not seating themselves in deference to Natasha.

She told the men that the dinner was on the kitchen table and for them to bring it out. It was her way of making her point and they brought out the serving plate of rockfish and bowls of boiled potatoes and fresh cooked greens. She continued her unofficial scolding by leading the blessing, closing by asking the Lord to help both Shorty and Josh have more respect for her than to be tardy for a well-prepared meal.

Once she announced she was over it and hoped both men had learned something, dinner was wonderful and she was back to her usual charming self. Natasha found the beautiful rockfish at her favorite fish market, deep fried it in pieces and thought the combination was a good one with the potatoes and greens. Plus, there was corn bread and plenty of it.

"These greens came from either Princess Anne County or Moyock down your way, Josh", she said, "I know you're anxious to have some of your kind of cooking and this will show you I can cook like that, too."

Josh thought it to be perfect and said so, enjoying it immensely and both men told her they were sorry for being late. As Natasha brought coffee while they were finishing their meal, Josh asked her a question.

"I met a pretty girl who knows you today, Miss Natasha," Josh said. "Can you guess who it might be?"

Natasha looked puzzled for a minute, then replied, "Well, since you were going downtown and I know you weren't in a ladies' shop, the only place I can think of is the coffee shop down near the waterfront. Did she have soft brown hair, pretty blue eyes and a beautiful smile?"

When Josh shook his head yes with a big smile, she just responded, "Annie, Annie Pickett. Wow, Josh, she's a wonderful girl who would be a great match for you."

Shorty was not paying too much attention, sipping his coffee and thinking about the next day's run, but when he heard her response, he perked up. He looked at Josh with a big smile and told him he'd be a lucky fellow to catch Annie.

The three of them enjoyed their coffee as they talked about Annie, teasing Josh just for fun, but he just laughed and even volunteered to do the dishes. Natasha nodded yes and told Shorty to help him, that he might learn something. As the two men worked in the kitchen, Josh washing and Shorty drying, they talked about Annie. Unknown to them, Natasha was in the next room nodding her head in agreement with Josh's assessment as she relaxed with her unexpected free time.

After Josh turned in, Natasha and Shorty continued the discussion about Annie and Josh. They agreed that if Josh were to court Annie, he'd be even that much happier to have to spend so much time away from Currituck. The ultimate win-win situation was advancing rapidly.

The next morning bright and early, Shorty and Josh were off to check in at the shipyard, pick up their two deck hands and head out. They were hopeful that this would be their last journey through the Dismal Swamp before the schedule change. When they arrived at the loading dock on the canal to pick up their shipment, Josh was pleased to see that the overzealous corporal was no longer on duty. He was relieved and replaced by a Sergeant who apologized to Josh for what had taken place. Josh just told him that he had forgiven and forgotten, but inwardly he felt like justice was served.

Over the next ten days they continued on the route as the schedule change was delayed, completing three more trips before they were finally finished. On that last day, Josh was unaware of the good news yet as he finished supervision of unloading on the run made in record time. He jumped aboard the Miss Margaret and while a dockhand secured her to the dock, Josh unhitched the barge and awaited departure to their overnight berth. Soon, Shorty approached, walking at double-time with papers in his hand and a big grin on his face.

Shorty was exuberant as he said, "We're done with the Dismal Swamp Canal, Josh. Day after tomorrow we'll start the first run of commercial goods for the Corps. I meet with them tomorrow with Mr. Watson and then we're ready to go. So, on Friday morning we're off with the first run via Currituck. We only have two stops before Elizabeth City, Currituck Courthouse and Coinjock, perhaps an additional one as well along the way. The return load won't be ready to load until Sunday, so we'll stop at Currituck and you can see your parents while I watch the boat. How does that sound?"

He told Josh to take the day off the next day, Thursday and he even suggested that he go see Miss Annie. Josh enthusiastically agreed. He also told Josh that when he returned, they would meet and set up a pay plan for Josh so that both understood what the arrangement was.

Josh was full of energy and excitement when he awoke. He even was up before Shorty and made the coffee, then looked around at a few minor maintenance projects that needed to be done. The kitchen window needed calking and he wanted to fix the gate out front that Natasha complained about.

After coffee with Shorty and Natasha, he went to work on the small projects. There was a method to his madness. He wanted to show his hostess how appreciative he was for allowing her to stay in her home while also while killing a little time before walking to the coffee shop. He wanted to be sure that Annie's workload was light when he got there so they could talk.

A few hours later, Natasha came out as Josh was finishing up the fence. He looked up and smiled but she looked angry.

She sounded stern as she said, "You better get a move on, young man, if you plan to see that little girl of yours during her free time, Now get going," were her final words as she broke into a grin and walked back inside.

Josh paid heed, quickly finished his work, made a note of other things he wanted to do and headed to town. About twenty minutes later he saw the coffee shop and walked inside. He was disappointed that he didn't see her, but decided to wait and see. Ten minutes later Annie entered through the back door carrying a bag of supplies from the bakery next door. She broke into a big smile when she spotted Josh.

Josh stood up as she approached, anxiously saying, "I just had to give you the good news. The skipper has been awarded the Currituck route and we'll start tomorrow. The best part for now is that I'll get to see my folks tomorrow for the first since I went to fight in Petersburg. I'm excited."

She looked slightly puzzled, then said, "Well, congratulations, Josh, but will I ever see you again?"

Josh showed concern as he said, "But, of course, Annie. Don't you remember I said that I'll be based out of Norfolk at least three weeks out of five. We'll be back in town at least twice a week and I can take a day or two whenever I'm free to see you. Plus, probably one day before long I might want to take you down to Currituck to see my folks, if you would join me."

At that, she broke into tears and ran up to Josh and threw her arms around him. He didn't know what was expected so he just hugged her, but not too tightly and patted her on the back.

"I'm sorry, Josh," she said, "I know we hardly know each other but I really want to know you so much better. I never told you this, but I fell in love once and he jilted me and now Grandma says I'll probably just be a spinster living with her as I get too old for anyone to want me."

Now Josh hugged her more tightly and said, "Well, Annie I wouldn't be talking about taking you home for a visit if I didn't feel something strong. We just have to let nature take it's course as I also start building a nest egg. Being almost twenty isn't old, you are only a few years younger than me. Everything will be okay."

They talked for another ten minutes and Josh said he'd see her early next week when he got back. He gave her a handkerchief and wiped her tears away. She smiled they embraced again and he departed.

That night after dinner, Shorty made a pay offer to Josh which the younger man quickly accepted. He would be paid a daily rate of three dollars per day for work days and one dollar per day for downtime since even then he was considered on-call for emergencies. A monthly pay of over fifty-five dollars per month was good money back then, but the shipyard rewarded their tug crews who faced demanding time schedules. Besides, Shorty was on contract long term since he was buying his own tug and they knew that once he owned it outright things had to remain attractive. It was also important that he had at least one crew member who was smart, wanted to learn and had a future in the business. Shipping Manager David Watson had observed the quick development of the young man and was impressed.

When Josh turned in that night early, he really couldn't sleep because he was so excited. He was excited about the excellent opportunity that Shorty gave him and that very soon he would see his parents again and see how they were and what help they needed. He would be able to help them both with their homestead on his time off as well as provide financial assistance that they might need.

He was excited also about that lovely young lady who he was so quickly falling in love with. It stirred feelings in him that he couldn't explain. There were the physical feelings which he knew about and had acted on a few times when war allowed. He was ashamed of that and wanted it out of his mind, but with Annie, it was a feeling of so longing for her that he never wanted to let her go. Smiling to himself thinking of her, he fell asleep with visions of her lying in his arms.

Shorty and Natasha were excited, too. They were glad Josh had accepted his offer and Natasha knew that would make her husband's work much easier. An able-bodied right-hand man he could count on was a luxury Shorty never had and even Shorty was relieved. He looked forward to the new route and the better assignment. It would be a new adventure starting tomorrow and he couldn't wait to get started. After all the lean war years and the uncertainty of it all, things appeared to be looking up for all of them.

SEVEN

On a beautiful Saturday morning as the sky was just beginning to show the transition from darkness, Josh and the Skipper fired up the steam engine on the Miss Margaret and headed to the Navy Yard. They would load private business goods for the Currituck area, check the manifest and make sure that the Elizabeth City lumber yard would be ready for them on Sunday. Sunday runs were the exception, but due to the lumber yard's late delivery from the Corps of Engineers, milling of the final product was delayed.

Once underway again, they passed the Deep Creek entrance and continued on the southern branch of the Elizabeth River until coming to the entrance to the new Albemarle and Chesapeake Canal. Josh remembered when it was completed, just two years before the war but had never seen or experienced passage on it. Compared to the rather dilapidated Dismal Swamp Canal it was a beauty. It was much wider, deeper and was shored up properly to eliminate shoreline collapses so prevalent in the swamp. And as they began the journey toward the North Landing River and the Currituck Sound, a beautiful orange sun was rising as if from the canal directly to their east.

Josh remembered hearing about the construction of the canal as a boy. While the Dismal Swamp waterway was built with slave labor and hand digging, the Albemarle and Chesapeake Canal was a marvel in advanced technology of its day. The most difficult part of the digging, removing tree stumps and roots for the new canal, relied on nine pieces of steam powered equipment called the "Iron Titans." The machinery dug out the stumps and roots and was used to clear the canal and right of way. The rest of the digging was much easier as much of the base came up with the stumps and roots. After that, it was more like digging a broad and wide ditch. It would have probably never been finished, however, had the line of sight requiring digging been more than fourteen miles due to financial constraints. Most of the route was on existing waterways, including the North Landing River, Currituck Sound, the North River and then into the Albemarle.

The project took nearly four years, completed in 1859, but with the war soon coming, it would not be an instrument for commerce until after the end of the war and Josh now saw just how valuable it became. Once reaching the North Landing River it was a clear shot into the Currituck Sound and then on to the southern cut across the Currituck peninsula at Coinjock. With a docking deck already in place there, it would be easy to unload goods for businesses. From that point, crossing the rest of that four-mile canal section, travel was easy down the North River to the Albemarle and westward to the Pasquotank River and Elizabeth City. Through local marketing, potential civilian markets could be developed in towns like Edenton and Plymouth on opposite sides of the Albemarle in addition to Elizabeth City. More would be developed in other towns as well. Transportation in and out of those places by land was difficult due to the many bodies of water throughout.

The two deck hands were, as usual, on the barge and as the canal moved into the North Landing River which after a time began to widen, they were amazed at the open waters of the Currituck Sound coming up ahead

Josh smiled, seeing the Currituck for the first time since that one weekend of medical leave before marching off to the battle in Petersburg and it excited him. He was interrupted by Shorty with a question.

He began, "Josh, what kind of dock is available in Currituck? I know it's not a port and I've never been there."

"Well, Skipper," Josh replied, "There is a dock but it's short. You'll have to dock the barge on one side and the tug on the other. That will work. So, what kind of maneuver will you use? And one more question, why do we always push instead of pull the barge?"

Josh always asked questions due to his inquisitive nature and Shorty liked that. He knew an inquisitive mind was one that was learning and Josh had the ability to easily take it all in. Shorty was the perfect man for him to work for in that regard for he loved to explain things about his work. He said he'd push the barge in, berth it, then back up and bring the tug round to the other side. He added that was the perfect situation since when it was time to leave, the barge would be towed. That would work in the Coinjock canal since the dock there was long and parallel to the canal. All they would have to do is shorten the length of the tow lines to ease control.

"As far as the pushing of the barge, Josh," he added, "just look at the blunt and wide bow on this tug. The newer, heavier duty tugs are stronger but they can't operate in the canals which are limited draft channels. To pull, which is usually for bigger or multiple barges, they have to have a more contoured hull and the distance from boat to barge allows for more slippage from port to starboard. It will work in a wide canal without significant turns but not in one like the Dismal Swamp. Even in the Albemarle and Chesapeake, it can be done but the approach is narrower and there is no point in switching back and forth underway."

As the North Landing River opened up toward Currituck Sound, Josh could see the starboard shore turn inland meaning Currituck Court House wasn't far off. As he spotted the familiar waters, he smiled, realizing at long last he'd see his family soon.

Shortly after noon, Josh saw the small village to the starboard side and pointed it out to Shorty. The skipper worked his magic to turn his payload gradually to port and in ten minutes they were approaching the docks. He slowed the engine to a crawl, then reversed engines as he pushed the barge to the dock in a manner that wouldn't crack an egg. Robbie and Zeke, the two barge workers, jumped onto the dock and quickly tied her up, then Josh unhitched the barge at the bow and rejoined his skipper in the wheelhouse. Neutral was shifted to reverse and they backed out, then swung the boat into place and Josh secured her on the opposite side of the dock.

Shorty said, "We'll have to see what we can do about them putting parallel docking up in that long open space along the shoreline seawall. It will speed up loading and unloading while allowing more boats to simultaneously tie up. Just thinking about the future when business picks up."

Josh agreed, finished securing the tug and joined Shorty on the dock as they walked to shore. They saw three local wagons and several men standing waiting for them. They knew it was the folks waiting for shipments on the barge.

A young man approached Josh and said, "Do you remember me, Josh, I'm Sam Jarvis. I'm here with our wagon to pick up Dad's shipment."

Josh smiled and said, "Well, Lordy, Lordy, Sam. Last time I saw you I could pick you up. You've grown and filled in."

Sam laughed and reminded Josh that he was about ten back then and was now seventeen. He also told Josh he would take him home if he wanted, since his folks lived less than a mile from Josh's family.

"Let's get you loaded up, Sam," Josh said, "then give me a few minutes to help the others and I'll be ready to go. I would appreciate the ride."

Josh and the two deck hands oversaw sorting out the ordered goods, got receipted signatures for the bills of lading, loaded the supplies and Josh turned to Shorty. He told him about the offer from young Sam.

"Here's what we're going to do, Josh," said Shorty. "You take a ride up with your young friend and if you can promise me you'll be back here by five in the morning, have a good visit. I'll keep these two busy here and we'll spend the night here. I've got my shotgun if there are any ruffians in these parts and we'll see you bright and early."

Josh was surprised and said, "Are you sure that will be okay?"

"If it wasn't, I wouldn't have said it," he responded but then he smiled. "Now go on, get out of here before I change my mind."

It was nearing three in the afternoon when Sam dropped Josh off at the Eldridge place located just east of the little town of Sligo, named for an Irishman of the same name. The man lived there in the 1700s but no one knew what became of him.

Josh sent a letter to his parents a few weeks earlier telling him he would be passing by soon, but he had no idea if the postal system was working very well. As he walked through the gate to the nearly bare wood picket fence, he saw his father, looking slightly bent over but still walking without a cane coming around the side of the house. The elder Eldridge looked, rubbed his eyes as if he was seeing a ghost before breaking into a broad grin. Josh then broke into a run to his father's side, put his arms around him and began to softly cry.

"We got your letter just yesterday, Josh," his father began, "but we had no idea when it might be. Let me look at you, Son."

They stepped back from the embrace and John Eldridge took a good look at his boy, then turned and yelled to his wife, telling her Josh was home. The two men heard a pot hit the floor and they correctly guessed that in her haste to see her dear son she literally dropped what she was doing.

Josh's mother, Emma came out the door, stopped on the porch and said, "Come to me, my boy, and give your ma a big hug."

John walked over behind Josh and then the three of them embraced with the parents now shedding a tear. Momentarily, they broke the group hug and Josh was peppered with questions about what he had been through.

Ma Eldridge led them to the kitchen and said she would prepare something to eat. She complimented Josh on looking so fit and he responded that he had been working hard but was well fed. He saved the best for last.

He began, "Ma and Dad, I am working on a commercial tug that is starting a route between Norfolk and Elizabeth City and while I'll be on the water and away for three or four weeks straight, I will then be able to come home for two-week periods in between. The schedule means I will be able to help you, Dad, with keeping the place up and with your work while also bringing home a good paycheck that will make things easier for all of us. My skipper is over at the docks and I have to meet him early in the morning, but in about two more weeks I'll be on my first free period and come home."

Father John followed up, "Do you like what you're doing, Son? I hope you're not just doing it to make money to help us, for you have to love what you do to be a success."

Josh assured them both that he loved it and explained how there is no way he could make that kind of money in Currituck while building a future. Then he told them about Annie.

"Well, Son", his ma said. "Before you make any firm commitment, just make sure you two really love each other. If you find that you do, we will love that girl like a daughter. It will complete your life and make you a full man."

They sat for over an hour eating and talking and John told Josh he'd get their cart horse Sally ready early and he'd give him a lift before dawn. John politely said that he would walk. He wanted his Dad to sleep well and explained he was worried about his posture.

"Dad," he explained," I spent entire days walking at the quick time. The walk back over to Currituck is nothing and the early morning fresh air as I walk fast will cleanse my spirit."

They sat up until about ten, late in those days, and Josh filled them in on everything that had happened since they last met when he was convalescing during the war. He told them that knowing they were waiting for him and loved him back in Currituck is what got him through at Point Lookout. When they finally turned in, John was sound asleep within five minutes.

Having trained himself to wake at the hour he needed to be moving, he arose at half past three, tiptoed around washing up and dressing and then slowly came down the stairs. He was surprised to see a lamplight from the kitchen and the aroma of fried bacon and fresh coffee filled his nostrils. His ma was working in the kitchen to surprise him.

She smiled saying, "I couldn't let you head out without something in your stomach. I'm packing a couple of my homemade biscuits with bacon; Josh and you can eat as you walk. Here they are wrapped up to stay warm, just put them in your pack and eat when you want. Take this mug of coffee, too, you might want to have a cup to use at work. I know how seamen love their coffee."

As he walked over to accept her food package, she began to cry. Josh took her in his arms and held her for a moment, then kissed her on the cheek and released her.

"Don't cry, Ma," he gently said, "You know what I'll be doing and that I'll be safe and, in a few weeks, I'll be back for the first of many long stretches with the two of you. And here, take this money for whatever you need while I'm gone. I know you can use it."

Josh handed her ten dollars and he knew it was more than her parents had seen in one place in a long time.

"You always were a thoughtful boy," Ma said, "and when you come back to stay, I'm going to make you the best seafood supper you've had in a long time. Your dad will be fishing for sure."

Josh turned, threw her a kiss and headed down the road.

Within five minutes, he heard a wagon coming fast from behind him. As he stepped out of the way to let the rig pass in the dark it slowed and stopped. It was Sam Jarvis, the young man who gave him a lift the day before, telling him to hop in.

Josh inquired, "Where are you going, Sam, in such a hurry at this hour?"

Sam laughed, responding, "I was coming to get you and was afraid I was too late. Dad told me to take you back since you are a hero to us after what you've been through."

Josh pulled out his package of biscuits and offered one to Sam, saying that his ma always gave him more than he needed and the biscuits were huge. Sam, knowing what a great cook Mrs. Eldridge was, eagerly accepted and the two young men ate bacon biscuits as they made their way to the Currituck dock.

"So, what are you going to do with your life, Sam," Josh asked. "Do you want to be a fisherman or farmer or something else."

Sam told him he was thinking about joining the Navy. He was good with sailing and loved the water, could tie any kind of sailor's knot there was and had steady feet on a swaying boat. Josh told him that he might be able to help him and to come see him when he's off duty in a few weeks. He promised nothing but said he had something that might be good for both of them, saying no more.

They arrived at the dock when the sky was just barely turning gray. Josh thanked Sam and said he'd see him in a few weeks and as he walked on board the Miss Margaret, Shorty told Josh to stoke the coals in the fire to get the steam going, saying they'd perk a pot of coffee before pulling out. Shorty walked out to make sure the deck hands were up, but came right back saying they had taken their makeshift tent down and were ready to go.

"Doggone it, Josh," Shorty said with a laugh. "You almost caught me snoring. Good job of getting here so early, we'll be ready to go in about twenty minutes."

Right on schedule, Josh checked with the deck hands telling them when to release their lines. He waited for the steam engine to fire up, released the tug lines and Shorty shifted from neutral to reverse and slowly backed out. Then he brought the tug around the dock to connect the bow with the barge, then backed out again, this time to deeper water. Once sufficiently clear, he switched to forward and brought the barge around to head out into the open sound.

"You know, Josh," Shorty said. We'll have to talk to the county and get that long dock parallel to the shoreline approved. This current situation will be a problem when it gets busy."

This was the second time in two days that Josh brought this up. He decided to write a reminder to ask his dad how to go about it. He had forgotten to bring it up the night previous and was mad at himself for being forgetful. He quickly wrote the note, stashed it and moved on.

With a hot cup of coffee in his hand and the lightening eastern sky of the rapidly approaching dawn, they were off to their next stop, Coinjock. Josh briefly pondered how good it was to find his parents reasonably well. He knew his ma was okay but he also knew the rigors of a life of pig farming and now fishing was taking its toll on his father. Soon he would be able to help him in his off time and Dad shouldn't have to work so hard. There was much to be done but things were looking up. Josh at last was starting to feel some security in his life.

The first trip to Elizabeth City went well. They delivered their goods to Coinjock and even two packages to Edenton, received the lumber from the lumber yard in record time early Sunday afternoon. Monday morning bright and early they made the run back to Norfolk, even blowing the tug whistle at a fisherman Josh knew in the sound. Arriving at the Naval Shipyard late Monday afternoon, Josh knew Tuesday would be a day of routine maintenance and he would have to wait until after his next trip to see Annie. He was really starting to recognize the yearning in his heart for Annie. As August of 1865 came into full swing, he realized he had come a long way in just under four months. From prisoner of war to hard working tugboat man, he was thankful for his good fortune and his developing. Annie would have to wait and he knew the wait would be worth it.

EIGHT

By late August, Elizabeth City had effectively fallen in line with Union military guidance and as a community began to handle any issues diplomatically and with great respect for the occupying forces. One of the major reasons was because of their regional military commander. Colonel Ramsey had family ties in North Carolina and he recognized the strides that the citizens had made. He despised some of the harsh edicts coming out of Washington and he felt that more forgiveness and less punishment was in order. Despite the limits of what he could do, he thought a little bit of fun was in order. He decided to have fireworks one evening on the waterfront and invite the townspeople to a little party with a band and refreshments.

Josh and Shorty had spent the day making deliveries and arrived in Elizabeth City late and would spend the night. As they approached the city on the Pasquotank, a group of Union soldiers was celebrating with fireworks in the early evening. Josh was surprised to see townspeople joining them but he was glad. It was a sign of a semblance of normalcy and he knew that was a major factor in how long the soldiers would stay and when the burdensome and growing Reconstruction would end. All Southerners yearned for a return to self-governance, yet they knew it would be years in coming.

Reaching the dock at the lumber yard, Josh and the deck hands quickly tied up the barge and they then moved the tug to a separate berth. The unloading wouldn't be done until the morning, so Shorty and Josh checked with the guard on duty and told him where they could be found. Then they headed to the seaman's boarding house, arriving just in time for dinner. They were in luck; fresh rockfish with hush puppies, collard greens and boiled potatoes made up the menu and they ate like they had never eaten before. Afterward, they walked out on the porch and fireworks could be seen over the river.

"You know, Josh," Shorty said, "after all the strife the South has been through it's good to see folks enjoying the fireworks. It's a sign that America is coming back together again."

Josh told him he had been thinking similar thoughts although after Point Lookout it made him look at things differently. It was, however, time to move on. Shorty said he was going to turn in, but Josh decided to walk to the small pub near the river for a beer. He reached in his pocket to make sure he still had the coarsely designed brass knuckles which he would only use if he was seriously threatened. Many seamen carried them in those days.

The little establishment was frequented by soldiers and seamen and, of course, wherever transient personnel were gathered with alcohol the ladies of the evening were present. Some of them looked really out of character, but Josh knew many were just trying to survive and it was the only way they could. As he thought about it, one of them approached him and asked if he would buy her a whiskey. He pointed at a chair and nodded. He knew a flirty comment would soon be coming.

She didn't waste any time before saying, "So what's a good-looking sailor boy like you doing alone in a place like this. My name is Rachel, would you like some company?"

Josh looked at her for a moment and responded, "Well, you don't look like the kind of girl who would be in here either. I'm Josh and why are you here?"

Rachel told him she was twenty-two, the widow of a Confederate soldier who was never found after Gettysburg. The last time she saw him was when he departed from Suffolk, Virginia back in early 1862 with a local militia. She ended up in Elizabeth City after her baby died of the fever and she couldn't face that town again. Her parents were dead and she had no one to turn to and another girl was coming to Carolina, so she tagged along.

Josh looked at this tired young woman, very pretty but without light in her eyes and he realized she reminded him of Annie. He was lonely and he knew she was willing but, no, he wouldn't allow any physical yearning to cloud his judgment. After all, it was just that very feeling that he succumbed to on a weekend away from war and he regretted it ever since. He had been taught that some things were meant to be shared with just one person and that was a loving wife. He was ashamed that he would never be able to give that which he had lost.

He looked sad as he said, "Isn't there some other way for you Rachel? Do you like what you're doing? After all, it could be dangerous for you physically and for your health. Do you have any work skills that someone might need?"

She told him that she hated what she did, but she saw no other way. She had applied at a number of shops, including the store down by the piers but was told there were no vacancies. She had prior store clerk work at a general store in Suffolk and was pretty good at it. She was also earning room and board, or at least most of it, by performing multiple jobs at the boarding house where she was staying. They talked about things for some time and Josh even offered to walk her home, but she declined, saying she couldn't go home empty handed. He said he would inquire around and he gave her a coin, telling her to use it for something good and got up to walk out. He left her with some final words.

"I come in here for a beer in the evening's when I'm in the city. Keep an eye out for me and we can talk some more," he said before walking away.

He looked back once at her and she smiled, then she turned to talk with a young sailor who pulled up a chair. Josh just shook his head as he walked out. Life was, indeed, tough for a young widow of a soldier, particularly with no family to give her moral encouragement.

In the morning, Josh joined Shorty for a hearty breakfast before heading to the lumber yard. He told him of the plight of the young woman and how it touched his heart.

"Well, Josh," Shorty said, "there are many stories just like that one around us. It's admirable that you want to help her but she's got to be willing to take the lead herself. But I'll tell you what, I'll put in a word down at the dock store and we'll see."

When they got down to the dock, they received bad news. The finishing saw for the big lumber went down the night before and they were not ready to load. They would need the day, meaning the Miss Margaret would be here for another day.

"So, Josh," Shorty said with exasperation on his face, "what are we going to do now? I don't want to waste a day for time is money."

An idea came to Josh and he responded "Why don't we take the Miss Margaret and make some sales calls. Wherever we go they'll know we're serious. We have the tug and I know a couple of places that might be good targets for more commercial business."

Shorty perked up and said, "So what do you have in mind, Mister Salesman, show me what you're made of."

Josh explained that since their contract now included private business commercial shipments, the idea of building a market was a good one and he knew some communities that would probably offer customers. He suggested that they steam first to Edenton to see if they could find more customers to add to the list there. Then they could steam to the other side of Albemarle Sound and make stops at Columbia, Plymouth and even East Lake. They could be back by dark and the visit would hopefully sow the seeds of business growth.

"Just think, Skipper," Josh said with excitement, "later we can probably add Roanoke Island and perhaps even Nags Head and Kitty Hawk, but that's a longer run."

Shorty liked what he heard and told Josh to stow some more coal, get the steam up and they would head out. He said he'd be back in a minute; Josh didn't know he was going to the port store to see what he could do for John's newfound friend, Rachel. As he returned, walking up the dock, he gave Josh the circular motion with his raised hand which meant to get ready to bring in the lines. Josh followed him on board, ready to release the line in his hand.

Shorty had a smile on his face when he said, "When we get back, go tell your new young lady friend that Mrs. Willis will see her in the store for an interview. She needs to get there in the next few days as she's decided to fill a position. I just hope this doesn't mean something more than you told me, Josh, because I think you and Annie are a match and she's a really good girl."

Josh assured him that he just wanted to help her since she was a widow of a fellow Southern soldier. He would have hoped somebody would have been so kind to his young wife if he died in battle as a married man.

"So, Josh," Shorty followed. "Stand and watch close as I put old Maggie out, we're going to teach you how to skipper a tug today. When we get out in the channel I want you to take the helm and you can take her across the sound if you know the way."

Aye, aye, Captain, I know the way," he said with a big grin.

Josh knew it well. As a boy he sailed with his dad and others across the sound and knew where all the entranceways were for the three small ports he suggested. All had small general stores with a need for goods and he doubted they had a commercial delivery. It was largely swamp country on the southside of the Albemarle and he knew getting supplies in or shipping things out wasn't easy for the locals.

Reaching near the south shore Josh veered slightly starboard and paralleled the shoreline, making sure he stayed far enough out to avoid the shallow bottom. He knew Shorty was a little concerned. It was obvious by the tension in his jaw caused by clenched teeth.

"I'm following the shoreline so that I don't miss the narrow entrance channel," he said. "It's a little tricky getting into Plymouth as we have to go up a quite narrow waterway. If you'd feel better taking over, I'll stand up here with you and talk you in."

As Shorty took the wheel, Josh told him the first river of three is the Roanoke River and that's where they wanted to turn in. He warned him of a sand shoal near the mouth and to stay to the port side of the river to avoid it as it wasn't marked.

"Unless the other channel markers were destroyed", Josh advised, "they'll start showing up and just follow them. There is a small river that goes left but stay straight ahead. And right up ahead, there's the entrance."

Just as Josh said, the sand bar was on the starboard and Shorty slowed forward speed and headed in. With Josh finding the markers in place, they made an uneventful run to the Plymouth docks where they eased in and tied up.

Josh suggested that Shorty stay with the tug while he found someone to keep an eye on the Miss Margaret. He wanted to make a quick run to the general store and see if there might be an interest in their service.

Within fifteen minutes, Josh appeared from the little town with a young man, probably mid-teens, accompanying him. He introduced John Moore, who worked at the general store and would watch the boat while the two men made a few calls.

"John," the young tugboat man said as he returned with his boss to the store, "this is Captain Weston, my skipper, I wanted him to meet you."

Josh led Shorty to the store where they met the proprietor, Mr. Green. The three men discussed things and when the store keeper realized he could send things by water from the dock to Norfolk, he was ecstatic. There was a cannery nearby that he worked with and they had canned goods in demand in Norfolk and Baltimore. Since the war, any transport was sporadic and he was looking for regular, reliable transportation. He also referred them to the local boat yard which also had need for building items from Norfolk suppliers, so they now had sufficient interest to start a trial run.

To celebrate their good fortune, Shorty told Josh to take command on the way out the river and he stayed at the wheel for the two follow-on visits to Columbia and East Lake. They also found an interest there. So, now they had commercial interests in Currituck Court House; Coinjock, Edenton, Plymouth, Columbia and East Lake. Each potential customer was given instructions on how to set up an account with paperwork provided and they said they would pick it up on their next trip.

Back in Elizabeth City as darkness set in, they learned the lumber load would be ready in the morning and they decided to celebrate. Shorty was going to spring for a steak dinner at the only real steak house in town and they ate their fill. Afterwards, Josh said he would go and pass the message to Rachel about a job interview. Shorty told him to be careful; he remembered his younger days and the weakness of a young man alone with a pretty girl.

As he headed to the small pub, Rachel appeared out of the dark and ran to him and hugged him. He held her close for a little too long, but then when he released her, he suggested they sit on the bench over by the water front and talk. He recognized his weakness yet he also knew he couldn't allow it to take charge.

When they sat under the gaslight, she put her hand on his, but he gently removed them and said, "Rachel, I can't get close to you. You are very pretty and I am flattered, but I can't. I have someone else in my heart and I must be true, but I do have good news for you. Go down to the shop at the dock tomorrow. They want to talk with you and they are hiring."

She smiled broadly and went to hug him again as she said thank you, but he held her hands and shook his head. He looked her directly in the eye with a tinge of sadness and thought for a moment about what he would say.

Finally, he spoke, "You are a beautiful woman, Rachel, and if things were different, I could fall for you. And it isn't easy to just get up and walk away but I must. I have someone I love and I can't, and I won't, hurt her. You've had it rough so go get that job, get yourself away from this awful mess and start your life over. Someone, believe me, someone will want you, but it can't be me."

As she cried, he gave her hands a squeeze, said good bye and just walked away. Despite his growing love for Annie, it wasn't an easy thing to do.

The next morning, Shorty woke him up with a loud banging on his door. He was startled until realizing he was late waking up. He let his boss in to talk while he got ready to go. He told him about the night before and Shorty applauded him.

When they arrived at the dock, each munching on a sausage biscuit they grabbed before leaving their lodging, the loaders were ready to get to work. Josh got his two deckhands in order and they directed the placement, properly weighting the barge for the long push home. Once done, he took on coal for the tender and then Shorty fired up the steam engine. Within fifteen minutes the pressure was up and they dropped lines and headed out, pushing the barge from the dock parallel to the river out the channel before turning starboard. Once in the channel, Shorty gave Josh the helm and walked out on deck, stoking a pipe for a morning smoke.

It was going to be a hot first of September day but out on the water there was a nice easterly breeze. It would slow their progress until they got to the Coinjock canal but from there on it would be an easy trip. They dropped off some finished lumber at Coinjock for a local builder, then at Currituck they left several postal packages that had missed the Elizabeth City mail a day earlier. Young Sam was there, doing a minor repair job on the dock office and he waved at Josh. Tooting the horn and waving back, Josh remembered his promise to the young man just a few days earlier and as the Skipper returned to the wheelhouse, his younger assistant decided to ask him about Sam.

"Skipper," he began, "When and if you decide you want any changes on your deck hand group, young Sam will make a great replacement. He is smart, understands how to operate on the water and is looking for a future other than local fishing or farming. I was hoping you might consider him sometime in the future."

Shorty looked interested and told Josh he would be making changes. He encouraged Josh by saying if he hired someone Josh knew then he was sure the question of work ethic would not be a concern.

"I figure, Josh," he said, "that if I hire someone you want, they will be like you or you wouldn't want them. A close-knit work team is always good on the water. Maybe we can arrange a meeting on our next trip south.

"Speaking of our next trip south, when we get back, we'll work and perform maintenance and get things ship shape on the boat tomorrow, but we'll go in late. I want you to go see that pretty little Annie in the morning so you'll forget you ever met that other girl. You're soft-hearted, Josh, and sometimes that's good, but sometimes it opens you to trouble."

Josh thought about that the whole trip home and as they walked from the boat back to the Skipper's house, he learned that they were taking the weekend off, waiting until Monday for their next trip. So, if he saw Annie in the morning, he could maybe make some plans with her for the weekend.

Bright and early Friday morning, before Shorty or Natasha were stirring, he headed out the door. He knew Annie worked early getting things ready and she took her morning break around nine. He'd order coffee and a roll and wait for her, then tell her what he wanted to do. As he walked into the coffee shop, Annie was bringing a tray of rolls up to the display case and she almost dropped it when she saw him. He was so happy to see that beautiful smile.

He enjoyed his coffee and roll, especially seeing her nearby and she had to avoid his eyes to keep her business head straight. Finally, her break came and she told him her boss gave her an extra twenty minutes and they walked two blocks over to a small park. As they approached the park bench, unobserved by others under a big magnolia tree, they embraced and kissed passionately for the first time.

"You don't know how glad I was to see you come in, Josh", Annie said. "I've missed you and it was almost like I've known you all my life. I just feel alive when you are here."

"Well, young lady," Josh responded, "you've truly gotten into my heart very quickly. I thought about you a lot while I was gone and, guess what, we won't be working this weekend and I want to see you."

They talked about it and Annie took the lead. She knew that if she was getting attached, then she had to introduce him to her grandmother. She told her about him but until she laid eyes on him, she would be skeptical. So, Josh would come over Saturday afternoon and have tea with her. Then he would join them in church Sunday and after that, the afternoon would be theirs. She knew that once her Grandma met him, she would be impressed, for what she wanted for her granddaughter was a good man at her side.

As they got up to leave the park, they again embraced tightly and Josh was embarrassed by the reaction he felt in his body. After a passionate kiss, Annie just giggled and blushed and he knew she noticed his reaction. She told him not to be embarrassed for that was natural and meant he was attracted to her. She had feelings, too, but she was fortunate that they didn't show outwardly. He was surprised, but she said her grandmother told her when she was growing up about men and how they were.

They walked back and said goodbye and Josh headed on down to the boat for he knew the skipper would already be on board. They worked for about four hours non-stop, cleaning, making a few repairs and Josh observed as Shorty taught him about the steam engine and how to perform preventive maintenance. He wanted to make sure the young man learned all facets of boat operation so Josh would be prepared to handle any situation. The older mentor marveled at how quickly he picked things up.

"Josh, I thought about what you said about your young friend, Sam," Shorty offered. "There is a family named Whitehurst down the street going to Currituck by buckboard to visit their family tomorrow. Would you like to send a message by them to Sam and tell him we'll be stopping at the dock on Tuesday? I talked with Mr. Whitehurst early this morning and he said he would gladly deliver it. He said his family is right down the road from your family home."

Josh replied that he would write the note and said he knew the family. Like clockwork, when they returned from work, he did so and took it down the street. John Whitehurst and his wife were very cordial and he appreciated their help.

When Saturday morning came, Josh walked into the kitchen where Shorty and Natasha were having a leisurely cup of coffee before breakfast since they had the luxury of some quiet time. They were shocked, pleasantly so, when they laid eyes on Josh. He was freshly shaven with trimmed hair and looked like a picture.

Natasha smiled and said, "Why, Josh, aren't you the handsome one this morning. You must have something special planned with Miss Annie today. Am I right?"

"Yes, ma'am," he said. "Annie wants me to meet her grandmother this afternoon and I will be going over for tea. I have a few chores to do finishing the fence work first and wanted to get the hard part out of the way. What is her grandmother like, Natasha, will she like me?"

Natasha just laughed and told him Miss Hilda was a sweet older lady but manners counted to her. She eased Josh's mind by telling him that if he behaved there like he did here she'd love him. And then she added something nice to know.

"Josh, Miss Hilda only wants her granddaughter to find a good man who will care for her and love her," she said. "And if you two decide to marry, she will likely have her younger sister, also widowed, come live with her so the two of you won't feel guilty for leaving her alone. The only thing you have to do is decide if you two want to make that kind of commitment."

Josh thanked her for those comments and it made him feel better. It also gave him something to think about while he repaired the fence and fixed a front step. Then he went to his room to get ready to go meet Miss Hilda.

Checking himself out in a mirror, he felt shipshape as he bounded down the steps in a crisp fancy white high collared shirt with a waist coat, he found in immaculate condition at the nearby Methodist thrift store. Walking in the kitchen to say goodbye, Shorty whistled.

"Well, young man, you are what we call all slickered up," he said with a wink. "Natasha, I do declare, old Josh here looks pretty spiffy, doesn't he?"

She and Shorty both laughed and wished Josh good luck and he was off. He found himself whistling as he walked and he stopped at a small flower shop and got some flowers for Annie's grandmother. He surely wanted to impress her and in so doing win Annie's heart. Of that he was now sure.

As he walked through the gate and started up the steps to the porch, Annie walked out of the house and smiled broadly at him. She stopped, looked him up and down and told him he was handsome.

"No wonder I'm growing so fond of you," she said. "How could I not be."

Annie showed him to the parlor and went to get the tea and sweet cookies that she had just baked. Then she brought in her grandmother, a tall, stately looking woman of immaculate dress. She smiled at Josh and offered her hand and they were introduced.

Mrs. Pickett pointed to the sofa for Josh and then sat in a soft armchair beside it and said, "Annie tells me you are from Currituck and you just came back from war. How are things going for you, Josh? I worry about our heroes coming home."

Josh told a short version of his story in the Army and how he lucked into his job on the tugboat. They quickly hit it off and Annie just sat nearby smiling. She knew her grandmother didn't spend much time with someone in conversation unless she liked them and they were talking like they knew each other for a long time.

Later, when the older lady grew tired, she told Annie that she and Josh could have the parlor to themselves to visit and what's more, she and Josh could go to church without her in the morning. As she walked out of the room, Annie rushed out with her for just a moment.

Miss Hilda told her granddaughter, "He's a keeper, Annie. He's not one you want to let get away. I can tell he's fond of you and will take care of you. You two have my blessing for whatever plans you may have together."

Now alone with Josh, she told him what Miss Hilda said and they embraced with passion. On the spur of the moment, Josh asked Annie if she would be his wife and she accepted without hesitation. They both knew that they had been through a difficult time in history and they wanted to have something to really live for and that would be each other.

The following day, Sunday, they went to church, had dinner with Miss Hilda and her sister and then they went for a stroll down to the park. They sat hand in hand on a bench, talking about their dreams for the future and what they must do to get there.

Josh gently kissed Annie and said, "After my run to Elizabeth City tomorrow and Tuesday, I will be going to Currituck to spend some time with my folks, Annie. I have to help Dad with some things on the house and I will be telling them about you. On my next period of time off I want to take you to meet them. While I'm gone, I want you to look at rings and when I come back, we'll go and purchase the one you choose and make our engagement official, but I want it to be very short. I want to marry you just as fast as we can."

They embraced and kissed again and then headed back to her home, with Josh bidding adieu and heading back to Shorty's.

Upon arrival, Natasha took one look at him and said, "Why, Josh, you have definitely fallen for Annie and from your look Miss Hilda approves. Am I right?"

Josh told her she was right on the mark and then he told her that he and Annie would someday soon be married. When Shorty said he thought that was too soon, Natasha looked at him with a smirk.

"Why, Shorty Weston," she scolded, "you only knew me three weeks when you proposed to me or was it not that important to remember?"

That did it, case closed and Natasha promised they would do anything to help Josh in making plans. With that, he was off to bed for they had an early start on the tug in the morning. He fell asleep dreaming about his wife to be. He knew they would be together until the day they died. What he didn't know was all of the big and small trials they would face together in their lifelong relationship. That would come later, but for now he was overjoyed at the thought of making this beautiful young woman his bride. For now, he would live for that moment.

NINE

Josh completed two more round trips to Elizabeth City before finally getting home for a break. The trips were profitable and showed great growth potential. On the southbound circuit they were adding both deliveries and pickups for Columbia and Plymouth to their schedule. Shorty also had a great interview with young Sam and the young man would begin as a deckhand when they started service again after Josh's return from time off.

Before leaving by steamer for Currituck Courthouse, Josh visited Annie to tell her goodbye and it was then that he presented her with an idea.

"How about if while I'm in Currituck, Annie, I tell them I want you to come down to meet them?" he said. "I can come up the second half of the final week, take you down by steamer and the two of us can return to Norfolk together on my way back to work."

Annie was skeptical, saying, "Isn't that too much of an imposition on them, Josh. I don't want to put them out."

He shook his head, saying, "Nonsense, Ma will put you up in my room and I'll sleep on the sofa downstairs. It will be like old times when I was a boy and couldn't sleep. It will be a challenge, however, knowing that my beautiful bride-to-be is upstairs all alone in my big bed."

She gently punched him on the arm with a shy grin and shook her head no, letting him know there would be none of that. Deep in her heart, however, she wished they were already married.

Just after noon on his travel day, a Friday, he was off on the small steamer, following his customary route to Currituck. As he came off the boat with a sea bag over his shoulder, he began the two- mile trek home as the dropping sun neared the tree line. By the time he reached home, the crickets were chirping and the whippoorwills were delivering their timeless tune.

The lamp was lit on the front porch and he knew his parents were anxious to see him. As he started to knock on the door, his dad opened it. He went from looking as if he was in deep thought to an expression of great joy and he grabbed his boy in a big bear hug.

"We've been anxiously waiting for you, Son," he began. "You look extremely happy and I'm glad after what you've been through. Now come on in, settle down and Ma has some fresh fish and cornbread just about ready. And I remember you love fresh greens cooked in ham hocks. We've got that, too."

Josh hugged and kissed his ma and they all sat down at the dinner table to chat while they awaited the tenderizing of the steaming greens. His parents wanted to know everything about his life.

"Well, Ma and Dad," he began. "I've mentioned Annie before and we're now making plans to marry. I want your blessing on the marriage and would like you to meet her while I'm off. I'm doing better than I've been in a long time and I'm saving up and have some money for you. Things are really good."

His parents told him they still had some of the money that he left a few weeks back but he insisted and gave them another ten dollars. He told them if they didn't need it, save it for a rainy day and they were pleased to find out he was so good with money.

Over dinner they discussed Annie and they both agreed they'd love to meet her. It was settled and a week later Josh would hop the passenger steamer back to Norfolk and return with Annie. He had their schedule and it was perfect for his schedule.

The next day, Josh went around the homestead to determine what needed to be done. The door to the barn needed to be rehung and was missing a hinge, some fence posts needed replacement and whitewash and so did the house. Otherwise, it looked in good shape. Dad's carpentry skills had kept up with any bigger problems; he just needed help with the heavy tasks and no longer wanted to climb without help.

Josh made a list and father and son took the buckboard and headed to Moyock, an unincorporated but prosperous community just below the Virginia line. Because of its location on the road to Norfolk it was

quite popular and had the best hardware supply in all of
Currituck County. Their travel was on a hardpan road for
the approximate nine-mile one-way distance.

As they walked in to the store, the elder Eldridge, John,
spoke to Mr. Aydlett, the proprietor. His brother ran the
other family store south of Currituck in south county. It
was the first time since he was a small boy that Josh had
been to this store. He presented the list to Mr. Aydlett
and went to look around while the two older men
renewed acquaintances.

The proprietor said, "John, do you know anything about
how supplies are getting to Currituck without coming
from me. I'm starting to lose some business to a water
route which goes directly to Currituck and Coinjock.
Maybe the Yankees want to run me out of business."

Aydlett had been a diehard Confederacy supporter and
was fearful he was now being blacklisted. John Eldridge
looked at his son as if to say he needed help.

"Well, Mr. Aydlett." Josh intervened. "The Navy has
started servicing this area at the request of localities.
How do you get your deliveries?"

Aydlett replied that he sent a buckboard up to South
Norfolk to make pick-ups as needed, but that it was
really a hassle.

Josh had an idea and decided to try it out, saying, "What
if you could get your supplies more easily and closer. Is

Panther Landing still useable? I used to go fishing near there and the water was pretty deep."

Aydlett had a smile on his face and said, "Well, Josh you know more than anyone else about that water service so are you involved? Actually, if it could be delivered to Panther Landing it would save me time and money. I have to wait for the ferry to cross the Northwest River and then the same at the canal to get to South Norfolk. If you can arrange that for me at a decent rate, I'll sign up right now."

Josh told him he was working with the tugboat that delivered the supplies by barge and yes, he could do something but it might take some time to establish.

He added, "While you and dad talk, let me run down to the Landing and check it out. Then I can tell you something when I get back."

John and Walter Aydlett walked over to a local café for coffee while Josh went to the landing. He found a good, sufficient dock and there was enough room to maneuver, so it could be done. When he returned, all of the hardware was loaded and they were ready to go. He told Aydlett that it looked good and Aydlett said the water was over eight feet all the way to the Northwest River, then deeper from there to the sound. John told him now to place an order and get a credit slip from the Navy Department and plans were set. He'd need his first delivery in three weeks with a monthly order thereafter.

As they headed home, John looked at his son and said he was proud of his business sense, that he was quite the salesman. Josh grinned, pleased with himself for finding another customer where he least expected it.

Over the next week, his mom fattened him up and he couldn't remember when he felt so well fed. He made all the repairs needed on the house, whitewashed it, making it look like a new home and time was quickly coming for his trip to pick up Annie. On that afternoon when his dad returned from putting out his nets, he couldn't believe the difference in the house. That night, the night before his travel to pick up Annie, Josh and his parents sat on the porch and just talked about how the future looked so much brighter.

"You know, Josh," his dad began, "just months ago we figured you were dead and we'd never see you again but here you are looking really good. Your mother and I are pleased that you've met a nice young woman and we look forward to meeting her when you get her here. I only ask that both of you be sure it's what you want, for a lifetime with someone is wonderful with the one you love but if it isn't, it will be a really tough life."

Just then his ma chimed in, asking, "Where do the two of you plan to be married, Josh? In Norfolk? Down here? When?"

John replied "Why don't you ask Annie when she gets here Ma? I've left that up to her. It won't be a large wedding but it will be in a church and the sooner the better as far as I'm concerned."

The moon was coming up over the open fields across the road that ran to the sound. It was a beautiful sight on an early October night and Josh knew he would be glad when the day came so he and Annie could live nearby. Shorty even talked about getting out of the city when and if the time was right, so he'd have to be patient.

That night to the sound of the late season chirping crickets, Josh fell into a deep sleep dreaming of being with Annie on their wedding night. He had a smile on his face in his dreams which told the story.

In the morning, John came from the barn and told Josh they had to get moving if he was going to be on time for the steamer. He threw his sea bag in back and they were off for the Currituck docks. As they pulled up to the docks, there was a nice breeze blowing in from the ocean and small whitecaps foaming on the sound. He hugged his dad and ran up the gangway just before she was pulling out. He stepped over to the rail on the starboard side and looked eastward toward the Outer Banks, wondering what the Atlantic looked like this morning. He truly was hooked on the water and the sea.

A well-dressed man stood smoking a cigar at the rail and spoke to Josh, asking what brought him to Currituck. Josh told him he was visiting parents and was now going back to Norfolk. He learned the man was a planter from near Edenton and was heading to Baltimore. He had business dealings with a vegetable broker there.

"Well, young man," said the planter named James. "You must have something to do with boats because your ruddy complexion gives you away. I love the water but spent most of my time working the land. Joseph Hewes was my grandfather, are you familiar with the name, he was involved with the Revolution?"

Josh knew he was being tested, but he knew the answer and said, "Yes, sir. They taught us in history class that he signed the Declaration of Independence and was the first Secretary of the Navy. Some say he was a driving force in making it important."

James Hewes smiled and said, "You learned your lessons well.'

They talked for over an hour out on the rail and when Josh told him about his tugboat work, Hewes asked him about carrying perishables to Norfolk. Josh took his card and said he'd check things out and write back.

Arriving in Norfolk in mid-afternoon, he decided to go by Shorty's house and see if they were home. They wouldn't be expecting him but in the worst instance he could spend the night at the seaman's hotel down near the water. When he found them not there, he just headed over to Miss Hilda's house and found Annie and her grandmother sitting on the porch. Annie ran to him and threw her arms around his neck and hugged him tight while Miss Hilda just chuckled and shook her head.

She commented, "Okay, you two lovebirds, what will the neighbors say? Come over here Josh and say hello to me, too."

He gave her a hug and then the three of them sat down on the porch. They were drinking fresh squeezed lemonade on a mild October day and Annie poured a glass for Josh. He told them about his visit home and how excited his parents were about meeting Annie tomorrow. Then he said he'd better go to Shorty's and see if he had a place to stay. Miss Hilda surprised him when she said they had a third small bedroom behind the kitchen on the first floor that he was welcome to use. That way they'd be ready to go in the morning together and could be on their way. He was pleased and then that wonderful older lady bid them adieu, telling them to enjoy the rest of the afternoon but not be late for supper at six.

Then, with a wink, she said, "And you two get the clean-up honors after dinner. I love to cook but I'll warn you, I'm messy."

The two lovebirds cleaned up, then sat on the porch enjoying the afternoon. They talked about the trip in the morning. Annie was especially excited, not just about seeing her future in-laws but also her first real boat ride. Oh, she had been on the ferry across the river, but never more than that and it would be her first time ever out of

Virginia. Her entire life thus far was spent between Richmond and Norfolk, quite common in those days.

Later, after dinner, clean up and a pleasant walk hand in hand around the neighborhood, they both decided to turn in since they had an early day coming. After thanking Miss Hilda for her graciousness, Josh stopped at the stairwell leading upstairs and kissed Annie with passion. Then Annie headed up and Josh walked to the small bedroom behind the kitchen. His accommodations had at one time been the quarters of a slave girl who was the housekeeper. Thinking about those days, Josh was glad to see that not all slaves were quartered in places of squalor. Miss Hilda had even taught the young girl to read and write, something that could have sent her to prison had anyone become aware.

In the morning, Josh had breakfast with Miss Hilda but Annie was nowhere to be seen. Hilda laughed, telling him to relax that she was dressing up for her trip to meet the parents. He couldn't wait to see her and as she walked into the living room, his breath was taken away.

She wore a flowered dress with a tight bodice that showed her figure tastefully, but with feminine grace. Her hair was up and her face was radiant, holding a bonnet in her hand to put on when they left. She just had a small bite to eat and they were ready to go. Much to their surprise, Shorty Weston was at the door with his buckboard waiting like a rough version of Cinderella's carriage.

"We set this up with Miss Hilda, Josh," Shorty said. "Natasha and I were home but we just followed Miss Hilda's lead. You don't think any one of us would let you walk that gorgeous Annie all the way to the docks in her finery, do you?"

They were off and arrived at the dock ten minutes early, with Shorty giving them a wink as he headed home. Boarding was quick and they went in to the dining galley for coffee. A few passengers who had been onboard overnight from Baltimore and continuing south were gathered for breakfast. Josh noticed that all of the men in the room did a double take when they saw Annie. Josh was proud, thinking to himself that they could eat their hearts out.

Soon, they cast off and Josh asked Annie if she'd like to go on deck. They stood at the rail on the trip down the Elizabeth River and Annie was impressed by the canal, pleased to know that her husband to be knew how to maneuver a tugboat and barge. She knew what a good teacher he had.

"I've got some good news for you, Annie," Josh said. "After we get back next week and when we have our first day off, Shorty is going to sponsor me for the tugboat Captain's license. That means if he ever needs time off, I can make a run myself. With a sharp young fellow like Sam added to the crew, we can really get things done. Meeting Shorty was the best thing that has happened to me after you, other than my parents."

She was so happy and he pulled her close and kissed her, noticing two older couples watching. He apologized for his public display but one of the older ladies smiled and said they had been young once. For show, Annie swatted him gently on the arm and shook her finger at him, winked and then smiled at the ladies.

Later, near the end of the voyage when she saw they were headed to shore, she sounded nervous as she said, "Josh, I guess this is it. Is that your dad on the dock waiting?"

Josh squeezed her hand and said, "Yes, and he's going to love you. Relax."

They docked, the gangway was lowered and Annie and Josh went ashore. Much to Josh's surprise, Ma was sitting in the buckboard while his dad was coming down the dock to them. Josh knew this was an important moment for her if she came to meet them. Josh introduced Annie to his father and he smiled broadly and gave her a hug. Then they headed to the cart. It had front and back seats, and Josh and Annie hopped in back and he reached over and hugged his ma from behind while kissing her on the cheek. They all just chatted and got to know one another on the ride home. So far so good, thought Josh.

As they walked in the house, Annie commented on the wonderful aroma emanating from the kitchen. It was a pork roast with vegetables with a side dish of late season greens. It would be topped off with an apple pie just out of the oven with freshly whipped cream for the special occasion. Dinner was just about ready.

Dinner was delicious and, after having an after-dinner cup of coffee together, the two ladies went in the kitchen while the men walked outside. Josh's father was anxious to show him something. There in the barn was his fishing boat modernized. A new working shelf had been added, the keel reinforced to better balance and he had new sails.

"Tomorrow I'll take you and Annie for a sail if you'd like," he said. "I'm very excited. The new mainsail and jib make it so much easier to catch the wind and the new rudder makes control better.

"And Josh, that Annie is a very pretty girl and has such a nice manner. We like her already and you have all the blessings you could ever want from us. I know, however, that your ma is going to want to know when and where you will get married."

Josh told him Annie knew that and she would let them know while she's here. Josh left that to her and father John agreed that was best, that when it comes to the marriage plans, the women are going to do what they want to do.

The next day, father, son and future wife took the boat out with Annie for her first taste of Carolina fishing. Josh brought a single fishing rig, it was not going to be a long trip and they wanted Annie to experience it as they sailed to a spot near the rocks below Currituck where there was a deep hole near the entrance to a creek. He pulled out cut bait, rigged the hook and dropped the line into the hole. Only one rig was planned for the hole to avoid the inevitable tangle two might cause in the tight water cavern below where the fish had a great hiding placed from predators. Then, surprisingly her, father John handed his pole to Annie.

"Just hold it, Annie, and wait until you get a good hard tug, not a nibble and then pull back and we'll see what you've got," John said with a smile. Josh just sat back and watched. He wanted to see how she would react.

About five minutes later, the fishing pole wiggled, yet Annie didn't yank it hard, she just gave a little pull back. John was impressed with her finesse, but then the fish hit hard and she gave it a hard yank. Father John then took charge and it was an easy catch. The fish was hooked and hooked for good. When it was over, they had a nice striper and both Josh and John gushed over Annie's natural instinct as a fisherman. She was grinning from ear to ear.

By then, the wind was whipping in with small whitecaps from the southeast and John suggested they take a zig zag course back home and see what the improved sailboat could do in the wind. Annie loved it, she just held her head back and let her hair blow free as they zipped along, cutting through the small waves of the Currituck Sound. She felt like she was flying and it was an experience she never had before. Josh and his dad loved to see her laugh and smile.

When they got back to the dock, they let Annie off, then went over to the launching ramp where they'd bring her in. Using a hand winch, they retrieved the boat, swung it over to the utility cart and pulled it up behind the dock shed and locked it down. All the local fisherman kept their boats there and two local boys living in a nearby house were paid to keep an eye on things. One of them approached and when he saw John Eldridge, he tipped his hat and went back inside. The house was no more than one hundred feet from the dock. They tied the furled sail down and tarped it, covering the open boat as well and went to the buckboard where Annie awaited.

Josh was pleased with what his father had done with the old dug out boat and said, "Your hunch was right, Dad. That modification was perfect with the better sail and keel, and the new rudder worked like a charm. Now it's both a workboat and a pleasure craft and Annie, watching you finesse the setting of the hook was amazing. You must have been fishing before?"

Annie confessed that she had fished off a dock but never did she hook a large fish before, but she knew you had to make them want the bait to snag them. With that, both men heartily concurred.

On the way home, they discussed fishing and John told his son that he would soon give up the commercial part. He planned to start devoting his time to building and repairing boats, something he was a natural at and something that should be a money maker. He knew that Currituck would change and become a sportsman's area for both hunting and fishing and the money was in equipment, like boats, and being able to guide. Tourism would definitely be important.

They had a nice leisurely ride home and enjoyed the afternoon. Annie spent a lot of it talking with Emma Eldridge for she knew it was important to get off on the right foot with her future mother-in-law. It was easy, however, because they had similar personalities and views. She told Emma that they hoped to be wed over John's next free period from work and she wanted to be married in the Methodist Church on Church Street in Norfolk near her grandmother's home. She said she hoped they could come and she would make arrangements for them to stay in her cousin's house. They had plenty of room and offered it. Being a Methodist herself, Emma was pleased and said they would be there, that nothing would keep them away and that father John would be so pleased. Little did she know that Josh was always planning to book them on the steamer for the trip both ways. He thought an added touch would be good for them and he knew his dad would love it.

In the meantime, John and Josh went back to his work room off the barn where they discussed boat building and maintenance. It was where the boat had been stored before they took it to the dock where it would now stay under tarp until winter passed. John told his son how boat repairs would be his major emphasis, but if he had the chance to really get into something new and if the money was right, he would love the challenge. It sounded as if he wanted to do something where he could still be close to Emma and Josh thought that would be great for him. Being out in the water often alone could be challenging and Josh knew it was best for a younger man. Josh was proud of his father and his plans. He knew it was a niche market where he could excel.

They all turned in early as Josh and Annie would journey to Norfolk at eight in the morning. Sam would be coming to drive them to the dock as it would give him time to talk with Josh about upcoming work. Josh drifted off, dreaming of Annie and the life they would have together. She was like a vision in a beautiful white gown in the distance and as he approached her, she kept drifting farther way but then, suddenly she turned smiled and walked into his arms.

TEN

The next three and one-half weeks were non-stop work.
Josh's marketing had paid off and orders were coming in
from all of the new towns on the Albemarle route both
for deliveries and shipments. There was a lull in the
lumber for shipbuilding which was a blessing, for they
were swamped. With the shipyard enjoying a profitable
business with the new private sector transportation
provided by the Miss Margaret, the Navy was more than
happy with the current arrangement. Josh was also
ecstatic when Shorty presented him with a ten-dollar
bonus on his next payday, assuring Josh that it would
only get better.

Josh wrote to his parents and sent them instructions for
their voyage. They were pre-paid for the trip and all they
had to do on the day of voyage is present the slip
included in the letter. He would meet them on arrival.

As the wedding day neared, Josh and Annie finally
picked out the ring and since Shorty was going to be his
best man, he would keep it until the day Josh put it on
her finger. It was a simple gold ring with a modest
diamond that would serve as both an engagement and
wedding band. Josh would wear a simple gold band
Being of a thrifty nature, Annie loved the idea of
simplicity. What was important to her was the
symbolism of the rings showing the two of them being as
one. She did, however, nearly drive him crazy with the

plans but he knew a wedding was for the bride. So, he happily went along with all of her wishes, including the obligatory meeting with Pastor Willoughby at the Methodist Church. It could have ended badly but John handled the strict minister very well.

A tall, thin confident man with a strong voice, Pastor Willoughby grilled Josh pretty hard, asking him how often he attended church and why he was missing so much. Josh was honest, telling him of his work schedule, but also telling him of his daily prayers, his knowledge of the Holy Trinity and reciting the Apostle's Creed, the Twenty-third Psalm and the Lord's Prayer as evidence of his belief. The pastor than smiled, relented and said he hoped that both husband and wife would be in church together as often as possible.

The day before the wedding, John and Emma Eldridge arrived on the Norfolk docks and Josh met them with Shorty's new buggy. He took them to Miss Hilda's house where Annie and her grandmother met them. Lemonade and fresh baked cookies were served as Josh's parents met the wonderful lady who played such and important place in Annie's life. All were right at home together quickly, realizing their values and faith were so similar.

"Now Emma," said Hilda. "You and John will be staying with my sister, Harriet, right up the street. She is expecting you and Josh will take you there. I want you to come back in the morning for breakfast and we can talk before the big event. Josh will be there, but then he will disappear for we will be getting Annie ready and he can't see her again before the wedding. You can ride with us to the church."

Josh kissed his soon-to-be bride and carried his parents by buckboard up the street and got them settled at Miss Harriet's home. He then told them goodbye for the night and went to Shorty's house. After securing horse and buckboard, he was surprised by the number of waterfront friends assembled with Shorty to take him to dinner, or so he thought.

The place they chose was a little bawdy for its day with dancing girls like those in a wild west saloon, holding their skirts up to show a little calf and lots of cleavage as they moved sensually close to Josh and those at his table. They would smile, flash an ankle, sit in his lap and whisper in his ear, then return to the stage. It was harmless compared to the ladies of the night working in many places, but it was considered risqué and Josh felt uncomfortable. All he wanted to do was go back to Shorty's and get some sleep but, alas, it was not to be.

Suddenly a sack was placed over his head and three of the burliest men in the group gathered him up, tied his hands and legs behind his back and put him in the back of a wagon. Josh knew it was a prank, yet it was still unsettling as the horse drawn wagon moved for some twenty minutes. Finally, it pulled up on the waterfront, recognized by the sound of bells and lapping waves and

Josh was taken on board a vessel and placed in a hold with the lid closed. Then there was silence, complete silence except for the sound of footsteps above him. Someone was with him.

At what must have been sunrise as he heard a rooster crow in the distance, the hold cover was removed and he felt himself being lifted out. With the sack removed, he was surprised to find Shorty looking at him with amusement along with one of the deckhands. He was on a small cargo schooner docked not far from the Miss Margaret.

"I'm sorry, Josh," Shorty said, "but if I hadn't let them do this, they would have tried something more drastic. I'm here because I wanted to make sure you are out on time for what you need to do. Come on, we'll take you home and get you ready for breakfast with the wedding party."

Josh acted angry but then he grinned, knowing that he would have participated in such an event for someone else. All was made well when they got to Shorty's and Natasha showed him the outfit that she had for him to wear to the wedding. It was an 1860's style tuxedo, complete with top coat of blue with a silk collar, white waistcoat and gray angora trousers with the silk striping on the outside of the legs.

"I hope you approve, Josh," Natasha said. "My cousin is almost exactly your size and he only wore it once and said he'd never use it again. Go wash up, try it on with

Shorty's help and then let me look at you. I can make any change measurements and then you can leave the outfit here while you attend your wedding party breakfast. It will be ready for you when you come back."

Later, when he returned, Shorty helped him get ready and then let him look at himself in a full-length mirror. Natasha's adjustments were perfect, he looked like it was made for him. Before the three of them headed to the church, Natasha checked him out carefully and told him that Annie would be beaming when later she would be looking at him while walking up the aisle.

When it was time to go, Shorty and Natasha escorted him by buckboard up Church Street to the church. As he walked in the door, he saw Sam Jarvis, smiling at him and nodding approval as he went to the pastor's study to get final instructions. Pastor Willoughby said he could always tell a groom who really wanted to be married at that moment and Josh filled it to perfection. He told Josh to just sit down and relax a moment and Shorty would take him to his place momentarily.

Shorty soon entered the room, smiled at Josh and led him to his designated place below but near the pulpit where he would watch his bride-to-be on her way toward him, then stand beside her for the ceremony. He looked out at the gathering and was pleased to see the shipyard's purchasing officer, a Navy Commander, present in the audience as well as his civilian subordinate, Dave Watson. He felt it was quite the compliment to an ex-

Confederate soldier who only a half year earlier would have been a mortal enemy.

The organ began and he looked down the aisle and there was Annie, all beautiful in a crinoline lined white gown with tight bodice and a veil that covered all of her head but her face, held in place by a flowered head band. She took his breath away as she smiled just like Natasha predicted, returning it with a look like the cat who was about to catch the canary. Her Uncle Isaiah was giving her away and he looked at her with a smile as they made their way up the aisle.

Pastor Willoughby's words were clear and deliberate as the couple stood side by side taking their vows. The rings, fumbled for just a moment by Shorty but delivered as required, were exchanged and when Josh was told they were married and could kiss the bride, he did so with gusto. The attendees enthusiastically responded with cheers and laughter and the party moved to the social hall in the basement for a reception. Food and spiked punch were offered, the punch courtesy of Shorty and even the Pastor partook, not knowing it was spiked. As he loosened up from the spirits, however, he asked him for the recipe with laughter.

On that Sunday afternoon, November 26, 1865, Annie and Josh became Mr. and Mrs. Joshua Eldridge. Neither Josh nor Annie had any inkling of what they would do for a honeymoon, but Shorty, the waterfront boys and even a few of the shipyard crew chipped in to give them two nights at the Bayfront Hotel in Ocean View. Even in colder weather, it was a popular place with the inviting fireplaces and view of the Chesapeake Bay and panorama of the northern half of the Hampton Roads harbor. As they thanked some of those very same folks who kidnapped Josh the night before, the happy couple exited under a shower of rice and hopped in Shorty's buckboard for a ride to the railroad station. They would be riding the new train designed to shuttle city folk to the bay beach for daily or longer excursions. On arrival, Shorty gave Josh their tickets and room reservation and payment slip, and the couple boarded the new Ocean View train, travel bags and all.

Shortly before dark on a chilly but not icy night, only four days before the recently proclaimed Thanksgiving Day, they were checked into their special room with a gorgeous view of the harbor and a warm fire roaring. It was the exciting start of their new life as husband and wife.

Josh was nervous as he waited for Annie, who went to freshen up before lying with her new husband. Would he be good enough for her? Would she regret marrying him later? When she came out in a beautiful nightgown with her hair down and a dreamy look on her face, all worries were over. She came to him, kissed him softly and asked why he wasn't ready for bed. His dreams were met a thousand-fold as they melted into one another's arms and consummated their marriage. An hour later she fell asleep cradled in his arms and the couple slept soundly through the night. They didn't even hear the bellhop knock on the door, leaving behind a bottle of bubbly.

When the newlyweds awoke, both were famished for in their hurry for one another the evening before they had eaten nothing since snacking at the reception. Josh put on his robe, went to the door and found the bottle of bubbly and an envelope which listed the times of service in the dining room which was already open. They cleaned up, put on fresh clothes and went for breakfast, served on an enclosed porch with view of the ocean. Looking out the window it was dark and dreary and very windy.

Their waiter in a white top coat approached with hot coffee and said, "Sorry for the bad weather for your honeymoon but a nor'easter started building late last night and is passing by slowly not far out to sea. The water is pretty high but by afternoon it should start clearing and you might enjoy a walk then as long as you wrap up. The hotel has some slickers if you'd like. As long as the tide isn't too high, a rough sea is beautiful."

After breakfast they walked onto the porch overlooking the bay and saw that the water was within thirty feet of the steps and the waves looked more like the ocean, rather than the bay. They could see in the sky, however, a few breaks in the overcast and decided they would walk later. They went back to their room, closed themselves off for the rest of the morning and experienced the bliss of married love again. They then dozed off and awoke in about an hour. Josh kissed his wife, told her how special she was and got up and looked out the window. It was approaching early afternoon and more signs of the storm breaking up were showing and the tide had dropped considerably lower. Shortly thereafter as they headed out for the beach, a uniformed staff member told them when they returned the bubbly would be in a bucket with ice.

The beach was beautiful in the now partly sunny mid-afternoon and they walked west toward the tip of Willoughby Spit. From there they looked across the Hampton Roads at Fortress Monroe and Fort Wool, two posts that were designed largely by Robert E. Lee back in his days as a Union Army Engineer. The water was calming and a number of large sailing vessels were returning to port after going out to sea to ride out the storm. Josh momentarily thought of the Miss Margaret and hoped that she had not suffered damage from the waves on the pier.

That night they enjoyed a romantic candlelight dinner to music by a local musical quartet, with dancing later. Part of the wall separating the dance floor from the porch area could be opened and the cool air filtering from the enclosed porch felt good after working up body heat whirling around the dance floor. Josh loved holding Annie close and feeling every move of her body as they danced the night away. He was so glad that she would be with him for the rest of his life.

After breakfast the next morning and a leisurely last walk on the beach, they returned to their hotel. They got their things in order and told a bell hop they were ready to depart. It was fun but they just wanted to get on with the rest of their lives. The hotel coach took them to the train and they were back in downtown Norfolk in just under two hours and hired a driver to take them back to Annie's grandmother's house. Miss Hilda was eagerly awaiting the news of their short but very special honeymoon. Josh fell asleep in the big easy chair while the two ladies talked and Miss Hilda laughed, figuring out what Josh's sleep told her about the honeymoon. For a split second, she thought of her life back in those days and she was glad that Annie made him so happy. She knew that they were a match made in heaven and that Josh would take good care of her special granddaughter.

The next morning, a Wednesday, Josh was off to the tugboat early in the morning and Annie was back at work in the coffee shop. It would be different now, however, since they would be looking forward to coming back to one another at the end of the day or one of Josh's trips and life was truly enriched with God's blessing. Unfortunately, Josh's day would be anything but routine, for instead of heading out on another round trip to Elizabeth City and the Albemarle, they were instead facing repair issues from the damage to the port side of the vessel pounding against the dock. The rising of the tide had loosened the lines and allowed enough slack to allow for the beating. Fortunately, the damage was above the water line and they could do it with self-help. Josh made the run to the marine self-help store with measurements and was back in two hours and they started repairs. As darkness arrived, they completed the task at hand and she was now seaworthy, a little unsightly until painted, but workable until their next free day.

"You know, Josh," Shorty said, "this means we'll be doing a couple of back to back trips. Are you up to it?"

"As long as the money is good," Shorty, "no problem. I'll break it to Annie when I get home but she'll stay busy. Besides, she hasn't had the time to learn any bad habits I might have."

They laughed and headed their separate ways, knowing it would be a short night and a Thanksgiving Day and then it would be a true time test of the couple's love for each other. Josh and Shorty would be working heavy duty on the waterways right through Christmas. Josh truly loved the work and the water, but he loved Annie with all his heart as well. He would just have to figure out a way to balance his time for both.

Over the next several weeks it was almost non-stop work, but they couldn't complain. Josh learned the meaning of "absence makes they heart grow fonder" and his step was lively when he finally got home. Then, following one two-day break for Christmas, work requirements grew even more demanding over the next six months. For the first half of 1866, Josh only had about one week of free time and he knew that was not a good omen for his family life and it troubled him.

The silver lining in his demanding work schedule was that with the extended hours and repeated bonuses as the money rolled in, he knew the money he sent to his parents and gave to Annie meant they could have things that they otherwise couldn't afford. He also knew, however, that with both his parents and Annie being frugal, most of it would be placed in savings. It was good for financial security but not conducive to happy family life.

Josh was fearful of what his current situation would do to his marriage, but he had no idea of the turn events that was about to come. He would soon find out.

ELEVEN

The mid-fall of 1866 was a strange one. The weather was unseasonably wet and cold and sickness was on the rise. Influenza was always dangerous with no relief in those days. The shortages faced by many due to strict rationing and other controls meant that diets for many were deficient. Flu congestion often led to pneumonia which was a big killer of the times.

By mid-October, pneumonia was on the rise in both Norfolk and Currituck, but Norfolk felt it worse due to close proximity of citizens to one another. Caretaker government officials made it worse by prioritizing the limited fuel supply for heating homes to their cronies. Living in a large family home like Miss Hilda's without adequate heat to even break the chill was a major concern. Josh was fine but both Miss Hilda and Annie came down with pneumonia and needed care, but Josh couldn't stay away from work without losing his job. He and Shorty were needed and both would end up penniless if they couldn't report as needed.

Natasha came to the rescue, she closed up her home when the men were gone and went to care for Josh's Norfolk family. Both women came to the brink of death but somehow Annie pulled through. She would need weeks for recovery but being younger and stronger made the difference. Miss Hilda died after a hard struggle and was laid to rest in the family vault next to her departed husband in Cedar Grove Cemetery.

Josh was able to attend the funeral, but not Annie, ordered by the doctor to stay home as it was a cold November day with sleet falling. Natasha stayed with her and when he came back, he found Annie crying. She did, however, force a smile that brought a light to his eyes.

"I don't know what I'd do without you, Josh and thanks for being there for me. I was thinking we should move out but she left this place to me, free and clear. Her sister, Aunt Harriet, said she wanted to move to South Carolina where their younger sister asked her to come live. She thinks it might be warmer there."

Natasha told Josh that Annie needed her rest, so he went to Shorty's where he would stay until Natasha came home. He appreciated her stepping in but, at the same time, he hated not being the one to care for his bride. He was right there in Norfolk and yet he might as well be a million miles away, so the only thing to do was throw himself back in his work. He was thankful that at least he had the resources to keep his family together when so many others were less fortunate.

On the next trip south, Shorty stopped in Currituck Court House for the night so Josh could see his folks. Sam was now part of the crew and he volunteered to watch the tug so that Shorty could join Josh for the walk up what is now NC 168. It was cold, but not icy and they were glad to warm themselves by the hearth when they arrived at the Eldridge house.

Emma Eldridge welcomed them, remembering Shorty from the wedding and she thanked him for the opportunity he gave Josh. The older skipper just grinned and said that Josh made his own opportunity, that he was a go-getter who made his life easier. Sensing the proper moment, Josh beamed as he showed his mom his Captain's license. He was now afforded full authority to run a tug with proper crew in the event that Shorty couldn't made a trip.

"How's Annie," his ma asked. "She is such a lovely girl and her grandmother was so gracious to us. Your wedding was wonderful."

"Annie's sick, Ma," he said. "She came down with pneumonia and it was touch and go for some time but now she's starting to recover. Shorty's wife is caring for her since we can't stop work and I stay at Shorty's house when we're in Norfolk to keep the house quiet.

"Miss Hilda also caught it but didn't make it. We buried her just a few days ago and it was sad. The lack of heating coal is what I blame much of it on and that's on the Yankees. I know many of them are nice and I'm over the war but they have people who are getting rich off of our people and it's not right."

Emma Eldridge hugged her son tight and told him to put things in God's hands just as Josh's father, John walked in, rubbing his hands together. She told them to sit at the table by the hearth and she would bring them hot coffee. The aroma was present throughout as it was still perking. John Eldridge, on hearing Josh's bad news, expressed his sorrow and told Josh to take care of his bride who he quickly had grown very fond of. He then turned to Josh's boss and spoke.

"Captain," John said, "Glad you could drop by with Josh. We enjoyed speaking with you at the wedding and appreciate your transportation to get Emma and me around while there. It was a wonderful event.

"And I want to show both of you something I'm doing. I've given up commercial fishing, now just fishing for subsistence meals, for the arthritis flairs up and I just can't do it anymore. I have, however, found a great boat building niche that is in big demand. Dories are wanted by everyone, yet there aren't enough builders. While they've been around these parts for thirty years, they are just now growing in popularity and I developed a design, a modification of a style in New England that is easy to follow. You are familiar with the craft, I hope."

Shorty nodded yes and he and John carried on quite a lively conversation while Josh went into the kitchen with his ma and asked her how things were. He wanted to know if he provided her enough money to make ends meet.

"Heavens, yes, Josh," she said. "We were able to get Dad a small start from your generosity and now his business is taking off. He has a young boy, one of the Gallop boys from down the road, to help when needed and he's doing well. He couldn't have made the change in his life without your help. And now when he wants to fish, Billy Gallop goes with him, but it's good to have him right here in his woodshop working instead of out in the sound alone which worried me so."

Josh apologized for not being back since the wedding due to work and Annie's illness. He assured his ma she was okay but they truly missed her grandmother.

She wisely said, "Remember what I taught you, Son. Life can turn quickly and you must be ready for it. Any of us can die at any moment and God wants us ready."

He agreed but felt a bit guilty for not being in church more frequently. He knew he needed it to boost his spirits and keep them high always. He must work on that.

Now warmed, they took a walk out to the shop and Josh was amazed at what his dad was accomplishing. He had one dory just completed, another well underway and enough material for several more. It looked like he found his calling and it comforted the younger man, knowing that his folks were now more secure. He knew he would always try and look after them and Annie concurred. Josh also learned that his father was now designing a modified dory that would result in the sail option, with an easily added mast, specially designed sail with an upward sloping boom for ease of coming about, a rudder with more exacting response to the touch and a retractable centerboard which would allow for boat use in both deep and shallow water. The removable centerboard would, of course, allow for control of slippage underway when inserted while removal would allow very shallow operation of the craft.

Josh was amazed at the sailing option, saying, "Wow. Dad, where did you get the idea for the modifications. A sailing dory would allow for so much variation in use."

"Honestly, Josh," replied his father. "A potential customer, a wealthy planter from Edenton, James Hewes, contacted me wanting to know if I could build one. He said he knew who you were. He referred me to a Boston boat builder who graciously provided the information. He had so much business in Boston that he was happy to give it to me, provided I told no one else, so mum is the word. I did make a few modifications but the plan is largely the same."

Josh was glad to know that his dad had James Hewes as a customer. That could only lead to building business in the future.

They looked the plan over at his small study desk in the corner, then returned to the boat under construction. Josh was so pleased with his father's good fortune and his much more positive outlook and couldn't wait to get his hands on one of those boats in the future. Shorty was also impressed, saying that he saw a new customer in the offing for delivery options as well as for supplies. He would soon find out how correct his assumption was.

Within a few months, Father John would soon need the Miss Margaret to deliver supplies as well as carry off boats. It meant an extra trip for Josh and Shorty between Currituck and the Albemarle at times when boats were ready for delivery, but it was profitable. The Navy contract gave them freedom to do what they wanted as long as the shipbuilding lumber deliveries were on time. John's boats were becoming so popular that he had a back order waiting list for two to four boats routinely. He started planning for a larger shop and a few additional workers.

By the end of June 1867, Shorty had some unexpected good news. It would enhance their profits and give Josh an even greater opportunity. After completing another successful trip, Shorty asked Josh to join him at Waterman's Pub before heading home. With Annie now back in full swing, he wanted to be home with her as often as possible. He knew, however, that when Shorty was this excited, he must pay attention. So, they sat down at a reasonably private table in the waterfront watering hole and talked.

Shorty opened the conversation by saying, "Josh, we have done so well in the last year that I am only about two payments away from owning the Miss Margaret free and clear. And I think that the shipbuilding business will be slowing down as the demand for Navy ships decreases. That means our new commercial customers will likely be the heart of our business in the future and I owe most of the credit to you for finding it. For your hard work, you deserve a special reward and I think it's only appropriate that I give you part-ownership in our assets. Right now, it is set up with me owning sixty percent and Natasha forty and in the event that I died, my shares would go to her. Do you follow me so far?"

Josh just nodded yes and Shorty continued.

"I've talked to Natasha and she has agreed with what I want to do, so here it is. I am proposing to lower my ownership to fifty percent and split the other half equally between the two of you. She knows that if something were to happen to me, she needs someone who could keep the business alive, so I am also proposing that if something should happen to me, my fifty percent would go fifty-fifty to each of you. That would make you co-owners, protecting her for her future financial needs while giving you all the incentive in the world to keep things profitable. Now I have to warn you, as a partial owner, you always have the possibility of failure and losing your time and effort. The sky is the limit on the up side, however, and with your drive and ambition I can't imagine you failing at anything. If you survived Point Lookout you can survive anything. If you agree, I have an appointment with an attorney tomorrow to draw up the papers and when you sign off on the document it is done. What do you say, Josh?"

Josh was speechless for a moment, but quickly recovered and with a wide smile said, "Where do I sign, partner? Yes, I want to be part of the team, it's beyond my wildest dreams at this point in my life."

They shook hands, headed their separate ways and Josh was whistling all the way home. They wouldn't be working the next day, so Josh looked forward to spending the day with Annie, who was still not back at work. She was well now but took all that time to fully recover and it was something she needed. The next day, the two who were still only in their first year of marriage, didn't venture outside all day. They were overcome with their love for one another and the joy that had suddenly been added to their lives. It was a wonderful intimate day together and as they drank tea sitting up in bed that evening, they knew their love was forever.

The next day Shorty and Josh sailed over to the shipyard to review their contract and while not having an order ready yet for delivery, they were asked to handle a shipment to Newport News Point and Fortress Monroe. The tug that normally handled that contract was down for major engine failure and the deliveries were critical. There was no way the Navy wanted to miss an Army delivery and have to deal with the fallout.

Before departing to load and deliver the goods, however, Shorty told them of his new business arrangement and they talked about terms of any new contract, since the current one would end at the end of the year. They were assured everything was okay but the Navy didn't want to commit to anything yet and both Shorty and Josh left with a strange feeling concerning about what they had been told.

Shorty didn't look happy as he said, "You know what, Josh? I think they just told us there will be no follow-on contract without saying so. What do you think?"

Josh nodded in agreement, adding, "I think you are right but look at it another way, Skipper. It means we're free, free to handle the business we want and I guarantee you that all of our newfound customers in Currituck and the Albemarle will stay with us. We just have to let them know on our next trip what the future might bring. They like our service and trust us. Also, a local native commercial ship chandler is coming back to Norfolk, a man who went north during the war since he had experience in Baltimore. He can handle the follow-on shipments and we'll just have to find a commercial dock in Norfolk to berth the tug when in Norfolk. There is, however, an option that would only be for overnight stopovers. Why not move the operation to Currituck? You said you wanted to get out of the city. You and Natasha should think about it."

Shorty rubbed his chin and said, "I'll do just that. It is actually a fairly intriguing thought. All I would need is about ten acres and close proximity to the water, which Currituck easily provides."

Perhaps he is serious, thought Josh as he enjoyed the change of pace of a trip across Hampton Roads. He thought back to the first time he saw it and liked the hustle and bustle of the harbor which was now really getting back in the commercial swing of things. As the sun finally broke through the overcast, the sunlight signaled a bright future as they docked in Newport News and the stevedore crew came to unload under Josh's watchful eye. One man in the crew stood out and when they finished, he pulled him aside.

"You look familiar but I can't be sure," Josh said. "Were you one of the prisoners from Petersburg?"

He looked at Josh and said, "Yes, I was in that Maryland hell hole and I remember you there. I am George Wilson from James City County. I work here because my wife is from Newport News. Glad to see you are doing so well for I know you, like me, will never forget that place."

Josh knew the work foreman was watching so he just told him good luck and they shook hands. He was glad to see that another man survived the ordeal and finding his way home to live another day.

Once the unloading was done, they took on some shipments for Old Point Comfort and headed east. Josh was glad to see the Army camp had been reduced in size. All Southerners looked forward to the day when the uniformed Union troops were sent back home. It was like a festering wound that would never close as long as they were there.

With the trip over after delivery at Old Point, they headed back to Norfolk and the Elizabeth River. Before heading back to the shipyard with the deliverables picked up, Shorty decided to stop at the commercial docks and put out feelers about dockage. He found out it was available, the price was reasonable and if he wanted it, to let them know. That took care of things for now but in the back of his mind he was thinking about Josh's comments about Carolina. He would move in a heartbeat but he wasn't so sure about Natasha. He would have to gradually work on it which, thankfully, he had plenty of time to ponder.

On their next trip south, they visited all of their existing customer stops combining marketing for the future with handling deliveries and pick-ups. Every existing customer said they'd rather deal with them directly instead of the Union Navy, plus they knew there was more business available. On a hunch they also made a stop at Roanoke Island and found that there was potential there, plus even at Nags Head and Kitty Hawk. The Atlantic beaches had already attracted a number of wealthy planters who built cottages on the ocean and on the sound. The area was definitely starting to receive some attention. Josh told Shorty that growth was inevitable at some point and it would be smart to get established as a reliable goods transporter ahead of the growth.

On the way north, they stopped at Currituck Courthouse for a visit with Josh's family. The subject of Shorty finding property for a home was broached and John Eldridge said there was property close to the Court House with direct waterfront access.

"I know the landowner, Captain," John offered, "and if you wanted him to put a dock up fit for your tug and barge, he would surely do it for you with a lease to own option. And the land adjacent is quite high by Currituck standards so you likely wouldn't have any significant flooding problems unless it was the Big One, which would flood all of them."

Josh just added that they could build it on stilts the Outer Banks way, placed deeper in the ground with exterior heavy shingles with an extra nail in each. Shorty was smiling and Josh could see he had things rolling around in his head, taking it all in. He was definitely interested.

When they returned to Norfolk, Shorty asked Josh if he would run the next two weeks without him. He had spent very little time with Natasha since Annie fell ill and he wanted to cater to her for a while. Josh was agreeable, grateful for the trust of his new partner. He also knew that Shorty wanted to broach the subject of moving with Natasha and he wanted to do it cautiously. While Josh was handling business, Shorty was catering to his wife's every wish. They took long walks, visited cafes and Annie's coffee house on numerous occasions and were inseparable.

One afternoon over tea, Natasha looked her husband directly in the eye and asked pointedly, "Why are you coddling me so, Shorty? Don't get me wrong, I love what we're doing and we're spending more time together these weeks than we've likely had together in years. You want something, I know it and would you please tell me honestly what is on your mind. You know I love you and want you to be happy."

Shorty knew it was time to come clean so he just blurted out, "I want to move to North Carolina. I want to find some land on the water where we can operate our business from our own dock."

Natasha just looked at him in silence for a moment, then responded, "I'm not opposed to that. Tell me what's on your mind."

Shorty explained what he and Josh talked about and the issues they potentially faced at the shipyard. Natasha listened closely and merely responded that she liked it and there was work to do. She said they could sell the house and with Norfolk growing it would be a money-maker. She also offered that she knew Annie would gladly sell her Norfolk home or even rent it out for top dollar if necessary. She wanted to be away from the city and near Josh and his folks since they were already so close.

When Shorty went back to work, he and Josh discussed the best ways to accomplish the move and in late September they again approached the shipyard management about the contract. There was still no answer, so they decided that by the November fifteenth deadline they would give their notice of ending service on the last day of the year. If the shipyard wanted to end the relationship, they would still have to pay for the unexpired term, which meant the average monthly earnings for the final six weeks.

On a return trip to Norfolk with their new commercial market growing, including two customers in Manteo, they laid over for a day at Currituck and John Eldridge accompanied Shorty to the properties available adjacent to the water. One was a large vacant lot and there were two other existing homes only a short way beyond, but easy walking distance to the courthouse. Shorty was going to look at both but when he set his eyes on the first, he knew he would look no further. It was well cared for and with the perfect spot on the water for a suitable dock. It was an indented sound front lot where a partial deep-water canal was protected from the open sound, almost like a small cove. There was an old rotting dock present which could be torn down and replaced, the perfect solution.

He made the landowner, Mr. Creef, an offer contingent on the sale of his Norfolk home and it was accepted and a deposit to seal the deal was made. The arrangements for the dock were also included and things were set.

A week later, Shorty walked into his home and Natasha greeted him with a huge smile and warm hug. She told him they had a buyer, a former Union Army finance officer who was coming to Norfolk to manage a downtown bank. Sadly, the rising Reconstruction-driven entry of carpetbaggers bankrupted an old Southern bank, but the event was a godsend for the Weston's plan to relocate the entire business. It was like a sign that Josh's plan was coming alive sooner rather than later. God had truly blessed them all and the icing on the cake was that payment would be made in cash. The funds were sufficient to pay for the new house, property and dock free and clear and still leave them with some working capital. It was one of the advantages of moving to rural land in a time before its value went through the roof.

Shorty strapped a small leather satchel to his thigh under his trousers for the trip south. Meeting Mr. Creef, the landowner and his wife with Josh as his witness, he reviewed and signed the legal documents and received a bill of sale and the deeded note. Payment was made in full and on the way to the dock they stopped at the court house and registered the sale. On the arrival of the Miss Margaret in Elizabeth City, Shorty went to the bank, deposited the remainder of his money and left a happy man.

Back in Norfolk, a similar transaction took place when the men returned from Carolina. Shorty and Natasha paid the banker's real estate agent the rent they owed for the time spent in the house after closing. They moved in with Annie until things were in place for their move. Annie's house was attracting potential buyers and she and Josh knew they wouldn't be far behind. All was happening much faster than they ever dreamed.

As if the two families had a guardian angel, a wonderful offer was made on Annie's inherited home in mid-November and the closing was scheduled within the week. An industrialist from Boston who saw the advantages of Norfolk for future development agreed to a high-end price and the plan was complete. They used the tug to move their belongings and went to live with Josh's parents until other arrangements could be made. Josh and Shorty stayed at the seaman's boarding house in Norfolk as needed and when November 15, 1867 arrived with no word from the Naval Shipyard, they made their move. Walking into the office of their friend, David Watson, the shipping manager for the shipyard, they gave formal notice of their plans to tender their option to end the agreement as established at the end of the calendar year. It was actually a good meeting and they learned that Watson had nothing to do with what was going on, but he was sworn to secrecy. He decided instead to let them know since they provided such quality service.

On their way out of the office, Watson said, "I hope you two wonderful men know it wasn't my idea. The shipyard commander made the decision, citing his desire to bring a crony from New York down to operate the business you have built so well. I hope you fellows keep the business you have developed and I will do nothing to help them do anything to slow you down. You deserve the best and I'll make sure you are fully paid for the final six weeks. They don't want you here. I wish you well. If

I can do anything personally to be of service, please don't hesitate to let me know. I'm going to miss you fellows because I know no one else will give us such great service."

Shorty stopped, started to shake hands with his friend and then hugged him instead, saying, "I appreciate your candor, Dave and we knew it wasn't you. This much I'll tell you, though, but it's only for you. You can bet on this, we will retain all the business we have built and the shipyard will soon realize the mistake that your boss has made. We both wish you well and we will be fine."

Josh and Shorty never looked back and they knew they had made the right decision. A brighter future was unfolding before their very eyes.

TWELVE

While Josh and Annie were figuring out their long-term
housing arrangements, they packed up their belongings
and moved in with his parents. Father John had a large
storage building on the property and Josh and Sam
stowed most things away. Josh knew the living
arrangements were temporary and was already looking
for property in the area. He was ready to act quickly
once he was sure the Norfolk house was sold. His father
insisted he not panic, that giving that lovely old house
away would be a silly thing to do and both Annie and he
agreed.

While Josh was off working, Annie pitched right in and
made life easy for mother-in-law Emma. She knew that
Emma rarely got a break and she wanted her to have
some time for herself and perhaps have some fun with
John. His business was going well and he had perfected
the sail opt ion for the dory. Emma even took an
afternoon sail with him on an unseasonably warm day.
When she was free, Annie spent time with Natasha who
was turning their house into a wonderful home.

Meanwhile, Josh and Shorty were busy. They delivered
two dories for John, then took up new orders before
running to Norfolk with shipments ready to go. The new
arrangement with the ship chandler was working well
and Josh and his business acumen allowed them to take
orders both for shipment and deliveries through the

chandler. He could handle business from Boston, New York, Philadelphia and Baltimore to the north, plus Charleston and Savannah, as well as locally throughout Hampton Roads.

On a visit to Edenton, Josh ran into James Hewes, the Edenton planter he previously met on the schooner run from Currituck to Norfolk the prior year. He inquired about his dory, aware that it was a slow process but just wanted a status.

"Dad's got it on order, Mr. Hewes, and it should be the next one starting production. Dad takes his time to make them perfect. I hope you understand," Josh replied. "He's looking to add a few artisans to his staff to speed things up but, at the same time, he wants to insure the quality is up to his standard. There will be no shortcuts and it is clearly first come, first served."

Mr. Hewes nodded in agreement, saying, "I don't mind waiting, I am told the boats are that good, so just keep me posted. I want to use them for some hunting trips and such for business acquaintances. In good weather it might even be fun to sail to Nags Head on one. They are fun to operate."

John Eldridge now had a staff of four plus a part-time bookkeeper and was building a large extension of his design room to handle the volume. He was fortunate to find a number of local sailors who were also quality carpenters and they jumped at the opportunity to help build boats, especially in the cold winter. The work of a waterman in the winter was never fun and it was also quite dangerous. One slip in the water and you might not make it back out.

On a trip in late March of 1868, Josh got word that the Navy had called on several of the Miss Margaret's customers in Coinjock. Edward Bell, a local feed store operator told him when he made a delivery.

"Josh, I don't want to concern you," Bell opened, "but a civilian working for the Navy Department came by the other day and wanted to know why I wasn't placing orders through the shipyard. I told him I found another transit service and he wanted to know who. I told him it was none of this business and he left. Since then I've heard that a few businesses around the Albemarle had the same visitor. I guess he's going to all of your accounts and trying to claim they have a binding order. They tried that on me and I just told him that my orders were explicitly non-committal other than the single order in question. He's probably trying to scare people, using the Navy as his weapon. Just be careful, Josh, I thought you ought to know."

Josh appreciated the information and would do a little searching on his own. Shorty said their commitment was over with the Navy and there was no special requirement in the contract other than fulfilling its length of term, which they did. Checking around, they found out the man was named Chowning, he was a civilian working under contract to the Navy, had been an enlisted Union soldier during the war and was in marketing and sales. Most of his earnings were a commission from initial and continuing sales from existing sales, explaining his forcefulness. He obviously had learned of Josh's customer list and was following around behind them trying to cajole the customers with a mild insinuation of a threat. Shorty told Josh to let him handle the Chowning matter and Josh left it with him. He had concern about what Shorty might do but he decided it was better to let the older man take whatever action he thought appropriate.

By mid-April, the closing on the Norfolk house was done, money awaited Annie at the Norfolk bank and she and Josh made a quick trip to receive the funds. They would be deposited in Elizabeth City on the next tugboat run up the Albemarle.

It was at this time that Josh also learned that Annie was two months pregnant. He was excited and now he knew making housing arrangements was of paramount importance. They needed their own place. He didn't want to be an imposition to his parents and he knew they would never say so. He chuckled to himself as he remembered those cold dark nights of the winter now ended and it made sense that she was in a family way.

He enveloped Annie in his arms, saying, "Well, I'd better get a move on about finding a home or we'll be run off from lack of sleep by Mom and Dad."

Annie laughed, knowing full well that Emma was already ecstatic knowing that her son would be a father and she and John would be grandparents. She had told Emma to keep the secret, but she wanted her to understand why she had been a little under the weather at times. So, they shared the news over dinner with Josh's parents and Emma winked at Annie, already aware but acting as if she just got the word. Josh and his dad really celebrated the joys of knowing they would be a father and grandfather.

On one of their rare days off, Shorty invited Josh to come down to his house for the mid-day meal. He wanted to talk with him and he had some good news. Josh arrived on a beautiful spring day in early April and he met Shorty who was sitting on the porch with Natasha. Looking out from the porch, the sound and the boat dock were readily visible and things were turning green and fresh. It was truly a beautiful setting.

"Josh, I have good news and also a good idea. Actually, the idea came from Natasha and that's why she is waiting here for you. By the way, congratulations, for Natasha told me you are going to be a father. It will change your life but I think you'll make a great one."

He looked shocked and said, "She already knows, too, Shorty? I just wonder why I am always the last to know anything."

"Because you are the father and she wanted to make sure before she told you; it's supposed to be that way,"

Natasha interrupted with a laugh. "Now I want you to take a walk with Shorty and he wants to fill you in on something. Lunch will be ready when you return."

As she got up and excused herself and walked back into the house, Shorty led the way down the steps and then turned south on the dirt road.

"Josh, there's no way that you can buy property and build a house in time for the baby," he began, "and Natasha's idea is a great one. I know you don't know but almost a stone's throw down this road beyond this thin stand of pines is a house quite similar to mine. It's in good shape, is owned by the same man who I bought from and it's directly back from the sound with an existing useable dock. I want you to look at it for it would be ideal. Annie and Natasha can be neighbors and not feel lonely when we are gone and you are close enough, but not to close, to your ma and dad when you want to visit them or have them visit you."

As they passed the thin stand of trees, there to the right was the house and the property owner was sitting on the porch waiting. It was Mr. Creef, the man Josh met when he witnessed Shorty's property closing.

Shorty said, "This is the other house that Mr. Creef owns and now that your home sale in Norfolk is nearly done, I think you should look at it. I'll sit on the porch and enjoy the fresh air while he shows you about. Take a look at it and see what you think, but I'll now be quiet and let you ponder for yourself."

Josh and Creef shook hands, remembering one another and the landowner went inside while Shorty made himself at home on the porch. The site was similar to his own property and he was sure that John would fall in love with it. It was owned by another brother of the former owner of Shorty's house, both now dead. Creef was next of kin to both, inherited both properties. He lived just down the road himself in another house and all had originally been on one large property plat. Since the buyer would be his neighbors, he wanted decent and hard-working folk owning them. He knew that Shorty and Josh filled that bill and he was willing to make a good deal. That would leave only one other nice additional family home open and he would look for a similar additional purchaser.

Shorty could hear the two men laughing as they walked about the house. He took that as a good sign they would live close together, yet with sufficient privacy, where they would dock right at home.

When the two men emerged from the house, Josh invited Shorty to join them on the walk down to the dock. It was located in a cut in the shoreline that acted like a small protective cove, blocking heavy wave action which could come in a nor'easter. The dock was sound, needing only minimal repairs. Then Josh asked Shorty to take a walkthrough with him while their host waited outside.

When finished, he looked at Shorty and said, "What do you think, Skipper, it looks good to me. Of course, I want to bring Annie down to look at it and check the underpinnings carefully but it looks like it was well cared for."

"I think you are right and I would suggest you try and do it tomorrow," was Shorty's response. "We can hold off a trip for another day and I think you should bring your dad, too. Remember, he's a good carpenter and might think of things to check you'd never consider."

The following day, the inspection of the house was done and father John found a few minor issues that needed to be taken care of but, all in all, it was a great buy. Annie made a complete walkthrough and fell in love with the house, too. Mr. Creef offered a good deal and, with everyone happy, an agreement was reached. Josh quickly made arrangements to go to Elizabeth City, draw out the funds and on May 16, 1868, he and Annie had their new home. Josh and Annie moved in the next day. As spring turned into early summer, Josh and Annie were all set to welcome their baby to a new home.

Summer went by fast, Josh and Shorty were swamped with work, Annie was busy getting the new house in order and planning for her baby with the help of Natasha. John Eldridge was busy making boats. The sail option was a big hit and he had all the business he could handle and then some.

Josh and Shorty also made a big business decision; it was time to consider another boat. They were looking at a schooner for passengers and small shipments. It needed to be big enough for larger hunting and fishing parties who were learning of the rich wildlife and the high volume of fish available in the local waters. They were considering a four- year- old schooner for the following spring which could carry people and goods from Elizabeth City to Nags Head. The housing market for summer places with cool ocean breezes was expanding, so a mixture of sportsmen and summer tourists would need support.

By October, life was settled and they were appreciative. To show their gratefulness to God for their good fortune, on the upcoming Thanksgiving Day they sponsored a community celebration of the holiday at the court house. Two large tents were put in place with a turkey feast and a short thanksgiving service planned by Mr. Whitehurst, the Methodist minister from Moyock who was glad to attend. The party was complete with a quartet and the community responded by bringing covered dishes. There was enough food to go with the turkeys provided by the fortunate seafaring duo to feed an Army. But as the party broke up and the two couples told each other goodnight before walking to their respective homes, lightning was about to strike.

Simultaneously, as the two couples approached the walkway to their front doors, Pinkerton's agents approached out of the dark wearing their distinctive top hats and topcoats emblazoned with badges, telling both men they were under arrest. The charge: suspected foul play in the case of the missing Josiah Chowning, shipyard marketing representative.

A coach with barred windows arrived and both men were taken into custody and carried to Elizabeth City, leaving Annie and Natasha alone and in the dark. The two women ran toward each other and the tears flowed as the carriage disappeared down the road. They went to Natasha's kitchen, trying to figure out what to do next. They were both afraid of what was going to happen and they were concerned about what tomorrow might bring, so they stayed together that night to comfort each other and both prayed ardently for a better day tomorrow.

Both women knew that something was seriously wrong and they also knew that their husbands could not be involved, but tired after what had been a long but enjoyable day, they couldn't think. They decided that at first light they would seek John Eldridge's help for they both respected and trusted him and they knew he would know the right course to take. In the intervening hours, no sleep would come.

THIRTEEN

Shortly after dawn, Annie and Natasha called on John and Emma Eldridge for help. They gave them a quick rundown of what happened and John calmly listened, then rubbed his chin before speaking. First, he patted Emma's hand. She lost her composure and sat there sobbing deeply, much out of character but understandable. After what her boy previously went through, this was inconceivable to her.

"Ladies," John began, "We need to go see Sam Pratt, a lawyer in Elizabeth City who can help us. I met him years ago and he also helped me on a property issue once and he was very helpful in straightening out a misunderstanding. Let me go by myself on this first visit, but be ready to go with me again within the next day or two. He can get me into the jail where I'm sure they are holding Josh and the Captain, but I know they won't let you in until this gets sorted out. Fill me in on the details as exacting as you can be and I'll be off right away."

The ladies gave him the details on what transpired and he was quickly off. Annie and Natasha would stay with Emma and console her and to make matters worse, Annie went into labor. She was already late and Ma Eldridge, a woman who had birthed children before in emergencies, took charge. There was no time to get the doctor as the labor advanced rapidly and in just two hours Annie delivered a bouncing baby boy. Both mother and child were doing well. He was a big one but when the doctor arrived later, he said he misjudged her state of pregnancy earlier. He examined mother and son and confirmed that all was well, then advised he would make a follow-up visit in a few days.

While a tired but happy Annie, Emma and Natasha were all joyous over the new baby, they just wished the circumstances were better. They were very sad Josh missed the occasion. The ladies also knew that life didn't necessarily work the way you want it. The baby would, however, help keep their minds off of their other troubles and they were thankful for that. They were resolved to stay together until news was received from Elizabeth City.

Meanwhile, John's buckboard ride to Elizabeth City was just over fifteen miles and he went a bit faster than he normally would. Luckily, it was a beautiful day and he knew on this Friday after the holiday, Sam Pratt would be in his office finishing things early so he could hunt over the weekend. He was a duck hunter supreme and he and John met about twenty years earlier when John served as his hunting guide in Currituck.

Arriving in the city, John walked into Attorney Pratt's home office which was as quiet as a church mouse and called out Sam's name. He heard a response from upstairs telling him to come on up. Sam had converted the first floor of his in-town home into his law office and he and his wife, Sally lived upstairs.

As John reached the top of the stairs, Sam bellowed, "Well, if it isn't John Eldridge. What in the world are you doing here on a Friday after Thanksgiving? I know it is important if you came all this way"

As Sally motioned to the big table and brought in her coffee service, John filled Sam in on the details. He said he had no idea why his son and Weston were picked up but he was concerned.

Well, you should be, John, "Sam responded, "because they don't use the Pinkerton guys for the small stuff and those guys are rough. The first thing we have to do is go to the jail to see if they are there or have been taken somewhere else. If that fails, we can go to the federal marshal's office which is here to make sure we Southern fellows follow the rules to a finite degree. Finish your coffee while I get my satchel and we'll be off."

On the way to the jail John filled Sam in on what Josh was doing with his life and how he couldn't believe he would be a lawbreaker. He also told him about Weston and Sam had questions. He wanted to know if the Captain had a past or was prone to violence.

"No, Sam, not that I could say," John said, "He's been very good to my boy and has a lovely wife and works hard. I like him and can't believe he would harm anyone other than in self-defense."

"Well, first things first, John," he began. "We want to first make sure Josh hasn't been beaten and I'll ask to talk with him as his lawyer. Then we'll check on his arrest warrant."

As they entered the jail, John recognized the sergeant at the desk. He told them why they were there and was told that yes, he and another man had been brought in the night before. He was allowed to see no one right now without a judge's order. Sam then stepped into the conversation and said they would be back with one, but that it would be much easier on the officer if he let him in now.

The sergeant looked at John, then back at Sam, looked around to make sure no one could hear him and then said softly, "Okay, Mr. Pratt, I know who you are and I'm not a big fan of the Pinkertons so I'll give you ten minutes. But you have to go in without John, I'll lose my job if I let him in."

Sam settled John and followed the sergeant through the secured doorway to Josh's cell. He was relieved to find young man looking grave but with no bruises or signs of a beating.

Sam introduced himself saying, "Son, my name is Sam Pratt and I'm an attorney who has been retained by your father to handle your case. Can you take me from start to finish on what happened to get you here? Try to be as detailed as possible.

Josh thanked him for coming and took him through the events of the prior night. He filled him in on his business and relationship with his partner and about the incident months ago with Chowning and the interface he had with his partner, Shorty Weston, regarding that matter.

"I don't believe the Skipper has done anything wrong," Josh exclaimed, "and we don't know what if anything happened to Chowning, just that he disappeared. And the goons separated us as soon as we got into the wagon so I don't know what they've done with him."

Sam responded, "I will find out, Josh. I also want you to know that your father is here with me but they wouldn't let him in. I'm going to the Sheriff now to see what he knows. I just hope they haven't silenced him. Since Union occupation began, the federals give a lot of leeway to Pinkerton's and I want to see your friend and make sure they haven't harmed him. You just hang tough because I'll be back soon. Don't tell them anything unless I'm here with you. Do you understand?

Josh nodded his head yes, then asked Sam to tell his father he was okay. He was at least relieved to know that his wife and parents knew where he was.

Sam and John Eldridge next went to the Sheriff's office. Sam knew the Sheriff well and they weren't close friends but they did have a relationship of respect. After telling the desk sergeant who they were, Sheriff Gray soon came out to the waiting area and walked them back to his office.

Robert Gray looked much older than his forty years. He had aged a lot since the beginning of the war, trying to maintain a balance between operating a clean department while having to also answer to the whims of the some more unsavory representatives of the hand-picked temporary government of the state. They were, in effect, lackeys of their federal masters. As they talked, Gray told Pratt and Eldridge that Weston was undergoing questioning over at the Pinkerton's office. He was able, however, to get them to approve having one of his deputies present. He didn't trust the detectives either since they had a clearly thuggish reputation in dealing with Southerners.

Sheriff Gray leaned over his desk to talk softly and said, "Sam, the Pinkerton's don't have any evidence to support the arrest. As far as I can find out, they have no clue what happened to Chowning or even if anything happened at all. Since he was working with the Navy Department, they have decided to play hardball with Weston. It sounds like a grudge."

Sam explained the situation between Josh, Weston and the Navy and the Sheriff nodded as if to say that the grudge now made sense. Before leaving, he told the two men he would find out from his deputy about the questioning and if any other information was available.

"When they have two partners involved, they try to play one against the other," the Sheriff said. "Don't be surprised if they interview Josh next and try to split the two up. They don't care who tells them what they want, just that they want to close the case with a win."

As requested by the Sheriff, John would stay overnight with Sam so that they could come back in the morning. The two men sat up half the night discussing what needed to be done and Sam's wife set up a spare bedroom for John for the night. He couldn't sleep, however, just lying awake in the bed worrying about his only son and his friend.

Morning came and John found Sam Pratt at the kitchen table with North Carolina law books. He also noted a book which covered the rules of the still developing Reconstruction, provided to him by the federal authorities.

"I hope you haven't been up all night, Sam," was John's greeting. "I must admit I didn't sleep well myself, but it was natural as a father that it would be a fitful night."

Sam's wife came out with a coffee service and poured each man a cup, looking rather haggard herself. John hoped he wasn't an imposition but he didn't know what else to do.

Sam told him he had been studying to determine what, if anything, federal prosecutors might do in a case like this without real evidence. He found what he was looking for in the Reconstruction literature and told John that it looked like Captain Weston and Josh could be held no longer than five days without formal charges. That would explain the intimidation tactic used thus far. It is common practice these days in the South, however, for them to stretch things out beyond the time limits, knowing that they can likely get away with it. It is my job to make sure they understand their own rules and politely call them out. I'll also try to get some support from some people in high places to make it high profile so the media can't miss it. Good reporters are always looking for a good scoop. I'm going to demand a charge sheet and push for an honest judge that I can verify.

"I think the Sheriff is telling the truth when he said they don't have anything, John," he informed the troubled father. "I think they are bluffing, figuring that Josh and Weston don't have the funds to fight the case. Furthermore, they are required by the rules to allow anyone held to be visited by an attorney of his choice within forty-eight hours of pick-up by authorities for suspicion. I will demand of the sheriff this morning that I be allowed to see Weston. We'll see how he responds. By the way, John, I know you are not a rich man and what I want from you when this is all over is one of those new sailboats you are building. I'll work as long and hard as necessary to make sure this case comes to the right conclusion. How does that sound, John?"

John had a relieved expression on his face when he said, "Agreed and done," then they shook hands to seal the deal.

Sheriff Gray greeted John and his attorney at the door to his office and took them inside where the three discussed things over coffee. He informed them that Weston was still under interrogation and he had no word of when he would be returned to his custody.

"This is highly irregular even under Reconstruction rules and I am afraid they may be trying to wear him down physically so that he'll cave in," the Sheriff said with apprehension in his voice.

Attorney Pratt informed him of the five-day rule, one hundred twenty hours, and that they were already nearly one- and one-half days in. He would be filing papers in the court house on Monday. Since the two were the legal responsibility of the Sheriff, he had until Tuesday evening to get them released.

"I hate to have to do this to you, Robert," Pratt concluded, "but I have no choice. You better get Mr. Pinkerton's boys in line or you are going to take the hit."

The Sheriff said he understood and that he had an idea. He would send a wire from the court house to the state court in Raleigh. It was quick, would get the message there fast and he explained his idea. He would ask the court to send the Confederate Advocate to Elizabeth City to step in.

John Eldridge was dumbfounded and interjected, "What do you mean by Confederate Advocate and wireless, Sheriff? I don't understand."

Sam Pratt turned and signaled for the Sheriff to explain. It was easy to understand why John didn't know about the wire communication since prior to the last year or so only large cities had such capability, sending Morse Code signals which were translated by code readers on the receiving end. Only in the first few months following the conclusion of the war did any town in mostly rural Eastern North Carolina have access to what was later called the telegraph. The Reconstruction made sure that even rural areas had some access and in Eastern North Carolina it was Elizabeth City and Wilmington.

The Confederate Advocate was the representative of the rights of former Confederate soldiers. The position was designed to assist them to become good and successful citizens after they took the oath of allegiance to the United States. In theory, as envisioned by Abraham Lincoln, the central government wanted these brave men to be leaders in making the South productive again because of their bravery and courage and the nation needed men like that. There were, however, many in Washington appointed to positions after Lincoln's death who wanted vengeance, not reconciliation. So, the Confederate Advocate was a position to try to work through that wide gap. In the case of Northeastern North Carolina and Southeastern Virginia, former Union Army Colonel Earl Winslow, the man who befriended young

Josh Eldridge on the sail from the Virginia's Northern Neck to Hampton Roads in the spring of 1865, was the Advocate. Neither Sheriff Gray or Sam Pratt had any knowledge of this, nor did Josh's father.

As Sheriff Gray completed his explanation of why he was doing what he planned, he added, "And now, Gentlemen, I am going to Pinkerton's and check on Captain Weston, make an official request according to law for his return to my custody and also tell them to leave Mr. Eldridge's son alone."

It was decided that the Sheriff would meet them three hours later at the downtown coffee shop. In the meantime, the Sheriff made arrangements for both John Eldridge and his lawyer to visit his son in jail. They both decided that Sheriff Gray was doing everything in his power to help them end the nightmare.

As the two men walked up to the desk sergeant in the jail, the same man who previously told John he couldn't see his son, Sergeant Hunt, was deeply apologetic and immediately took them to the visitors visiting table. It was divided from the prisoner seating by a heavy wire screen. As a courtesy, the sergeant did insure that no other visitors could use the room until they were done, giving them complete privacy for their conversation.

As John and Sam Pratt sat at the table facing the see-through screen, the side door on the other side soon opened and in stepped Josh, looking sad but showing no signs of mistreatment. As he came to the bench on the other side, John reached his fingers up against the screen so that Josh could touch them and the older man started to cry.

"Don't cry, Dad," Josh said. "It will be okay; we did nothing wrong and the truth will prevail."

"I'm glad you have that kind of attitude, Son," was John's response. "I know you did nothing and I believe that your skipper is also an honest and good man. Before we talk further, though, I want Mr. Pratt to fill you in on where things are. We're making some real progress on getting you out of here."

Attorney Pratt filled the young man in on the current status and told him about the matter with the Confederate Advocate. Josh interrupted with a question. He wanted to know who the Advocate was and where he came from.

"His name is Colonel Earl Winslow, Son, and he's being contacted," was Pratt's answer.

Josh was beside himself with excitement and couldn't keep it to himself. He just couldn't believe how fate was swinging his way.

"Mr. Pratt, Dad," he beamed. "I know Colonel Winslow. I met him on a schooner sailing to Hampton Roads after release from prison. I knew he was down here working to help us former soldiers, but had no idea this would be what he is doing. I even have his card in my money belt which the jailer is holding."

They visited for about twenty minutes, then left and went back to Sam's house before walking to the coffee shop to meet the Sheriff.

"I think fortune is shining on us in the form of Colonel Winslow," the lawyer said. "We just need to be able to ride out the storm until Tuesday. Pinkerton's is not going to give the okay to let them go until they are put under some heat and I think Winslow will be the clencher."

The Sheriff joined them at the appointed hour for a bite to eat and coffee, bringing some good news. Pinkerton's was getting cold feet and would release Weston back to the Sheriff's custody. While he couldn't put Josh and his partner in the same cell, he could assign them to adjacent ones separated only by bars and they could converse. He also told them that Pinkerton's would not interview Josh because they claimed they got all the evidence they needed from Weston, something Sheriff Gray sincerely doubted, saying they were bluffing.

When Sam Pratt informed him about Josh knowing the Confederate Advocate, Gray actually smiled. He knew that they now had an ace in their deck to hold until the right moment. He was also filing charges in court on Monday concerning the Pinkerton interference with his lawful duties. The judge couldn't refuse to act on it since as Sheriff, his constitutional authority had already been approved by the appointed Reconstruction managers gaining control in Raleigh. If they didn't maintain some semblance of normalcy returning even their Washington masters would be held accountable.

After the Sheriff left, Pratt gave some personal advice to John, saying, "Since it's Saturday afternoon, John, go on home and come back here on Tuesday morning. Nothing more will happen until then and your wife and Josh's wife must be worried sick. Go home and comfort them while I handle things on this end until then. It's what you need to do."

"You're right, Sam," John concurred. "They are likely worried to death, but please tell Josh for me that I will be back bright and early and that we are going to get him out of that jail and back home, both Josh and Captain Weston."

They shook hands and John headed to the livery stable where his horse was again bridled and hitched to the wagon for the two-hour ride home. As horse and driver crossed the bridge leaving Elizabeth City, the worried father said a silent prayer for God's grace. He knew the original meeting of his son with the Army Colonel was part of His plan for what was coming. He needed to put his faith in that plan and He who designed it.

When he drove up to his barn, Emma came running out and threw her arms around him. It was nearly dark and getting cold, so he put the horse and wagon away for the night and headed inside to the warm kitchen. He was glad to find both Annie and Natasha there and he would be able to tell them all what had happened. He was excited to learn about the baby and spent his first few minutes saying he had the best of both mom and dad. It was a special bright spot that was needed after the last couple of days.

Later, after dinner, he and the three ladies talked about all that happened since he left. Both Natasha and Annie stayed over and he took them back home in the morning, then went down to the dock to check on the tugboat. All was secure and deckhand Sam was cleaning some gear. John was glad to know that this industrious young lad was so diligent and reliable and the boat showed it, gleaming and ready to go whenever Josh and the Skipper returned.

There was no lay minister coming to the court house for morning worship that day as there were none available, so John decided to go and get Emma and take her to Moyock for the service there at the sponsor church. He spent nearly the entire service in personal prayer over Josh but he also prayed for his new grandson who was yet to be named. He felt reverent in the Lord's House and thought that was what he needed to do on this day. Upon return home, he and Emma spent a quiet day together, something they had not done in a long time. They spent time with the baby so that Annie could get some much-needed sleep, but she was physically in very good shape and would be up and about the next day.

Sunday night the wind picked up and the rain was heavy. A nor'easter had formed out of a system moving up the coast and by Monday morning it was blowing hard and steady. John walked outside and saw a few trees down but the barn, workshop and outbuilding were snugly closed and safe. He and Emma spent the entire day inside, talking about John's return trip to Elizabeth City the next day.

"Hopefully, this thing will blow out today and tomorrow will be okay," John said, "and when I get there, Emma, I'm not leaving until I have him with me. It might take a day or two, but be patient, I'm bringing him home while also making sure that Skipper Weston is taken care of."

Emma concurred with his reasoning and she was glad to find later in the day that the wind began to lessen and signs of blue sky were peeking through from time to time. By the time they turned in for the night, the wind was light and variable and the stars were twinkling in the sky. They talked for some time about the situation, but each committed to prayer for their son and for his quick release from confinement and return to home and family.

As they slept fitfully that night, both parents dreamed about their son but from a different perspective. Emma dreamed of Josh as a cute little boy, running to his mother for comfort when he cut his hand on a sharp piece of glass. John's mind traveled in a different direction, picturing him as a prisoner of war hanging on by a bare thread of life as he fought to survive his living nightmare.

John awoke, thinking how unfair life can be, especially his son who now was locked up for something that he clearly had no part in and for which there was absolutely no evidence. Then again, he did have a new baby boy in the family, a healthy and cute one and Annie had told him to get Josh's ideas for a name, for she didn't want their son with no name for long. Thinking of the little one eased his mind and allowed him to get back to sleep and that was a good thing, for he'd need his sleep to deal with the legal issues that were awaiting him. When he awoke, he was refreshed. Now it was time to move on and get his boy back home where he belonged.

FOURTEEN

John departed at daybreak on a morning which would be clear but extremely cold. A cold front filled in behind the storm and the temperature must have dropped over twenty degrees. There were patches of ice along the way and in puddles on the road. He arrived in Elizabeth City, left his rig and horse at the livery stable and walked over to the coffee shop across from the courthouse where he would meet Sam Pratt when he arrived. He was now warm from the hearth as he sipped his coffee when Sam walked in.

"Well, John, I'm surprised to see you beat me here this morning," Sam said, "I hope you've warmed up for that ride must have been cold."

Sam pulled up a chair and signaled for coffee and the two men took up where they left off Saturday. John did interject the good news about the new baby and Sam told him something as positive as that is what Josh needed to keep him strong. He needed to have something positive to cope with the ordeal he was facing. Sam also said Shorty was now back at the jail, he had a few facial bruises from his interview, but Sheriff Gray had filed a complaint against Pinkerton's with the court which would be added to the docket. What's more, Colonel Winslow was expected in town by noon and upon his arrival and meeting with the Sheriff, a court hearing would be scheduled.

John asked impatiently, "But I thought the deadline was today, so when will the hearing be conducted."

"Relax, John," Attorney Pratt responded. "Technically you are right but when Pinkerton's deliberately stalls on following the rules it doesn't mean they don't apply, it just means that they've successfully pulled off an illegal delay. They'll be cited for it but that's about all, but we'll get your boy back and that is what's important."

Just before noon, Colonel Earl Winslow walked into Sam Pratt's law office, an impressive trim and tall man dressed impeccably. He shook hands with Sam who introduced him to John Eldridge.

After shaking hands, Winslow said, "It's nice to meet you, Mr. Eldridge and I'm sorry to hear what happened to your son. In those few hours we talked on that schooner I recognized a bright young man who had been through a horrible ordeal and men like him are the reason I took this job. Lots of good boys were hurt on both sides by that war and we owe it to them to help them get on their feet without being terrorized by groups like the Pinkerton thugs."

John was impressed and felt like that meeting with Josh must have been godly inspired, for how else could he be here when Josh needed such a worthy advocate as this man.

The three men sat around a table in Sam's office and had a cup of coffee while Sam filled them in on the legal process. Winslow was also told of Josh's blessed event back home and he smiled, knowing how such a piece of good news can be just the morale booster needed at a time like this. Then they walked to the Sheriff's office, met Sheriff Gray and the four walked to the court house. Once there, Lawyer Pratt led them to the chambers of Judge Davis who would hear their argument in private. Pinkerton's was glad of that for they didn't want their mischief to be discovered by the general public.

Judge Davis was an imposing man, stout but tall with pure white hair and glasses down by the tip of his nose giving the appearance of a scholar. His desk was clear with papers neatly stacked and a library behind it full of legal books.

He was holding a document in his hand as he stood, shook hands with each and told them to have a seat. Then he looked very solemn as he began to speak.

"Mr. Pratt, I've read your brief and it has much merit," Judge Davis began, "but excuse me for asking this, Colonel, but why are you here?"

"Well, Judge," said   Winslow, "I met the young ex-Confederate soldier on a schooner bringing him closer home from federal prisoner of war status and he impressed me. Part of my job is to make sure that young former combatants from the Confederate Army are treated fairly. There is clearly no evidence of a crime and something is dreadfully wrong. Judge, I know you are well aware that there are some in high places in the federal hierarchy who don't want to treat these people as citizens. They are, however, citizens again and Pinkerton's, for whatever the reason, is always found in the middle of cases like this. Why?"

Judge Davis asked several more questions of Colonel Winslow and then John Eldridge, before turning to Attorney Pratt and saying, "I must take this under advisement and do some other questioning. Come back at ten in the morning and I'll have some kind of decision for you."

With that, the men were dismissed and returned to Sam Pratt's home office to continue their discussion. Sam asked both John and the Colonel if they could stay overnight and he was heartened by Winslow's statement that he would not leave until the problem was resolved. This case was his full time focus until young Eldridge and his partner got justice.

A short time later, John and Attorney Pratt paid a visit to Josh in the jail. They told him where things stood and that they looked good, but then John surprised his son.

"You have a baby boy, Josh, he was born right after I left to come up here the last time. He is beautiful, but Annie wants to know what you suggest for a name."

Josh broke out with a smile for the first time since his ordeal began and said, "I want him to be John Albert, John Albert Eldridge. The John is for you, Dad and the

Albert is for Annie's deceased dad. Tell her that's what I want."

John just said, "Well, you can tell her yourself for we plan to leave here tomorrow with you and Shorty."

They talked for a few more minutes and on the way back to Pratt's office, the attorney said, "Now that really gives your son something to look forward to in life."

The elder Eldridge just smiled, realizing once again that someone bigger than he was working some magic for Josh and it must be God.

At ten o'clock sharp the next morning, Attorney Pratt, John Eldridge and Colonel Winslow met Judge Davis in his private chambers. He asked a number of additional questions and then said he was prepared to announce what he decided.

"Gentlemen, after careful consideration and further discussion with the Pinkerton organization which is representing the Navy Department, I have decided to release Josh Eldridge and Captain Weston without bail while the investigation continues. There is one condition and it's a hardship I know. Neither man may leave Currituck County until further notice. The only exception would be to come to and from Elizabeth City as required but by land only. They are not to operate their tugboat transportation business until there is some resolution."

Attorney Pratt asked the judge how these men were supposed to be able to support themselves since work on the water was their livelihood.

The judge just looked at him and replied, "That can't be my concern, but hopefully this will be resolved soon. It was the only solution I could come up with quickly, otherwise motions and hearings would have gone on for weeks. Gentlemen, you know how the Navy could tie things up and they are willing to do that. It does appear that someone in a rather high place has it in for your client but I can't prove that. If you can find some solid evidence of wrongdoing, Mr. Pratt, I would be glad to evaluate it quickly."

As they left the chambers, there was both elation and gloom. They were happy that Josh and Shorty were being released but the issue of how to keep their thriving business alive was critical. The two skippers could financially handle the legal issue, but the long-term future was a different matter if this matter dragged on. They stopped for a cup of coffee to further discuss things while they awaited the wheels of justice to release the two men from jail.

Colonel Winslow offered one action that would be helpful saying, "I have a good friend in an important position with the Justice Department. I will wire him before I head back home and ask for his assistance in determining whether the supposed victim is actually missing. He'll put someone on the case to try and track him down. I think the whole thing is fishy."

John spoke about the tug business saying, "Perhaps Josh and Shorty can find a temporary skipper for the tug. With the top deckhand being a close friend, he could oversee the routes and keep things moving. At least they could avoid losing the business they have and I suspect that is what this whole exercise is about."

For his part, Sam Pratt said he would keep the legal motions and push ongoing. He knew the judge really didn't have his heart in keeping them ashore but Pinkerton's did have influence in high places and he wanted to avoid a political battle.

Two hours later, Josh and Shorty were released, all thanked Sam Pratt and Colonel Winslow and they boarded the buckboard for the ride back to Currituck. Colonel Winslow asked them to wait just a moment and he walked up to the buckboard.

"Josh," he said. "Keep this contact card with you. It has a code on it that, if used in correspondence or in a wire, the code will get the message to me with speed wherever I am. I am going to be doing some of my own investigating into this whole story. Remember, I have plenty of friends in high places in the Army, including the President-elect, General Grant who, although the Reconstruction candidate, does have a soft spot for anyone who fought bravely and honorably in war. He has some problems but is a decent man and he wouldn't take kindly to what Pinkerton's did to you fellows. He also needs to show fairness to the Southern states who have officially ratified their statehood return. North Carolina is one."

With that the Colonel stepped away, wished them luck and said he would be in touch and was off. The elder Eldridge was pleased and turned to Josh and told him he needed to get that name straight for his baby. He said no grandson of his was going around without a name. Josh grinned as he told his dad that the new parent would take care of that as soon as they got home. Then he just relaxed, enjoying the smell of freedom as they headed home.

Arriving home just before dark, the two Eldridge men were glad to see Emma and Natasha were both at Annie's place, helping her and settling things before the men arrived. All three men hugged their wives like they hadn't seen them in years and sighed with relief that a big part of their problem was likely over. They realized, however, that the livelihood issue had to be resolved in some fashion quickly or life would become very difficult in the future.

Before anything else took place, Josh took Annie by the arm, told the others they'd be back in a moment and went to see his son. He looked at the precious bundle, then looked at Annie and spoke.

"Annie, how would the name, John Albert Eldridge sound? I thought it would be great, John for my dad and Albert for yours."

She looked pensive momentarily, then broke into a big smile and hugged him, saying, "I love it."

They walked back in to the others with Annie carrying Little John and Josh said, "We have a name. John Albert."

John and Emma Eldridge were ecstatic and Shorty and Natasha grinned, then they all went with the new parents back to the baby's room to see how nice it looked. Little John was yawning, so his mom laid him down, wrapped up warm and he was asleep.

They all walked into the parlor, Annie suggested everyone stay for dinner and the three ladies headed for the kitchen while the men discussed the best way to solve the new dilemma facing the joint tugboat captains. At first, Shorty just listened quietly, but with an expression that looked as if he was somewhere else. Suddenly, Josh noticed that his partner wanted to say something and he asked Shorty what was on his mind.

Shorty stood up and said, "What if I can find us a temporary skipper to run the boat until this gets sorted out? You and I can run the business side of things from home, Josh. You need to be here anyway while Annie gets her full strength back and you get acquainted with your boy. Sam Jarvis has learned the routes and can be the new skipper's navigator. I know a couple of good captains in Norfolk and things are slowing down up there. I can write a letter to a pier manager I trust who can represent us and Sam can deliver it and be our interface. If he's too young to do the whole deal, couldn't we find a local businessman to do it. What about you, Mr. Eldridge, you'd be perfect?"

Josh's dad stepped in with a few words, saying, "I'd be glad to go with Sam. He's a fine young man and I would just be there to give him encouragement or to do whatever needs to be done to protect your interests. My business is slowing down until spring now and I have the time. Just say the word."

It was settled and the trip to the Norfolk tug docks would be scheduled for the following Monday. Josh and his dad called in Sam Jarvis and told him of their plans. They offered him a raise and said he would be accountable to them while working as the temporary captain's chief mate. He would be ready to go bright and early on Monday morning.

When Monday came, John picked Sam up at his small frame house adjacent to Josh's home and they went to the boat dock at the court house to board the schooner Lady Liberty and headed for Norfolk. Shorty had given John a letter for Frank Meekins, the dock manager at the tug docks and Sam was given it to read. They enjoyed the view along the way, wrapped up from the chill and by early afternoon they reached the Southern Elizabeth

River. The wind was brisk as the river widened and they were at the docks within another hour. They found Frank Meekins' office with a note on the door in the hallway that he would be back soon. They sat down on the bench adjacent to his office and waited. John told Sam he would take him to a nice steakhouse nearby for dinner and they would spend the night at the seaman's house before returning to Currituck the next day.

Soon a shuffling bespectacled man with a slight limp and a ruddy complexion approached. They introduced themselves and told him they had been sent by Shorty Weston. Meekins showed them into his office and directed them by gesture to the two chairs across from his desk. Sam handed him the letter.

He smiled as he asked, "How is Shorty and how is his young partner who is a fine worker? Those were two of the hardest working men I've ever seen on this waterfront and I see that you are Josh's father. I hope they are doing well."

John explained the details that were briefly alluded to in the letter and filled Frank in on the problem that caused their dire need for a temporary tugboat captain.

Frank rubbed his neck as he listened and then said, "We'll, I'm thinking of either of two skippers, both known to Shorty, who would be perfect and they are in a lull at the moment here. Both of them dock their tugs here and I will defer the extra charges when not in use for their boats when here.

John introduced Sam Jarvis, pointing out that he would be the owner's representative as assistant to the tug captain. He also explained why he was here instead of Shorty or Josh and Frank didn't looked surprised.

Frank replied, "I'm not surprised, Mr. Eldridge. The shipyard has become a snake pit and the only one over there I ever trusted was Dave Watson who loved both Shorty and your boy. There's been a big overhaul in management and they are now very hard to work with. Come to think of it, about a week or two ago a fellow who said he was from the shipyard dropped by and asked if I was working with Shorty. I told him to get lost but I can't remember his name."

John perked up on that comment and asked, "Was it Chowning?"

Meekins nodded and said, "Yes, and another thing. I didn't like the way the fellow looked. He looked like trouble."

John dropped the subject and they now talked about arranging for one skipper at a time to come to Currituck for an interview. John said if either wanted to come by tug, they had dockage but whoever they hired would be working on the Miss Margaret.

The dock manager said he could get John O'Brien down there before the week was out. The next week he could send Willie Talbot. John liked that, they could get a decision made right after Christmas and get the business going again. He knew Shorty and Josh were worried but the information about Chowning would be welcome to their ears. It showed the supposedly missing man was alive and in Norfolk about the time he disappeared and he either ran into trouble on the docks or his disappearance was planned. He would need to get in touch with Sam Pratt with this information.

John and young Jarvis were scheduled to travel back to Currituck in the morning and he took the young man to that wonderful steakhouse near the harbor park. Then they walked over to the seaman's home and received lodging for the night.

Arriving back at Currituck Court House in early afternoon the next day, they walked over to Shorty's house and were glad to find both men together. They joined them for coffee and filled them in on their successful trip, then gave them the information about Chowning.

"My gut tells me this is a set-up, fellows," John said. "I don't think anything happened to him. I think that since he had no success in getting your business back, he saw this as a way to force the customers to go back to the shipyard for service. I'll bet he's alive somewhere and I suspect it's not in Norfolk. I'm going to Elizabeth City to tell Mr. Pratt, but I'm going by myself. You boys relax, start getting ready for Christmas and get ready to oversee your new captain right after the holiday. I have a feeling that's going to be harder work than doing it yourself. The first candidate for your job is John O'Brien and he'll be here this week to talk. You keep an eye out for him and handle it your way. I told Frank Meekins he can dock here at Shorty's dock. Is that okay?"

Shorty said, "Is that okay? Are you serious, John, you've done all the heavy lifting and you ask? Of course, you've done a great job and more. Thanks for helping us get ready to put life back into the Miss Margaret again. This is going to be a special Christmas."

Right after sun-up only five days before Christmas, 1868, John Eldridge headed out in the buckboard on the road to Elizabeth City. His spirits were as high as they had been in years and he was singing Christmas carols as he went down the road. He arrived mid-morning and found Mr. Pratt as he expected in the coffee shop, enjoying a cup of coffee before his morning in court.

"Well, hello, John," the attorney greeted him. "You look like you have something important and I have about twenty minutes so join me for a cup of coffee and fill me in."

John explained about Chowning and how he had been seen in Norfolk no more than a week before Josh was arrested. He was sure that would show that if anything happened to him, Josh and Shorty couldn't have had anything to do with it. Sam agreed and said he would contact both a private detective in Norfolk who owed him a favor and Colonel Winslow.

"Either someone killed the man for other reasons or he is alive somewhere," Pratt responded. "Either way, my detective friend will find out and Colonel Winslow can put some heat on Pinkerton's for not thoroughly doing their job. Then again, they may have been told to do just what they did without questions. Give me a week with this John. By the way, have my clients found a way to keep their business operational? That situation really concerns me."

John replied, "No need to worry, Mr. Pratt. Yes, I think they've found a temporary skipper to run the boat for them until this is resolved. All I know is I just want Josh to have a good Christmas after what he's been through. He doesn't need this on top of what happened earlier in his life."

Sam said he'd be in touch, that he'd get his wires out today and he assured that justice would prevail. He got up and headed to court while John had some breakfast before heading back home. He felt very relieved.

While his father was handling the legal matter in Elizabeth City, Josh and Shorty were discussing their replacement skipper situation. Josh knew them both well and indicated his preference.

"John O'Brien would be my pick, Josh," he said. "John is still pretty young, maybe ten years older than you and he is driven by money. He loves to work hard if he is paid well and I know that business right now is down in Norfolk. Willie is also a good man, but he's a little more laid back and he has a pretty bad case of arthritis in his hands. I think he is also ready to retire. Both are totally trustworthy and honest so that's not a problem with either. But I'm thinking, if you like John when you meet him, we could get him to work quickly and that's all the better for us."

Josh said he'd leave that up to Shorty and as they were walking out to the tug to check on things, John's tug, the Lulu Belle was pulling in. Two boys jumped off to tie her fast and he came out of the wheelhouse with his customary corn cob pipe set in his mouth.

"Well, hello, Shorty," he grinned. "How do you like it down here in Carolina? It sure is easier to dock than in Norfolk. And you must be Josh, it's good to meet you as well. I am intrigued by you wanting to talk with me."

Josh stood back and let Shorty take over and he vigorously shook O'Brien's hand like an old friend. He was anxious to get this situation resolved so they could breathe a little easier. Then Shorty filled O'Brien in on things.

"We've got a little predicament down here, John," he said. "And I heard your business was slow and I thought it might be something you could help us with."

"I'm all ears, Shorty, please fill me in," he replied.

Shorty told him their predicament and that he needed someone he could trust. The two men knew and trusted each other and Shorty knew John would be worth every penny. Even if they merely broke even, keeping the business going until things would be resolved would work since he and Josh had been saving, but at least the fog of the future would be cleared.

They walked over to Josh's house where Annie and Natasha were fixing a meal. It was easy to make room for one more since they stayed ready for the unexpected visitor. It was the way with Southern hospitality. John knew Natasha since he had dinner on several occasions with the Weston's and he was the consummate gentleman.

The ladies decided to eat in the kitchen and let the men talk business and as John and Shorty talked, Josh quickly recognized that this man was top quality. He was ready to agree with Shorty that they need look no farther. After dinner they walked down to the dock where John checked out the Miss Margaret. He was pleased with what he saw and the only concern was paying his deckhand. Only one was working right now due to the slowdown but he was a quality young man.

"I'll tell you what, John," Shorty responded, "you can keep him with you as long as he's willing to work under Sam Jarvis. Young Sam is tasked with directing you where we are going since he's a local boy and knows the water well."

It was settled. Two days after Christmas, which would be the following Friday, John O'Brien would dock his tug in Currituck and begin a temporary assignment of unknown duration as Skipper of the Miss Margaret. They toasted with a shot of whiskey and after visiting for another hour, Captain O'Brien headed back to Norfolk.

Being it was now Friday, Josh and Shorty turned their thoughts to Christmas, to the special Christmas service that the traveling minister would deliver and the food they would serve for the occasion. Both couples opted against any Christmas presents, deciding instead to celebrate their freedom and the increasing likelihood that this latest ordeal would soon end. They had much to be thankful for in addition to the celebration of the Baby Jesus that year.

The occasion was a good one and they even used it as a special service to include the christening of John Albert Eldridge as a child of God. What could be more appropriate at Christmastime than welcoming a new baby boy into the Flock.

With Christmas quickly past, John O'Brien reported just like clockwork on that Friday after Christmas. With Sam Jarvis directing his way in the new waters, the backlog of deliveries was rapidly resolved since the man was a workhorse. He went non-stop for ten days when Shorty told him to take a day off, that things were going extremely well.

Josh's mind was spinning as he thought about John O'Brien as a logical candidate to lead up their expansion with passenger service. They put it in the back of their head, focusing on the here and now and were just thankful that money was coming in strong. With Josh's dad also doing so well in his boat building business, the three men were pleased. The only thing that would make it better would be a resolution of the Chowning matter and a lifting of that albatross from their back.

January and February 1869 rolled by quickly and business was booming, but Josh and Shorty were anxious to be done with the Chowning matter. John Eldridge also was concerned but he said that good things take time to happen.

On March seventh, Captain O'Brien was picking up goods for shipment in Elizabeth City when a well-dressed man approached him on the dock. Sam Jarvis saw him and waved. He recognized the man and he knew it was Sam Pratt. Pratt asked to come aboard, introduced himself to O'Brien and handed an official letter to him and asked him to deliver it to Josh and Shorty.

"Tell them it's important," he said, "and I think they will both be pleased."

As he departed, the barge was loaded and O'Brien pushed her out to the channel, and came about for the straight run to Currituck. He knew that several supply wagons were expecting the deliveries and that whatever the content, Shorty and Josh would be pleased with the letter.

As he maneuvered into docking position at Shorty's dock, he tooted his arrival. Shorty and Josh were both coming up the dock as he tied up. Coming ashore he waved the envelope and placed it in Shorty's hands.

"An attorney in Elizabeth City, a Mr. Pratt, gave me this for you," he said. "He merely said it was good news and that you'd be pleased."

Shorty tore into the envelope with Josh eagerly looking over his shoulder and said, "We're free, Josh, all charges are being lifted. There are more details about us having to be witnesses and you can read it for yourself. Sounds like we are going to be so busy that we need to keep John working. That's okay by me."

Josh and Shorty decided to look at the rest of the details later but, for now, they were going to gather the wives together and crack open a special bottle of bubbly. Meanwhile, Skipper O'Brien, Sam and Matthew, the junior deck hand, moved the barge to the main Currituck dock for unloading. It was much easier to use now since the long, shoreline-parallel docking platform was in place and loading and unloading was much quicker and more efficient. When finished, they moved back to Shorty's dock, cleaned up the boat and went home to the little house down the road they shared. It had been leased to own by Josh and Shorty as a trial before committing to purchase. Sam Jarvis was already living there and there was plenty of room for another.

That night, John O'Brien sipped a shot of whiskey while he contemplated his future. In just the short time he had been in Currituck, he fell in love with the place and really didn't look forward to going back full time to Norfolk. He knew he had enough business to survive, but he liked this quaint rural place and besides, his tug was paid up and he could work anywhere, even sell the boat if he wanted. He fell asleep thinking about his future.

Little did he know that Shorty and Josh were preparing to reactivate their dream for expansion and they would want O'Brien to play a key role. Even though they were now fully exonerated, they would be required to spend time in court with depositions on their case and make several appearances in court to testify for the prosecution. Not only were they free, but they would now be federal witnesses in the trial of several shipyard officials and Chowning, who was still not in custody but they were sure was alive. He would soon be found or tried in absentia. All of the defendants were culpable in the fraudulent attempt to punish the small tugboat operators. Even President Grant had spoken of the travesty at the request of Colonel Winslow. He knew good people in the South needed to know that not all hope was lost.

The tide had turned in the shipyard case and the only official at the shipyard who was truly trustworthy in the leadership were David Watson and his direct military leader, who believed in Josh and Shorty. The wrap up, however, would keep the two entrepreneurs busy until at least May, which would give them time to make their new plans. In the meantime, John O'Brien would stay on and; they would wait to tell him of their plans until all was ready.

FIFTEEN

Josh and Shorty spent most of the time late into May going to and from Sam Pratt's office in Elizabeth City, meeting with prosecutors and answering questions or filing written statements about the travesty against them. Now fully exonerated, they took their duty seriously and voluntarily made themselves available to the prosecution, but it was clearly taking its toll on them. It was especially difficult for Josh as a former Confederate soldier, feeling as if some of the officials were privately looking down on him.

Finally, the trial date came and as they hitched up the buckboard for the trip to Elizabeth City, they stopped by the dock for a short visit with John O'Brien.

"John," Shorty began, "Josh and I think we have an opportunity with us if you'd like it, but we must get through this trial first. We appreciate what you are doing to keep us afloat and we have some big plans. Do you think you'd be interested?"

John grinned as he told Shorty and Josh about his newfound happiness in the country and that if he could do something that would cover his needs instead of going back to Norfolk, he would jump at the chance. Shorty promised that they'd talk about details just as soon as they returned, but it might be a few days.

With that, Shorty and Josh headed down the road while Captain O'Brien, Sam Jarvis and the young deckhand Matthew headed by water toward the Albemarle, pushing a full load of supplies to deliver and shipments to pick up.

The younger Eldridge and partner Weston arrived at Sam Pratt's home office by eight and were surprised to find a full breakfast being laid out for them. Both Sam and Colonel Winslow were there waiting for them.

"Gentlemen," Attorney Pratt offered, "Today is the day we begin the process of putting a few tyrants in jail who belong there. The shipyard commander is charged as is his assistant and Chowning was as well, but events changed that. Colonel Winslow received information about where he might be and he sent federal agents looking. This came after the two or you were already exonerated. The agents found the scoundrel in a boarding house with a suitcase full of cash but he was dead. Someone got to him first to keep him quiet, so then murder came into the case. A few more months of what was going on and you two would have been in financial ruins.

"Now I've got a big surprise for you fellows, for there is someone you like in the study and he will testify as will you two and Colonel Winslow. He is the one with the testimony that will lock the case down solid. Please remember also that you have both been fully exonerated from the case, so just be relaxed and tell your story as you've told me before the jury. The military officers in question will be court-martialed later based upon the results of this civilian court."

Winslow nodded as Sam Pratt stood and walked over to open the door to his study. Josh and Shorty were quite surprised to see David Watson walk through the door. He looked very somber, but nodded at Josh and Shorty.

"I know you are well acquainted with Mr. Watson, Gentlemen," Colonel Winslow said. "When he found out about what was really happening at the shipyard, he contacted local authorities who contacted me. They knew I was working on your case."

Watson told his two friends how he just knew something wasn't right and once he heard about their plight, he had to speak up. As it turned out, Chowning was just the tip of the iceberg. Several senior personnel at the shipyard were submitting felonious documents and receiving kickbacks, not to mention trying to hyperinflate charges to billing on Albemarle accounts. When the shipyard officials realized someone was on to them, they took Chowning off the streets and were suspected of being complicit in the murder.

Sam Pratt entered the discussion, saying, "So, do you see, Gentlemen? This case not only involves felonies such as bribery and racketeering, but now even murder is involved and the entire management team at the shipyard is under scrutiny, except Mr. Watson here who came forward once he felt it was safe to do so.

"The good news for you, Josh and Captain Weston and for David here is that the Navy has agreed to pay for all of your legal bills as part of whatever is found out. Officials from Washington are now overseeing all operations at the shipyard pending finalization and replacement of all guilty parties.

"You three men are the key witnesses to a big enough part of the graft and corruption that was going on that it will blow the lid off the rest. But we must keep you in a hotel suite until your testimony is complete. I'm dispatching a messenger to let your families know and expect you to be here for at least a week or two. Your accommodations and meals will be first class, but you will be limited to movement with armed guard escort due to the seriousness of the case. Expect us to prepare and work with you for the next few days with the trial beginning next week. Do you have any questions?"

All three men were dumbfounded and didn't know what to say, but while they were disappointed about the separation from family, they knew it was necessary. So, over the next few days, when they weren't undergoing trial preparations, they ate well, slept well and killed their excess time playing cards.

The following Sunday all three men were surprised by visitors, approved and delivered by federal marshals. Annie, Natasha and Dave Watson's wife, Sarah were there to spend the afternoon. Each couple was given a private room for the afternoon with room service at their call. Even the federals knew that a witness who was sorely missing his wife wouldn't be the best presenter and the conjugal visit was a truly good idea. Having the opportunity for private time with their loved ones meant that they would be able to clearly carry out their testimony in a much better frame of mind.

After a final day of preparation on Monday, the trial began on Tuesday, June 8, 1869 and was expected to last four or five days. Josh, Shorty and David Watson would all be called as prosecution witnesses in the first two days, then stand by in case the defense wanted to cross-examine even after their first testimony was received. Judge John Wilson was the presiding judge and was brought in from Washington to insure federal rules were fully followed in the former Confederate stronghold community. He did have a reputation as being stern, but fair and expressed sympathy in earlier cases elsewhere for the plight of former soldiers on both sides of the battlefield.

On Wednesday, both Josh and Shorty testified, telling their story convincingly and in a straightforward manner. It was obvious during cross that the defense wanted to anger them, hoping that they would blurt out a response that would weaken their testimony. In Shorty's case, he was totally unrattled and sailed through, but the defense knew that Josh was less seasoned and a former Confederate soldier and they tried to get under his skin with some salacious terms about Confederate soldiers and their strength and honor. Sam Pratt, however, prepared Josh for just such situations and whenever he felt himself getting flushed, he just waited silently and when his internal anger subsided, he answered the question clearly and fully. He left no chance for misinterpretation. When completed, both men were told they were subject to recall and they retired to their lodging.

After they left the courtroom, Judge Wilson called lawyers from both benches forward. He told the defense that any further show of belittlement of a witness would not be tolerated and would be met with a contempt citation and possible jail time. That decision would prove to be a decisive action since it convinced the defense not to recall Josh or Shorty, though at the time no one would know.

David Watson also was masterful in his testimony. He had names, dates and places in response to prosecution questions and obviously had been keeping book on his superiors. William Hoskins, Shipyard Comptroller and Harold Ramsey, Head of Industrial Operations, were two of the defendants and the Commander and Deputy Commander of the facility, were both pending courts-martial (they were military men) depending on the outcome of the trial. At the end of day two, Sam Pratt met with the three witnesses and told them their performance was superlative and that the defense would begin its arguments in the morning.

"I know you don't want to attend," he acknowledged, "but it's important for you to hear their argument so you can help me take apart any discrepancies."

All three agreed and were escorted by the federal martial detail to the court in the morning as the trial reconvened. Only David Watson was recalled and the defense tried to hammer him repeatedly on several of his dates and places, trying to confuse them to weaken his initial appearance. Watson was steadfast in his resolve and finally the judge said that enough time was spent on the issue.

Another day of defense presentation came on Thursday with nothing of further substantiation and final closing arguments were heard on Friday. At the conclusion of those remarks, the jury was given instructions by the judge and told to return on Monday at nine in the morning to deliberate. He told them not to discuss the trial with anyone and also warned them about taking in outside information that wasn't in the trial.

Sam Pratt told his clients that it looked to him like a sure conviction, but that since it was a jury, strange things happen. In the meantime, they had to stay in Elizabeth City for another weekend and that meant more cards. By that time, even Josh had to admit that he was getting pretty savvy at something he previously never played.

The jury went into closed session Monday morning and shortly after lunch they sent a note to the judge that they had a verdict. They returned to the courtroom at two and announced that a unanimous jury had found all defendants guilty as charged. The judge also announced that murder charges were coming and that one of the defendants would be tried again but he refused to specify.

As reporters left the courtroom to file their stories, Josh and Shorty bid adieu to their friend Dave Watson and also said goodbye to their lawyer. They asked Colonel Winslow to stay for a moment until they said their good byes to Sam.

"Mr. Pratt," Josh said, "my dad asked me to tell you that he will start building your boat right away and he sends you his thanks. You have given us hope when all else was bleak and, besides, this way you'll have to come to Currituck. One of us will sail it back with you so that you can get accustomed to its handling and feel."

He thanked Josh, shook hands with both men and departed as the happy younger skipper turned to Colonel Winslow.

"Sir, for both the Skipper and me, I thank you from the bottom of my heart," he said. "You believed in us when no one else did and you went the extra mile. I hope one day you'll come to Currituck for a visit and see what kept me alive while at Point Lookout. You gave me hope when I needed it. We both wondered if you would let us treat you to dinner tonight. It's too late to start the trek home and the Downtown Steakhouse is very good. Since you saved our hides, it's the least we can do."

Winslow went back to his hotel, Josh and Shorty went to the seaman's home since their eloquent lodging ended with the trial closure and freshened up before dinner. An hour later they met the Colonel and sat down to a wonderful dinner of steak and all the trimmings. The Colonel even insisted on buying a fine bottle of wine and the men celebrated the end of their ordeal.

What they didn't know was while they were enjoying fine dining, Annie and Natasha were facing the scare of their lives. Both women turned in early, having been notified by the Currituck Sheriff that Josh and Shorty would be home and that the trial was over. The small Currituck courthouse had recently installed a wireless connection to Elizabeth City for just such reasons and it made the handling of emergencies easier.

As Annie began to drift off to sleep, she heard a loud shotgun blast coming from Shorty's home. She put on her robe, grabbed the double barrel which Josh taught her to use and headed out the door. Running in her direction was a figure dressed in dark. She yelled halt and received the response of a pistol shot, to which she returned fire. She heard a yell of pain as the figure ran up the road.

The two women hurriedly dressed as young Sam and John O'Brien ran over with rifles in hand. They escorted the ladies up to the Sheriff's office in the court house and stood guard at the door.

Sheriff Doughty met with them and listened to their story. He was concerned and asked them to excuse him momentarily as he went to send an emergency wire to Elizabeth City.

"Ladies, this incident must have something to do with what your husbands have been facing," he said. "I suspect that whoever it was didn't know that the trial was over and he wanted to send them a message not to testify. You two were likely his targets and if you had lacked firepower one, maybe both of you would probably no longer be with us. Annie, did you say that you winged him?"

"Yes, Sheriff," she replied. "I heard him howl as he ran off in the dark. I don't think I got him in the leg since he was running fast, but probably in the arm. With my lantern I think I saw a trail of blood so I definitely hit him."

"Well, Mrs. Eldridge," the Sheriff replied, "I don't think he'll bother you anymore, but the Marshal Service Office is sending two guards for around the clock protection for both you and Mrs. Weston. They will shift on and off and can camp out if you can't quarter them."

Both ladies said they would make sure they were given accommodations, but they didn't think they would need them after their husbands arrive. He reminded them that it was their husbands who were really their target, that the culprit came after them to send a message.

The two marshals arrived early in the morning, just as John O'Brien, Sam Jarvis and Matthew were pulling out on a business run. They would pick up Shorty and Josh, since the buckboard and horse had been previously retrieved due to the lengthy timeframe of the now completed trial. Then, with the once again legal skippers on board, they would make deliveries and pick-ups and have them home by dark.

A Sheriff's posse was assembled to look for the suspect from the night before. Ten men headed north toward Norfolk, four more went westward toward Elizabeth City and a local skipper said he would prowl around the waterways. No one in any direction had heard or seen anyone, and by seven when it was getting dark, they were about to give up the hunt when a young man in the northern group found a bloody rag in a ditch. As he and a few more searchers headed up the ditch they found a blood trail and there, under a pile of brush was a body of a man about thirty. Nothing else was done until Sheriff Doughty arrived. He carefully reached into the man's coat pocket and pulled out a satchel containing fifty dollars and identification. The dead man was Robert Chowning, the brother of the dead perpetrator. Why would he have been trying to threaten the two families? They would never find out but Sheriff Doughty surmised it was revenge. In his jaded mind he blamed Josh and Shorty for the death of his brother.

Two weeks later, Shorty and Josh were asked to testify in Norfolk at the court martial of two senior officers involved in the cover-up. Both were convicted and sentenced to dishonorable discharges, to become effective after five years in a Navy brig was completed. Their mission finished, Josh and Shorty were now totally free of any commitment to their case, fully exonerated. They went home to Currituck. There they would finalize plans for the future with their new additions to their growing business, John O'Brien and his young deckhand, Matthew.

When they met with O'Brien and told him of their wishes, he jumped at the opportunity and even offered to use his vessel to handle overload, for business was booming. They would spend the next three months operating in that fashion, handling a heavy volume of valuable business which gave them the seed money for their new passenger vessel.

That night, the last night of June 1869, Josh and Shorty went their separate ways to spend time alone with their wonderful wives they knew they had neglected. It was truly a good thing they lived in rural Currituck, for the joy and laughter in each household would likely have been heard throughout a city neighborhood.

Josh, however, despite the love of his wife and knowing that he was truly free, still had an empty feeling inside as if there was something more important that he was supposed to do. He wisely put it away for the time being, but he knew a time would come when he would have to address it. For now, however, life was truly sweet.

SIXTEEN

The mid-summer of 1869 was the beginning of a boom
period for Josh and Shorty. They had more work than
they could handle. Despite the expanding
Reconstruction, much of the nation was over the war and
railroads were building new lines as the country looked
to expand into the Western frontier. This was also good
for Currituck, since people of wealth were beginning to
recognize the potential of the Atlantic shore and
recreational activities like hunting and fishing for
pleasure were coming into vogue. This meant that the
tug operators had a great business to service customers
in areas where railroads couldn't run, such as marshy
tidewater lands. It was a mixed blessing, however, for
they just couldn't start the ferry system they wanted
without neglecting the commercial transportation needs
of the area.

They had a partial answer, however, using John
O'Brien's tug with a modified barge to ferry people to
and from the Currituck docks when demand warranted.
They did work it around the supply schedules and the
barge was not a luxurious ride, but it did work for
hunting parties to remote western shore locations on the
barrier island, Mackey Island and the now emerging
fowl-rich environs north of Kitty Hawk. With John
Eldridge's past hunting experience and his contacts, they
also found tour guides for small parties who could ferry

their clientele by way of sailing dories, which worked very efficiently. It was a win-win for the partners and Josh's dad as well as the locals who had great skill at hunting and needed work.

The modified approach to business had its drawbacks when the supply transit became extremely busy, but it did give them the opportunity to test the waters and see if a real market was growing for general passenger service as well. Besides, they had the equipment to try without any large cash outlays and Josh was sure it was helping them prepare for the future.

In the meantime, they were also picking up new commercial business in Manteo and added a few in Nags Head, Kitty Hawk and even in Stumpy Point on the western shore, their first venture that far south into Pamlico territory. All of their other ports of call were booming as well, but the workload was causing major strains on married life. By late October, the loneliness and strains of being in a rural setting began to be noticed by all in Natasha.

Natasha had always been a city girl as was Annie, but unlike Annie she had no relatives to ground her in the joys of simple living and being thankful for whatever life gave her. While Natasha loved Shorty, she wanted more than to sit home and wait for her man. She wanted him to do special things for her and not take her for granted and the strain it was bringing to their marriage was putting a divide between them. He tried as hard as he could but he knew if he slacked off, customers would seek other options that were sure at some point to surface. His younger and very attractive mate was allowing herself for the first time to grow resentful of him for the first time in her marriage.

Playing a part in it as well was the fact that she couldn't have children, so she naturally was a little jealous of Annie. She felt like the odd girl out when Annie was so often too busy to spend time with her since Josh's family was now her family as well. Annie felt right at home in Currituck and the rural setting while there were times when Natasha missed the hustle and bustle of Norfolk. She just wasn't thinking clearly.

Annie and Josh could talk over the issues and Annie recognized that it was important to maintain a good emergency fund. Natasha, on the other hand, had forgotten the recent bad times already and wanted more now. She wanted to go shopping and out to nice places and she kept telling Shorty that he needed to take off. She wanted him to take time to go with her to Norfolk for an overnight visit and a ritzy dinner. That just wasn't what Shorty was all about.

One evening after a long day on the water, Shorty walked in to a pouting Natasha who said she was going to Norfolk for a few days. He didn't like the idea but he relented, knowing that she would probably go anyway. He gave her some money, got her a round trip ticket on the schooner service, and she left the next morning. She did kiss him goodbye and said she loved him, but gave no inkling of how long she would stay or where. It was a day when they were performing engine maintenance at home and Josh first saw Shorty as he walked back from putting Natasha on the vessel at the Currituck docks.

Josh asked, "Where you been, Skipper? You look like you just lost your best friend."

"I don't know, Josh," he replied. "Perhaps I'm in the first stages of losing my wife instead. She's not happy so I let her take a little trip to Norfolk to visit old friends."

The two men talked and Shorty explained that Natasha felt neglected and said he was too tight with their money. Josh was just there to listen but it bothered him, for he and Natasha had been so good together and he hated to see that bond stretched. Of course, he knew that Annie being so busy with their little boy, John Albert, didn't help any since there weren't many younger people around Currituck for her to have as friends.

"Let me talk to Annie tonight, Shorty," he said. "We have our share of problems, too, due to our heavy schedule, but at least Annie has things to keep her busy."

Shorty thanked him and the two men went back to work, trying to figure out what was causing the strange hum in the tug diesel engine.

That night, Natasha was staying with two of her old girlfriends who lived near the Ocean View resort area. They were both single, a bit flighty and wild and they loved to party, so they took Natasha to a ritzy piano bar at the oceanfront hotel. It was the place to be to meet well-to-do visiting business executives if you were after a wild night. Natasha's two friends were sisters and they weren't prostitutes. They had plenty of money, the daughters of a Greek shipping magnate, but they had no interest in being monogamous and they saw nothing wrong with trying to lead Natasha astray. They saw it as a challenge.

That night as they walked into the classy piano bar, the two brunettes and a blonde captured the eye of every man in the place. Most were with women like the Theodofoulos sisters, out for a good time and whatever that brought. They made their way to a table in a location where they could see and be seen. The older sister, Stephanie, ordered three stiff drinks for the trio and told the waiter to keep them coming. She told Natasha not to worry, she was being treated to a night out.

Two drinks later, Natasha was getting quite tipsy and she started laughing at every joke, funny or not. The two sisters looked at each other with a devilish grin as if to say their plan was working.

Soon a distinguished looking man with jet black and perfectly coiffed hair and a very expensive suit walked up and asked Natasha to dance. She was inclined to say no but the now third drink was draining her inhibitions so she accepted. On the dance floor, he was a smooth dancer and held her just close enough, but not too much so as they wheeled around the room. He whispered words in her ear, words about her beauty and her poise and grace. She was enjoying what he said and he held her closer.

The sisters looked at her with smiles and nods as she started to melt into his arms. He led her to a private table and ordered champagne. He was charming and very handsome and Natasha caught herself thinking that she wondered what he would be like, but then she wiped it out of her mind.

He never tried to prod her to leave with him, but just talked about her beauty and how much he enjoyed her company and dancing with her. Later, when the sisters were ready to leave, he took her to them and said he hoped she'd return, that he would be there every night for five days until his business was completed.

That night, Natasha had a dream of the man, but she also dreamed of how heartbroken Shorty must be. In her dream, however, she just didn't care. So, when the Theo sisters asked her the next day if she wanted to go with them to Ocean View again, she followed her dream, readily agreed and off they went.

As she walked in, the same handsome man named Bill walked up to her and asked if she would join him for dancing, drinks and a bite to eat. Without hesitation she joined him and, once again, he made small talk and complimented her on her beauty. He never made a move at all, she did. Again after a few stiff drinks she asked him if he wanted to go somewhere more private. When he asked why, she leaned over and whispered in his ear.

All she said was, "I want you. I want you tonight."

Later, after letting her get anxious while he played her in a very gentleman fashion, he took her by the hand and led her to the stairway toward his suite. He smiled to himself knowing that his plan had worked like a charm.

Back in Currituck, four days passed and there was no sign of, or word from, Natasha. Shorty was really despondent. Josh noticed he was having trouble focusing on work, something alien to a workaholic like Shorty, so when he got home, he sat down with Annie.

He said to her, "Did Natasha ever confide in you about her relationship with Shorty? Did she ever mention she was unhappy and felt neglected?"

Annie looked unsurprised, replying, "Well, she did say that she thought he was taking her for granted and there were times when she wondered what another man would be like. I didn't think it was serious, many women have such thoughts at some time in their life but realize they aren't serious, just curiosity. Now that Natasha's been gone for four days with no notice, however, I'm getting worried."

Josh asked Annie if Natasha came back, would she talk with her. Annie offered a different suggestion.

She said, "Why don't you go to Norfolk and find her, Josh? She respects you and I think she would listen. She shouldn't be too hard to locate, her two girlfriends are the Theodofoulos sisters, you know, the ones with the rich Greek shipping father."

Josh thought to himself that Natasha was playing with the world party set and that wasn't good, but he agreed and said after the next run he would go. He also said he would ask Shorty first, to which Annie agreed that would be smart.

Shorty told Josh the next day that he thought his plan was a good one and he hugged him, saying he was not only a good workmate but a great friend. So, on return to Currituck and home, on the next day Josh boarded the schooner for Norfolk.

Upon arrival, he asked where the sisters lived. It turned out they were in the ritzy neighborhood walking distance from where Natasha and Shorty lived. He went to the house and a butler in a morning jacket answered. He told him who he was and who he was looking for. The doorman stepped out on the porch, closed the door and looked around him to be sure no one was listening and said he had seen Natasha.

"That one is a looker and if she hangs around with my employer very long, she'll get more than she can handle. I'll bet you can find her tonight in the fancy piano bar down at the Ocean View Hotel. Try it after eight, they go there almost every night looking for handsome men."

Josh's worst expectations were true, but a deal with his wife and Shorty was a deal and he would present himself at the appropriate hour. He did have a slight smile realizing that the beautiful Ocean View resort was where he and Annie consummated their marriage and he was so happy they were married. He'd have to remember when he got home to never allow what was happening to Shorty and Natasha to happen to them due to his lack of attention.

At half past eight he walked into the piano bar and took a seat at a small table that gave him a good view of the action without being too obvious himself. He ordered a whiskey and watched the entranceway. Sure enough, before nine three beautiful women, two brunettes and a blonde, entered in attire that highlighted their figures and beauty. One of them was Natasha and almost upon her arrival, a tall handsome man met her and she walked over to another table with him. As they talked, she nuzzled with him and kissed him twice and Josh fully realized that Shorty's concerns were real. Josh was actually embarrassed, for he had never seen Natasha like this and it troubled him.

The gentleman took her out on the dance floor for a number and they then returned to the table where he ordered another round. Josh figured it was now or never, so he rose from his seat, took a deep breath and headed toward their table.

As he approached, he said, "Excuse me, Sir, but may I have a dance with your beautiful companion. She is a friend of mine who I haven't seen in a long time."

Natasha looked shocked but quickly recovered, saying, "Hi Josh, it's good to see you again and of course I'll dance with you. Excuse us, Bill, we'll be right back."

Josh was not a good dancer, but he was adept enough not to step on her feet as he put on a smile and whispered into her ear, "Have you lost your mind, Natasha? What in the hell are you doing? Do you know that poor Shorty, your husband, can't eat, sleep or even work well?"

She began to softly cry, but then said, "But I can't live without something other than looking at the sound and pine trees, Josh. And I need him to take me in his arms every day and tell me how much he loves me. You know, Shorty, I love him but he will never be able to do that. I want to live and laugh and love. Don't you understand?"

Josh was sympathetic, but he also knew how much Shorty loved her and said, "There's a lot more to love than what you are looking for, Natasha. You are a very beautiful and desirable woman and if you don't mind breaking the heart of the man who would give his life for you, then go ahead. Now I am going to walk you over and return you to your gentleman friend, then I am going to walk out of this piano bar. I will go and sit in the lobby for a half hour and then I will leave. You do what you think you should do."

They ended their dance, he took her back to her table by the hand, looked her deeply in the eyes and thanked her for the dance, nodded at her companion and then walked out of the room. He waited in the lobby for an extra fifteen minutes, then left.

The next morning, he boarded the schooner for Currituck, arrived in early afternoon and went home to Annie. He told her his mission had failed but he also told her he would not tell Shorty the truth.

"I can't do it, Annie," he said. "I am afraid of what Shorty might do to himself. I will tell him I just couldn't find her."

She hugged him tight, thanked him for his efforts and told him he was probably right.

The next day when he met Shorty on the boat, he told him he didn't find her, that she had been several places he looked but no one would give him any information. Shorty said nothing except to thank him for his efforts and they were off for a two-day run. They went through Coinjock, called on Elizabeth City, Edenton, Plymouth, and Columbia, then ended the first day in their new port, Stumpy Point. The next day, a fairly choppy one, they crossed the expansive Pamlico Sound, making an added stop in Hatteras to deliver some building supplies that missed their regular shipment.

Heading north past Oregon Inlet with stops at Manteo, Old Nags Head and Kitty Hawk, Josh looked at the quiet beauty of those slightly inhabited sand bars and wondered how many lost souls lived on those barren isles. He had no idea what made him think of that but he was beginning to realize that he had a place in this life which far outweighed the life of a tugboat captain pushing barges. He still needed to figure out what was missing and how to find it. He had some soul searching to do.

Josh and Shorty arrived back in Currituck after dark, tied up and secured the barge. They would need sunlight and the supply wagons due in the morning to unload. The on-duty dock man would keep an eye on the supplies.

Josh invited Shorty to come over for a late supper but he was told no, that it would be okay. They went to their own homes and as Josh walked in, seeing Annie at the stove with John Albert nearby peacefully dreaming, he realized how lucky he was. He walked over to her, took the stirring spoon out of her hands and placed it in the steaming pot. Then he took her in his arms and kissed her with passion, telling her without words how much he missed her.

He looked her in the eyes and said, "I love you with all my heart and don't let me ever forget to tell you that. I am nothing without you."

She smiled deeply, then said, "Don't forget John Albert," as she went back to finishing the preparation of his supper.

Just down the road, Shorty walked into his darkened house, somewhat despondent, but not suicidal for he'd never take the coward's way out. He walked into the kitchen and lit a lamp, figuring out what there was to eat. He had an eerie feeling, however, that he wasn't alone and then he heard strange sounds. At first, he couldn't tell what they were but then realized it was someone sobbing softly. He turned around and looked at the kitchen table and there, leaning over the table bawling into her hands was Natasha.

He felt a feeling of anger at first, but then it turned into love, for he knew he still loved her. She looked up at him and continued to cry. Then she decided to speak. She asked for his forgiveness.

"Will you take me back, Shorty? I know I don't deserve it but I still love you. I don't want it to end. What can I do to make it up to you?"

Poor old Shorty softened like a marshmallow when he saw tears on her beautiful face. He walked over to her, gently grabbed her by both hands and lifted her out of her chair, then put his arms snugly around her with her head on his shoulder.

He spoke softly, saying, "How can I not forgive you if I really love you? I always will, but I don't want to hear about it, so here's what we're going to do. We will not talk about this ever again. I love you, Natasha, but I want you to only love me. If we can work together for that, we will be okay. Let's both give this marriage our all and we'll be better than ever together."

They kissed passionately and she took him by the hand and led him to their bedroom, closing the door behind them after they entered.

The next day when Josh and Shorty met at the dock, Shorty surprised him. He was whistling and was chipper and told him that Natasha was back and that he forgave her.

"I know you didn't tell me what you saw when you were in Norfolk," Shorty said, "and I don't want to know. I do know, however, that you have a gift with people of making them see the difference of right from wrong. You left your mark on Natasha in Norfolk and she thought about it after you left and came home. You are a great tug boat man but you also need to figure out a way to use your skill in other ways. You have something wonderful within you that a troubled world truly needs."

Josh thanked Shorty and pondered what he had just been told. Something was working on him and he was going to figure out what it was. He knew life was too short not to do what was meant to be. He would be thinking about it a lot in the days ahead.

SEVENTEEN

After the Weston's crisis, Josh and Annie went out of their way to be kind and help them come together in any way they could. Christmas was drawing near and the two men even cut back their schedules and their customers were supportive. It was a different time and everyone needed to put family first at Christmas. John O'Brien volunteered to handle any necessary runs for the holidays as he would be granted a special bonus for doing so. He loved the water and said he could always stop along the way for a little cheer with customers who were always generous at Christmas. Josh and Shorty also committed to taking a close look at their business plans in the new year, making sure that they remembered to put family first.

For Shorty's part, he went out of his way to try to show Natasha how much he loved her. On a trip to Elizabeth City, he found her a beautiful dress and Josh and he made plans to take a trip with the ladies to the city for dinner and a couple of overnights just for adults. Emma Eldridge coaxed her son along on this, knowing that it would be good for both couples and, besides, she could spoil John Albert while they were gone. She loved that little boy and welcomed time caring for him.

The two tugboat men were keeping their plans a secret and wouldn't tell Annie and Natasha until nearly the last minute, getting Emma and John to have them up at their house while they finalized a special touch. They decided to decorate the tug and use it for transportation. There was plenty of room in the wheel house and it was warm and it would give the ladies time to see why they loved being on the water so much. If the weather was good, they planned to make the trip beginning in the middle of the afternoon so the beauty of an Albemarle sunset on the water could be enjoyed.

Using the wireless at the court house, they finalized reservations at the hotel, decorated the boat and when their ladies returned home that afternoon, they sprung the plan on them. They would head for Elizabeth City the next day. The two men were pleased that the ladies were delighted and, of course, they went to get things ready for the trip. As the sun began to drop, they noticed how red the sunset would be and they smiled, knowing that good weather was coming. Reading the elements was important since weather prognostication was scant in those times.

Wednesday, December eighteenth dawned beautiful. The sky was cloudless and a deep blue, there was only the trace of a breeze and the sound was almost glassy. It was chilly but would warm up and as the ladies finished packing, Josh and Shorty got the boat shipshape. They had decorated the wheelhouse in red and green with a wreath on the cabin door and some mistletoe dangling just inside. They turned the wall mounted pull down bed into a sofa and were ready to go. Emma and John

Eldridge rode up to see them off and to pick up John Albert.

Josh beckoned his parents to the boat, saying, "Come on board and tell me what you think, Ma and Dad? Let me run and get Annie and John Albert. I know she's got a bag with enough for a month. Just stay here while we fetch the ladies and I can brew up some coffee if you'd like."

The older couple was surprised at the ingenuity of their son and his good friend. The wheelhouse looked like a cozy sitting room and they were surprised how effectively they used the space. Their attention quickly turned toward the house as Annie came toward them with the growing baby in her arms. Like Josh, Shorty soon returned with Natasha, loaded down with her traveling bag that he jokingly referred to as a steamer trunk. The two husbands, however, had planned things to perfection and the bags fit right under the now sofa and were out of sight.

The parents stayed long enough to have a cup of Josh's special blend coffee and they asked where he got it. He told them he'd bring them some home from Elizabeth City upon return and, with that, Emma took John Albert, was helped off the boat by the doting grandfather and the threesome was buggy bound for home up the road. It was now time to sail.

Shorty grinned as he said, "Now, I'll warn you ladies, when I fire up the diesel it will be quite noisy, but once we get to cruising speed it will calm down. Just stay seated until we get her out in the channel at cruising speed and then we'll walk on the deck. I have some deck shoes for both of you to wear so you won't slip."

As the powerful diesel engine started, it was loud and they waited for the steam pressure to build, then Sam Jarvis, who would be working with O'Brien, caught the lines on the pier and they slowly pulled away from the dock, then turned out toward the sound and headed to deeper water. Turning starboard, they began approaching cruising speed as they headed toward the Coinjock Canal.

The ladies were totally overwhelmed by the raw power of the diesel engine and the beautiful scenery passing by. The sun was just beginning its descent toward evening and seagulls were following them on the glassy sound, only broken by the wake of the tug. Josh and Shorty took turns at the wheel, alternating answering the ladies' questions. As they turned to starboard to enter the Coinjock Canal, slowing almost to a stop awaiting the signal to come through, they were fascinated. They had been standing at the makeshift rail, installed just for their safety, and stayed there until they completed the three-mile cut and entered the North River, now turning to port toward the Albemarle. They came in to rest and were amazed at how cozy the heat of the diesel made the cabin.

Natasha asked, "How do you stand it on a hot summer day? Don't you roast?"

Shorty showed the ladies the exhaust pipe that, while open to allow fumes out, can be helped by the blower motor which is used when needed during excessively hot weather. He also reminded them that when the pilot house windows are open as well as the door, a natural breeze blows through that clears the excess heat.

Later, as the sun began to slide downward, they entered the Albemarle which compared to the other bodies looked like an ocean.

Annie said with amazement, "Are you sure this isn't the ocean? This is so much like the Chesapeake Bay."

Shorty assured her it was the Albemarle. Then, as they turned to starboard to power their way to the mouth of the Pasquotank. Annie was awestruck by the sky. It was beginning the earliest late afternoon phases of color and she could tell it would be beautiful. Their next turn was to starboard as they entered the Pasquotank and the short final leg to Elizabeth City, the sky was now turning a beautiful red.

Josh and Shorty nodded with a smile and almost in unison said, "Tonight is a sailor's delight and tomorrow will again be beautiful. We'll sail to Edenton to see the beautiful town in its Christmas splendor."

The ladies just smiled from ear to ear, they were so happy for this little adventure with the men they loved.

Docking was fast, Shorty slipped some money to the dock foreman who provided nighttime security, and they were off, bags and all, to check in to the hotel. The ladies were so impressed when they entered their adjoining bedrooms with their soulmates and found fresh flowers with notes saying from the one who loves you.

Great minds must think alike because it was now after six but their dinner reservations were set for a fashionable eight-thirty. Both men, with devilish smiles on their faces, walked to their doors, locked them and took their beautiful wives in their arms. The shades of night were definitely heavenly at that moment.

Dinner was quite the occasion with patrons dressed up for a special seasonal dinner. Josh and Shorty had stopped in the bar for a drink since they knew if they stayed while the women primped and made themselves perfect, they would grow impatient. The restaurant and bar were owned by the hotel, but it had a separate entrance and Josh was slightly shocked as he walked up to the seating stand. There, looking resplendent in a red gown checking the seating chart was Rachel, the girl he tried to help.

She gave him a big smile and said, "Well, Josh, I took your advice and worked at the clothing shop for a year where a regular customer was Roger Baum, the owner of this hotel. He had a beautiful girlfriend who jilted him and over time he and I just gravitated toward one another. He hired me to manage the hotel front desk and now I am managing this bar and restaurant. Your advice was good and I turned my life around. Roger and I will be married in just a few months."

Josh gave her a gentle hug and kiss on the cheek, saying he was proud of her and she showed them to their table. Shorty, for his part, was ecstatic for he always feared that Josh might somehow be connected with Rachel again. He was glad to see her finding a man who helped her get straight with life.

A few minutes later, Annie and Natasha showed up at the doorway, looking resplendent and beautiful. Rachel glanced at Josh with a quizzical "is this them" look. He nodded and she brought them to the table. She suggested that they get another drink plus drinks for the ladies and said she would seat them shortly thereafter.

The dinner was wonderful, they had roast beef with potatoes and steamed broccoli with chocolate mousse for dessert. They enjoyed relaxing as they ate with a small quartet singing to a beautiful grand piano. Later they put on coats and walked out into the chill of the night, admiring the twinkling stars above. The moon began to rise over the Pasquotank as they walked a short distance to the water and Annie was pensive but smiling.

Holding Josh's hand tightly, she said, "You two fellows have been unbelievable this day. This has been the most wonderful day since our wedding, Josh and I wish it would never end."

Josh replied, "Well, if it didn't you wouldn't see John Albert again either, would you, Honey?"

They all laughed, with Shorty saying amen to that as they headed back for a special night's sleep. Each man dozed off smiling, looking at his beautiful wife with her head on his shoulder.

In the morning, they had a leisurely breakfast then fired up the Miss Margaret for the run to Edenton. The ladies were impressed at all the businesspeople near the docks who knew and liked their husbands and they were invited to lunch. While walking to the great little tea room that the townspeople loved, they passed James Hewes, the planter who was awaiting his dory from Josh's father.

"Hello, Mr. Hewes," Josh said, "We'll be contacting you right after the holidays and schedule delivery of your dory."

The locals went on, saying they would hold seats for Josh, Shorty and their wives while Josh introduced the successful agriculture tycoon to the ladies. Mr. Hewes congratulated Josh and Shorty for the successful outcome of their legal issues and invited him to stay on his plantation overnight when the boat was delivered.

"Your wives would, of course, be welcome as well," he said on departure. The ladies seemed enthralled.

The lunch was wonderful and they thanked their hosts profusely before heading out to let the ladies do a little shopping. They wanted to get back to Elizabeth City before nightfall as there would be Christmas fireworks on the waterfront, complete with a festival atmosphere and some Christmas libations. The townspeople were finally coming back to normalcy after the war and their lives showed real promise again.

The evening was wonderful and they were all a bit tipsy as they returned to their comfortable hotel. They all joined together for a nightcap before turning in. They would leave early the next day, run across the Albemarle to Columbia where a shipment was awaiting and then head back to Currituck. The ladies enjoyed the travel across the Albemarle, found the swampy yet beautiful environs quaint and loved the little town. The shipment would ultimately go to Norfolk and John O'Brien volunteered to take the final leg.

While steaming home, it got a bit windy and the whitecaps began. They weren't heavy but they were enough to cause Natasha to become seasick. Shorty went to her side and Josh skippered them all the way home while Annie enjoyed watching him work. Annie was unfazed by the chop and seemed to revel in it. She was proud of what he had made of himself and hoped they could always find a middle ground when she needed some attention. The pre-Christmas surprise trip certainly worked wonders for now and she was appreciative.

Making it safe and secure back home, Natasha quickly recovered and the two close couples and John's parents had a joyous Christmas together. John O'Brien took care of the shipments that had to be handled along with Sam Jarvis who both wanted the extra money, and life was good for everyone. Josh and Shorty were keenly aware, however, that they must make some changes if they were going to keep their families happy. They both recognized there was something in life more important than money. While it was certainly important, if they sacrificed those that they loved for it, they would lose the most valuable part of their lives.

Josh began to ponder his younger days back home growing up when he and his parents went to church every Sunday. While he remembered sometimes being bored and impatient, he also remembered how his days in Sunday school and church made him feel secure and safe. Why was that and why was it coming back into his thoughts now? He knew that he had to answer that question or he would never be satisfied.

On New Year's Eve the two couples and Josh's parents gathered together for a toast. It was a toast toward the future and one which would help guide them to where they needed to go. Afterwards, each of the three couples retired to their own homes. For Josh and Annie, it meant making sure John Albert was fast asleep and then they sat by the fire and just talked. It was open and honest talk and they shared their thoughts about what they wanted and needed.

Josh opened the conversation, saying, "You know, Annie, we are missing something in our lives and I think I am coming to grips with it. I want you to hear me out."

She was snuggled up next to him and she leaned over and kissed him on the cheek saying, "Please tell me what you think, Josh. I w ill respond openly and honestly for I also believe we have to focus differently on the future. I love you and whatever we do has to be something we decide together."

Josh began, "Annie, I have been truly blessed, blessed with you and John Albert, great parents and blessed by God to get me through the war and back home again. I am also blessed with a home that we own free and clear, thanks mostly to your inheritance, and a great business with a great partner. So, I feel guilty, I know that I must do something to repay God for His blessings.

"I grew up in the Methodist Episcopal Church starting with Grandma taking me to church. Mom went occasionally and I know both she and Dad say their prayers and read the Bible but I went all the time. And now it's coming back to me, but we don't have a regular church here. The little church closed when so many went off to war. That little church needs to be reborn and there is so much more that is needed for those isolated by water. I want to be a part of making that happen.

"In order to do that, I want to study and learn more about the Bible. I want to learn what God really wants me to do and figure out a way to include it in my life. I first thought of this when I was fortunate enough to survive Point Lookout but I just put it out of my mind. Now, however, no longer faced with the threat of not being able to earn a good living, I see people every day in my travels who need God's help. While I don't want to be a full-time ordained minister, there must be something I can do to further His work."

Annie hugged him tight saying, "Josh, I have some of the same feelings and if you want to do something, why don't we start by going to church regularly in Moyock. I know they would love to have someone like you for you have a great gift with people and Reverend Whitehurst could help you find the right place for you."

"Let's sleep on it, Josh," Annie said, "I want to think about it, too and we can talk some more tomorrow. Let's think about going to church in Moyock Sunday."

Josh reached over to turn off the gas lamp and Annie cuddled up in his arms and they drifted off to sleep. Both dreamed about exactly what they had discussed, for their minds remained active while they slept and would surprise them in the morning by what it brought out.

When they awoke, Josh jumped out of bed and decided to surprise Annie by getting the coffee ready. As it brewed, the delicious aroma made its way to the bedroom and Annie awoke to it. She noticed Josh was up and rose suddenly, donned a robe and headed to the kitchen. He was seated at the table with a cup of coffee in his hand. On seeing her, he hurried over to the stove to pour her a cup, brought it to her at the table and kissed her gently. Annie was looking at the paper and pen where he was seated and curious about what he was doing.

"I was making some notes, Annie," Josh said, "from what we were talking about last night. I was remembering what I knew about the organization of the church and I thought of the lay ministry. I could train for that while still working and work for becoming a lay minister in my travels. I know that since the division of churches after the war ministers are in short supply. What do you think?"

"Well, I know you have to get out of here today with a shipment for your customers," she said, "so let me think about it while you are gone and then we'll plan to talk with Reverend Whitehurst Sunday. I am curious about one thing, though. What made you decide you wanted to do something like this? What convinced you that you had a calling? You know, Josh, to really work for the Lord you must have a calling."

For the first time, Josh told her the details of his interface with Natasha in Norfolk and how he felt he was being guided by a strong force outside of himself. She had to admit, he must have said something powerful to her that made her soon come to her senses. Helping a friend to save a marriage without causing bad feelings certainly was a special gift.

As he got ready to go, Annie had an idea that she would carry out after he left. Mrs. Daniels up the road was a regular at Moyock and was influential in the church. She would talk with her and also with Natasha, gently getting her take on Josh's counseling skills. She walked with him to the boat to kiss him and say goodbye and would walk back with Natasha, who was already there, kissing Shorty goodbye. As the Miss Margaret sailed away with their men, the two women walked over to Natasha's house for a cup of coffee. Annie told Natasha what she wanted to know about Josh and his counseling and verbal skills and why.

Natasha smiled as she said, "Why, Annie, if Josh didn't do what he did, I probably would have never come home. I was ashamed and embarrassed at the same time and knew I couldn't face Shorty. Josh was insistent, however, and while I stubbornly didn't come with him back home that night, he really got my mind spinning. I know I can tell you this in privacy, but I was guilty of responding to my lust and not love. Shorty had grown so aloof and I just wanted to feel physically wanted, not realizing that I was just being used. Josh set me straight and it's why I came home. I will spend the rest of my life making it up to Shorty for I know he truly loves me. Things are now so much better and I am happier than I've ever been in my life. I can tell you that we will never take each other for granted again and I owe Josh a debt of gratitude for opening my eyes."

When the two ladies said goodbye, Annie was beginning to realize that Josh obviously had a special gift that needed to be shared. The next day she took the buckboard up to see Mrs. Daniels who lightened up brightly to what she said. She was a smiling older lady who clearly knew where her life would lead her.

"Annie, darling,": Mrs. Daniels said. "Let me talk with the Reverend and set it up. He is always looking for someone younger to help with the mission of the church and who could be better than a young man who has seen his share of suffering. What training he can't provide can be handled up in Portsmouth where training is conducted when they have a good candidate. Currituck is in the same church district. Let me get busy and I'll see you in church Sunday."

A day later when Josh and Shorty returned, Annie made a special dinner for her husband. A hunter down the road, a man Josh frequently did favors for, brought her some beautiful venison ready to cook. She made it into a wonderful stew with vegetables and a thick broth and had it piping hot when he walked in the door. She ran to him, threw her arms around him and kissed him hard.

Josh grinned and said, "Well, Annie, I guess you missed me as much as I missed you. What's that I smell cooking, it smells wonderful. Where did you get the deer?"

She told him and said she also had done some research and his thoughts for the future were doable. She told of her visit with Natasha as well as Mrs. Daniels and told him the more she thought about it the better it sounded.

"You know, as a father, Josh,' she added. "the best way to get your young son in the Spirit is through your example, just like your grandmother did for you."

He agreed and as they sat down for a delicious dinner, Josh said a beautiful grace for all of their many blessings. It was the perfect ending of a long but very productive day, for the two skippers made a great profit and they were glad that a Currituck entrepreneur started a teamster's group to haul supplies north to Norfolk by land. No longer did they have to make the Norfolk trip and that was a huge blessing in itself. The fact that Josh and Shorty had a nice stake in the business, having helped with start up costs, wasn't bad either.

It was Saturday night and Josh and Annie turned in early for tomorrow was a big day for him up in Moyock in the morning. As they were lying in bed, awaiting sleep, Josh began a prayer out loud, holding Annie's hand close as he said it. He asked God to guide him and direct him in whatever was meant to be for him and for his family and all needing Him. Then he kissed Annie and they heled each other, falling asleep feeling secure in their love.

Josh had a dream that night. In his dream he saw himself speaking publicly and using words that he could have never created on his own. He was receiving a subtle answer to what his future should and could be. All that was needed now was his commitment.

EIGHTEEN

Sunday morning came bright and beautiful and Josh made coffee and started getting ready for church before Annie awoke. The grandparents were coming to look after John Albert while the young couple would travel to Moyock to speak with Pastor Whitehurst and attend services. Josh was nervous but he was comforted by his dream and Annie walked into the kitchen, smelling the perking coffee she needed to start the day.

She saw Josh sitting at the table just thinking and said, "I noticed you were up awfully early, Hon. Are you worried about talking to Pastor Whitehurst? You shouldn't be, he's a very nice man."

Josh hugged her and said, "I'm not worried but I am nervous. I don't know why exactly but I think it's because I feel like I must not fail. It's just something I must do."

They sat for a few moments with their coffee at the table and Annie just encouraged him, telling him if the Lord has called him then he won't fail, just like he hasn't failed to become a good skipper in record time.

He laughed and acknowledged how silly he must sound, kissed her and told her to get ready first. Since he was already shaved and cleaned up, all he had to do was throw on his Sunday clothes which were ready. While he sat there, he thought about his dream again and realized that it was telling him in advance where he was headed with his life.

Shortly, his parents came in and Annie came down looking beautiful with John Albert in her arms. Grandmother Emma scooped up the boy and told them not to worry, she and John would love to care for him. She also told Josh she was very proud of him.

Annie wasn't one to eat much in the morning and Josh said he was too nervous to eat, so they headed out in the buckboard on an unusually warm January morning. Sixty degrees was almost unheard of, but here they were sunny and bright and it felt like a spring day. The trip to Moyock took just over an hour and they passed a teamster wagon headed south. Josh figured it was probably coming to take the final load of his shipment to Norfolk.

They arrived at the church at half past nine, about a half-hour ahead of time, and just sat in the buggy waiting for Pastor Whitehurst. Soon, he came in with a wave and invited them into his small office behind the sanctuary. He was a man about the age of Josh's father with a portly build but smiling eyes. He welcomed them as they sat on a sofa next to his desk.

"So, Josh," he began. "I know I've seen you here in church a few times and I also know you lived through a terrible ordeal during the war. The strength and courage you have is something that we always need in service to the Lord but tell me why you want to do something that will directly impact those around you for Him."

Josh was silent for a moment and then as if struck by Divine Providence, he just poured out his soul. He told Reverend Whitehurst that he had grown up in the church, had been absent from it during the war, but now his heart told him there was something he must do for God. It was like an awakening of his soul. He saw the futility of life just for the sake of living without meaning and that he knew there was something much bigger. Without being too informative, he told the story of dealing with the guard on the Dismal Swamp and how he substituted peace and logic for fisticuffs to solve his dilemma without incident. In a similar fashion, but without specifics, he explained his counseling with Natasha and how it had worked, bringing her to her senses.

They talked for a few more minutes and then the Methodist minister said, "Well, Son, you've convinced me and we always need traveling lay preachers to help spread God's word. God's business here is definitely in need of some willing souls to help. I know, however, that you have a busy and viable business, so I have to ask a serious question. Can you devote three weekends over three months for training either here or up in Portsmouth. I'll also give you Bible reading assignments to bring you up to speed on things, but I know if you attended Sunday school a lot of it will come back quickly."

Josh unhesitatingly said yes before Pastor Whitehurst continued.

"That's good, Josh, but now I have to ask about your commitment after you are trained. You can provide a great service since there are Methodists in many of the locations on your travels, places like Columbia, East Lake and even right there at Currituck Court House. You might even be able to help out on occasion with the Outer Banks since the Methodist Church in Wanchese leads that effort. While Methodism is the oldest Christian denomination on the Outer Banks, we are woefully short of manpower to fully meet our mission. Sadly, since we are part of the Virginia Conference, I sometimes think our Virginia brothers and sisters look at us as stepchildren."

The pastor was very honest and open, he told Josh that anything he did was strictly as a trained volunteer, but he probably could draw a stipend once fully involved for travel and incidentals. Josh realized that his commitment was one because he wanted to do something for God for all he received, not be an employee of an organization.

The pastor said he would set up a training schedule of one weekend a month for three months. Bible reading and study would also be required independently and he would be provided a suggested study format. Pastor Whitehurst would provide some of the training, the rest would be done at the Conference lead church in

Portsmouth. They would arrange accommodations for Josh provided he could get himself there. The next phase after that would be to give several training services in front of a congregation, either in Moyock or possibly Elizabeth City, then he would have the basics and would gain further knowledge from experiences he would undoubtedly face.

Reverend Whitehurst then rose, told Josh he would hear from him about scheduling in about two weeks and the couple was led to the sanctuary by the pastor. The sermon was about service, about what we give of ourselves to serve God in our daily lives and, at the end, he asked Josh and Annie to stand while he introduced them and told them of the plans they had. As the service ended and everyone departed, Mrs. Daniels, beaming, came over to Annie, gave her a big hug and then turned and put her arms around Josh.

She said, "I'm expecting great things from you, young man and I'm sure you will do very well. I'm hopeful that maybe this will be the start of getting the congregation active again down at the Court House."

Josh thanked her and said he would do his best and then they headed out, shaking hands with many parishioners who wanted to convey their best wishes. Feeling relieved that the interview went well and knowing in his heart that this was what he needed to do, he felt more at peace with himself than he felt since before the war.

On the way home, Josh and Annie sang some beautiful hymns beginning with "Amazing Grace." She held his arm the whole way telling him she was proud of him. She knew it was what he needed to do and she was pleased to be able to be part of it. A stronger relationship with God could help them weather any problems better than ever and she knew that since her childhood. Finally, they would refocus their family strength around their faith and raise John Albert with those same values.

While waiting for word from Pastor Whitehurst about his training, Josh and Shorty went back to work while also making some decisions about how to balance family and business to make life good for all concerned. One thing was taken care of largely by itself, for with the new commercial teamster operation land service from the Currituck dock to Norfolk, that leg of the work was taken excepting unique situations. Josh even got a letter from Mr. Aydlett at the Moyock Hardware thanking him for fixing his supply dilemma. This would also allow the flexibility to handle father John's boat delivery throughout the Albemarle without creating a shipment overload problem. They would now have the time to schedule a sailboat only shipment when a full load was ready.

With regard to family time, Josh and Shorty vowed to limit their service to two roundtrips a week, again excepting emergency needs. The roundtrips weekly would involve stops at Coinjock, Elizabeth City, Edenton, Plymouth, Columbia and East Lake with once monthly service to Stumpy Point, Roanoke Island and the Outer Banks. This should afford them three, sometimes four nights a week at home and overage would be handled by John O'Brien. John worked independently and just enjoyed being in a rural setting where he could fish and hunt on his day off. Occasionally he went to Norfolk when he had a few open days, for he did have a lady friend but he had never talked about any future plans with her.

So, things were getting better, business was still good and they each were building a rainy-day fund while enjoying family life more than they ever did before. Sometimes the two couples would go on a day off picnic or Josh and Shorty would go fishing and hunting for a great home cooked feast. Best of all, the ladies were feeling loved and wanted and even Shorty and Natasha started attending church with their younger close friends. Even John's dad said that when he was qualified and could preach publicly, he would be there with Emma.

Josh and Annie had established a daily devotional time, said grace at each meal and jointly tucked in their precious little boy after saying prayers. They felt better than ever for it and when Pastor Whitehurst rode up in a buggy, they knew John's new opportunity was about to begin.

On the second Saturday in March, 1870, Josh took off early in the buckboard for his initial training session in Moyock. He was refreshed in the Methodist order of service, memorizing it to heart, taught why the service was formulated as it was and was taught about John Wesley and why he developed Methodism. At the end of the day they reviewed some Bible verses, part of John's advanced reading and Mr. Whitehurst said that the next day session would be in the afternoon after church.

"We are having a little covered dish church meal after church, Josh, so you will be able to bring Annie and as long as she can wait around for you for no more than two hours we'll be done for this month. Wasn't that easy"

The Pastor realized that Josh had a gift and was a quick learner. He would go to Portsmouth the following month where the meeting would be led by a senior lay leader which would include several others in training.

After church and training the next day, Annie asked him on the way home, "So, what do you think, Josh? Is this going to be for you?"

"Yes, Annie, it is," he said "and I think the Pastor sees something in me. I'm just going to pray to God for guidance from now on in everything I do and he'll help me out."

On the first Sunday in June, John was announced at the Moyock Church as the new traveling lay leader. On the following Sunday, he would give his first sermon. His topic would be "Why We Need to Know God Better." He would burn the midnight oil all week to get ready and Annie was right there to encourage him. He passed his first test performance with flying colors and next, the following month he would preach before an even larger congregation in Elizabeth City.

With Annie sitting in the congregation and the minister evaluating his performance, as John spoke, he felt like the words were not his, but words coming from someone of much higher authority. He was pleased when the Pastor complimented him, saying that he had held everyone's attention.

"Young man," the seasoned minister said, "You have a gift and I'm glad Reverend Whitehurst saw it in you. You would be welcome to preach anywhere as far as I'm concerned.

The young tugboat skipper was now approved by the church to preach the word of God as a lay missionary for the Methodist Church. He and Annie were invited to lunch with one of the leaders of Elizabeth City commerce and he was complimented on being willing to give his time. It wouldn't be long before the young man who worked on the water would be known in local ports of call as the "Tugboat Preacher." He was on his way, both with a happy family, a decent and honest business and a much more open heart. He was grateful on all counts.

His first calling was to fill in for existing churches when their preacher was away, particularly the Moyock and Wanchese churches. He also spent time trying to get the community around the Court House organized so that regular services could be held. It was a different time then and the court house offered a large room in the basement for services on Sunday. Josh enlisted several local Methodists and other religious folks to help clean up and bring in benches. His father even offered to craft a wooden cross and a simple speaking pulpit from some of his leftover wood.

Meanwhile, Josh was still busy with Shorty and the boat, but he made sure not to overdo so that both of them returned home regularly. They were sticking to their vows on the subject. It was at this time, while guiding the tug into a port stop at Columbia, that the guidance of God was of great assistance to him. This incident would remove all doubt about his true purpose in life as God called upon him to act decisively.

As they were nearing the pier, Josh spotted someone in the water and struggling. It was a young woman and she was yelling that she wanted to die, yet seeming to be fighting to stay afloat. She obviously was barely able to swim at best. Josh told Shorty he was going in, kicked off his shoes and hit the water. Thankfully it was warm weather, but with the current and the weight of his clothes he was having trouble making headway with the hysterical woman. It was hard to keep hold on her and there was something very different about her. Fortunately, Shorty had managed to stay within close range and a deckhand threw Josh a lifeline.

Josh pulled the struggling young woman to the side of the boat and, using all the strength he could muster, lifted her high enough that Shorty could pull her over the side and onto the deck. He then climbed up the rope ladder that was dropped and climbed on board and checked her pulse and breathing. She was alive but her pulse was almost non-existent as he rolled her on her side and she expelled a large amount of water. She was shaking with chills and they realized she must be close to delivery time for her baby. With Shorty leading the way, Josh carried her ashore calling for help.

A lady at the first home coming off the dock responded. She opened the door and yelled to them, telling Josh to bring the woman in as she cleared her kitchen table and put a clean tablecloth on it. He placed her on the table face up while she called for her husband to get Ruth, the local midwife. The poor mother-to-be was quite young and the shock had thrown her into labor. The kind woman asked Josh to step out of the kitchen while she took the poor girl out of her wet clothes and covered her with a warm blanket and placed a pillow under her head.

"Okay, Preacher," she said, "You can come back in and pray."

Josh stood nearby to do whatever he could and then put his hand on her shoulder and began to pray out loud. He asked for divine intervention, for God to intervene in the heart of this troubled soul with his mercy and grace and give her another chance. He also prayed for the life of the baby inside her.

Suddenly, she opened her eyes and looked right at John and said, "I see Jesus, you look just like Jesus" and she closed her eyes.

By this time, the midwife, Ruth, arrived and confirmed she was in labor and that the delivery would be soon. She was worried about the health of both mother and baby but that the mother's life was most worrisome.

"That's Becky Baum from East Lake way," she said. "That sailor boy home on leave did this to the poor girl and her parents threw her out. I guess she decided life wasn't worth living and that the little one would be better off in heaven. I wish we could get her to the doctor but there isn't time."

Josh began to pray again out loud and when he did Becky once more opened her eyes and said, "Thank you, Jesus, thank you for saving my baby."

Old Ruth said, "Well, Preacher, Jesus, whoever you are come over here and help me. Her labor is fast because of the activity, but when that baby starts to arrive, we might have to intervene to help nature take its course. I want you to watch for the umbilical cord as it could be wrapped around the neck. If it is, you are going to unwrap it so that delivery can finish. Now wash your hands and bring some towels."

Becky was pushing and screaming and using some choice language when Josh saw the top of the infant's head. As it started to emerge, he said, "Stop," and he gently reached in and pulled the cord from around the child's neck and delivery took its natural course. The midwife lifted the child by the feet and gave her a slap on the bottom and the newborn baby girl proved that her lungs were strong.

He kept praying and, with the kitchen full, she again said, "Thank you, Jesus, you saved me."

Ruth turned around and told everyone they'd better tell the preacher that he has competition in town. The "Tugboat Preacher" had saved two lives and helped in a delivery. Everyone clapped before leaving.

Ruth told him before he left that she appreciated what he did. She also told him that she was very worried about the mother for she wasn't taking good care of herself, but despite that, the baby seemed fine. Ruth said she would care for them for the time being. She asked if he would check in on his next run to town because the girl would obviously want to talk with him.

She said, "You must have a special tongue, my boy, because she would believe anything you said. Thanks for your help.".

They were naturally late leaving and decided to put off the stop in Plymouth until next trip, but they did need to stop in Elizabeth City for coal. On the way, Shorty slapped Josh on the back and said something that would prove to be absolutely true.

"Josh," he said, "whether you know it or not you are now a legend in these parts and henceforth will be the Tugboat Preacher around here. On this day you showed all of us what your true calling is and, trust me, Eastern North Carolina will be better for it.

Two weeks later, Pastor Whitehurst stopped by unannounced on his way to lower Currituck. He handed him a copy of the Virginian-Pilot, the new Norfolk paper which had a feature story about the "Tugboat Preacher from Currituck." The Pastor smiled and confirmed what Shorty had said about his future. Mr. Whitehurst warned him of one thing.

"Josh, if you take your calling seriously and do it properly, you will never get rich from it financially, but spiritually you will be one of the richest men God ever placed on earth. Never forget that."

Josh never would.

NINETEEN

As the two skippers headed on their rounds on the Albemarle, Josh showed Shorty the feature article in the Pilot.

"Wow, Josh, that's a big deal," said Shorty. "That little title will now stick like glue. The Pilot is the main paper read down here as well as in the Tidewater. Just remember, don't get a swollen head or you will think you are much greater than you are."

"You know, Shorty, you are right," the younger co-owner replied, "but I still wonder how that got in the paper so fast for it was little more than a week to publication."

Shorty couldn't help but laugh and Josh knew something was awry and he gave Shorty a look that could kill.

"Okay, Josh, when we stopped in Elizabeth City for coal before heading home, there was a reporter on the dock interviewing someone about a marine accident. I suggested he hitch a ride over to Columbia and get a real story and I guess he did."

Josh laughed for despite his display of modesty about publicity, he liked that "Tugboat Preacher" moniker and knew it would attract people for the flock. He had a strong message to share and he knew these folks needed it.

On this trip they only had three stops, Columbia, Edenton and Elizabeth City and he decided to go in reverse order. As they docked at Columbia he walked up to the general store and asked the proprietor about Ruth the mid-wife and Becky Baum and where Ruth lived.

"Well, I saw you in action last week and you were working for God," the store owner replied. "Ruth lives down North Street, just go down Front Street and look for the street sign, then you'll see her midwife sign in the yard just down a bit. Ruth is looking for you, Preacher and Miss Becky isn't doing so well. Good luck, Son."

He told Shorty what was going on. Shorty said he would take care of deliveries and pick-ups and would wait at the dock. Josh followed the directions he was given and easily found the house. He knocked on the door and Ruth looked very relieved to see him.

"I never even asked your name that day, but am told you are Josh, Joshua," she said, "and I'm glad you are here. Becky isn't doing very well. Since she wasn't eating well during her pregnancy, she has developed pneumonia and the doctor said he's done all he can do. She is in the back bedroom and wants to talk with you, she says it's important."

Ruth led Josh to the room and showed him in, standing back to let Becky say whatever she wanted. Josh pulled up a chair and sat close because she was weak and couldn't speak loudly. Her face was pale, her eyes showed no life and she spoke through a rattle in her chest. Josh knew it wasn't good.

"Miss Ruth says you want to talk with me, Becky," he said. "I'm sorry you are so sick but will try to help you if I can."

She cast her gaze on him, trying to force a smile and said, "I'm glad you came, Pastor Joshua and I have a big favor to ask. Will you pray with me for my soul?"

He knew that she knew her life was going to end and he reached over, held her hands and asked her a question.

"Becky, do you believe in God, the Father, Son and Holy Spirit and do you repent your sins before God and want to go to see Jesus if you die?"

She said, yes and told Him she had seen Him in her dreams.

Josh began to pray, asking Him to look after and care for her while he also praised God for the gift that he had given her in that gorgeous little girl. He prayed for Becky's soul and the care of her little girl and for his grace and love. Becky thanked him and he noticed a tear in her eye, a mixture of sadness and joy. She was sad about losing her new little girl and the part she played in causing her own demise. She was happy, though, because she saw the Light.

Josh asked, "Becky, do you have a name for the child."

Becky said she wanted to name her Rachel, for her grandmother and for her middle name, Yehoshua, the Hebrew name for Joshua which means God is salvation. He was amazed she knew so much about the Bible but questioned using the Hebrew in such a rural place. She said if she had been a boy, she would have named him Joshua, since Joshua saved his life. Josh had some concerns but then he thought of something that would work and also be easy to use.

"Why don't we call her Rachel Salvation Baum, Becky? If anyone asks, it can be explained with the link to Joshua. That way it will be easy to remember and say and it could even be used as a nickname, Sally. I think God himself would smile approvingly at that name."

Becky just smiled weakly, tired from the conversation and Josh could lip read the name Sally being repeated without sound on her lips. He realized that this young woman's heart was in the right place and that Jesus was indeed smiling down on her. He excused himself to go and speak with Ruth who was standing right outside the door.

Josh asked Ruth if Becky had any family who would raise her child. She said her parents wanted nothing to do with her or the baby.

"Can you keep the child temporarily, Ruth, while I work this out. I've got to talk to my lawyer for advice and I'm sure it will require contact with the parents and the father as well. We'll find her a decent home, it just has to be done legally."

Ruth patted his arm, amazed at his generosity and said she would care for the child as long as necessary, then Josh went back to the dying young woman.

She actually smiled as Josh said, "Becky, Miss Ruth will keep the baby until I can get things worked out. We'll find her a good home. I won't let her end up in an orphanage. I was an orphan myself and a wonderful man took me in as his own. Do you like that idea?"

Becky asked him to lean over to her and she kissed him on the cheek and smiled, then she looked toward the ceiling with her eyes open as if in wonder and breathed her last breath. There was a smile on her face.

Josh thanked Ruth and said he'd visit again within a week or so and left, hurrying to the boat to make their port calls. The stop in Edenton was uneventful, he had Mr. Hewes sailing dory to drop off, and several large crates which he assumed were agricultural equipment. He loaded up shipments and they were off to Elizabeth City. On the way, both men noticed a building chop on the sound and made note of it as they arrived in the City on the Pasquotank.

Josh told Shorty he had to see Sam Pratt about the matter of the baby and would hustle back. The dock master told them the shipment would have to be tied down for storm conditions as a nor'easter was brewing.

Josh caught Sam Pratt in his home office, explained the situation and Sam said he'd research the issues and be able to help him in a few days.

The attorney said, "I'll wire you the information, Josh, so when we next meet, we can deal with it. I'm sure there will be a few tricky issues but we'll get it taken care of. By the way, I love the boat, please tell your dad. Now, get out of here before the storm hits."

They loaded up and all gear was stowed, but before beginning their trip, they moved the tug from push to tow mode. Then they headed down river with smooth sailing for the wind was pushing the water behind them but that would soon change. Turning to port in the much larger Albemarle, the wind and waves were now coming directly at the bow, creating a roller coaster effect with water rolling down the deck. Josh was watching the barge closely and was pleased to find that the additional tie down measures were working well.

By the time they reached the Currituck cut, they slowed and brought the barge in a little tighter for the canal. It was quite calm since it was narrow with just some small swells but the closer pull cut down on the chance of getting boat and barge out of alignment in the narrow channel. It also required cutting forward movement to a crawl. They stopped momentarily for some additional coal as Shorty said the added power fighting the Albemarle had burned a lot of coal. The last thing they wanted was to be in the sound with no power. As they neared the sound side lock, Shorty gradually allowed the towline to unreel just before the turbulent Currituck.

As John powered up into the open water, he swung wide, allowing the barge to avoid the impact of the rougher open water until it was clear of the canal. As they turned to the north, Josh had to steer to the starboard to allow for the impact of the waves now coming in at a slant instead of head on. He would maintain that direction until they passed the town, then swing to port so that he could be pushed directly past the blocking jetty where things would be more easily handled. Shorty was pleased to see his younger partner perform so well. He couldn't have done better and it was Josh's first on water experience with such a strong storm. It was blowing hard with some nearly fifty knot gusts on the water with four to five-foot seas, not ideal by any means for towing a heavy barge with a valuable cargo. Shorty would remain silent unless he saw something out of the ordinary that needed his attention.

Josh made the turn at the exact right spot, maintained the proper separation from the barge and safely cut the engine way back as he passed the jetty, then headed slowly for the long dock, reversing engines briefly so that Shorty could bring the barge close to allow better control. This also slowed the tug significantly allowing him to angle in to let the barge reach the dock. The barge deck hand jumped on the pier and secured the barge as Shorty released the tow lines, freeing the Miss Margaret to dock separately.

Both Annie and Natasha were there in foul weather gear, glad to see their men safely home. Sam Jarvis and John O'Brien had been keeping things secure as they scrubbed their scheduled Roanoke Island trip earlier in the day.

The Tugboat Preacher and his older partner had done well, they hugged and kissed their wives and told them to get out of the rain, they would be their soon.

"John O'Brien spoke up, saying, "Go spend some time with your wives, fellows. Sam and I will make sure all things are taken care of. We can't unload until the weather calms and the wagons come tomorrow. We'll take care of everything and make sure things will be fine for overnight. The storm is already starting to lighten up."

They accepted his offer and ran to catch up with their wives who were half way home. When John and Annie got in the door, he immediately hugged her tight and kissed her with vigor and she responded like a woman who was worried about her man. He told her he was safe and all was fine and life on the water has its perils. Then, after changing to dry clothes and washing up, he came back to tell her about his trip, but she wanted to scold him first.

"Josh, I was worried to death about you," she said. "I know Shorty is used to bad storms but you've never been through one like that."

He responded, saying, "Well, Shorty said it was good practice and I was at the helm the whole way. He said I handled things just like he would and here we are, safe and sound, cargo as well. I'm not going to do anything foolish, but I'm sorry I worried you so."

They kissed and made up, not that it was really a fight, and now he told her about his trip to Columbia. She was nodding her head in agreement as he explained the situation with young Becky and how Mr. Pratt in Elizabeth City was trying to help him.'

Annie surprised him when she said, "If nothing else works, John, we can take the baby. Try to find a suitable situation but I can't see putting a beautiful baby girl in a place where they really don't have the resources to do the job right. We are so blessed and you don't know what would have happened to you had that wonderful man you call your father not taken you in."

"I was thinking the same thing but I wasn't sure how you would respond," he said. "Anyway, things will be in limbo for awhile and Ruth said she will keep the little one until things are properly in order. I gave her some money to help and will check on her every trip."

On his next trip, Josh gave a memorial service at Becky's grave, paid for by an anonymous donor. Ruth held no service at the time for she wanted the Tugboat Preacher to handle it. Her parents back in East Lake had no interest whatsoever. Josh told the attendees, a surprisingly large group of area citizens, that Becky never had a real chance for a good life, but at the last moment when she fought to save her child, God was smiling down on her troubled soul.

In his closing he said, "You know, when she realized that she was still alive she looked at me, she thanked Jesus for saving her. She wasn't talking to me, she thought I was Jesus in her mind. And before she died, she said that she believed in Him and her baby girl lives and is healthy. I am sure Becky loves Jesus and is now in His loving arms."

A close friend of Ruth's, her next-door neighbor, held a small reception in her home and attendees thanked the "Tugboat Preacher" for officiating. Even Shorty came to the reception, but he said the only memorial service he would ever attend was his own since he had no option.

After the reception, Josh stopped with Ruth at her house to see the little girl who was cooing and smiling. He gave Ruth the status, telling her he would check in on every stop to see what she needed and told her a home would be found, but that the legal issue needed to be resolved first.

As he went to leave, rough and tough old Ruth hugged him and told him he was a fine young man. It touched his soul and he knew he was meant to do what he was doing. She also told him how upset she was about Becky's parents who claimed they had no daughter. John shook his head, telling Ruth that the world has good and bad in it and sometimes it looks like the bad is winning.

Then with a wink he said, "But we're working on it," and he was off to the dock stops in Plymouth, Edenton and finally, Elizabeth City. On the final stop, while awaiting the unloading and loading, he went looking for Attorney Pratt. His office legal assistant said he was in court but that he was making progress on the baby and would be contacting Josh within the week.

The young bespectacled man said, "Mr. Pratt said he thinks they know where the father is located and he has someone going to visit him and that the young woman's parents have agreed to waive all rights. They have an appointment next week. If they don't show he'll have to get the Sheriff involved. He'll be in touch."

With everything that could be done finished, the final leg of this trip was wonderful. It was partly cloudy with just a wisp of a westerly breeze and the two skippers were jovial. Josh got his ministerial things done and the partners had made a smart profit on the trip.

In the few remaining months of 1870, things were coming together regarding young Sally. The father signed over all rights as did the maternal grandparents and Christmas was anticipated to be the best ever. The Eldridge family was very appreciative of their good fortune and decided to file papers to bring little Sally into their home and adopt her. There was, however, a nagging little issue that wasn't going away.

Young John Albert had acquired a nagging cough which was commonly known as the croup. It was always worse at night and although the country doctor told them it normally runs its course in a few days, it wasn't improving. About ten days following its onset, one night his fever went higher and he showed difficulty in breathing. Something was dreadfully wrong.

They were fortunate that at first light it was not bitterly cold like normal December days, so Josh and Annie wrapped him warmly and took him to the Elizabeth City hospital. The young doctor was fresh out of training, examined the young boy and had a bad report.

He asked, "Has your son had diphtheria, Mrs.Eldridge?"

"Not that I know of, Doctor," she said with concern. "Doctor Mann gave him something for his sore throat which reduced the swelling in his neck and things seemed to get better before the cough got worse."

The doctor told the couple his diagnosis was croup brought on by diphtheria and that was a concern. While croup by itself usually runs its course. If it comes after diphtheria it could be very dangerous. John Albert was very sick and would be admitted.

Annie told Josh to go do what he had to do for the family and come back. He protested but she said life couldn't stop and she'd stay with him. The hospital moved a small bed in so she could stay with him if she wished.

"I will go and send a wire to Currituck for Shorty, Annie," he said. "He's my boy, too, and I'm staying."

She relented and the two of them sat together, only leaving one at a time for the necessary room or to eat. They knew letting themselves get rundown wouldn't help anything.

On the second day Shorty showed up with Pastor Whitehurst. When he came looking for Josh, Shorty told him what transpired and offered him a tugboat ride to Elizabeth City. He sat with the family and Shorty and prayed, asking for God's grace on this poor little boy who was suffering. Shortly after Shorty and the pastor left and with Annie and Josh at the bedside with the Doctor showing concern, the little boy's chest expanded as he desperately gasped for breath, then he exhaled hard and breathing stopped. His suffering was over.

Annie and Josh just sat there for about an hour. Annie was angry and for some time so was Josh, but then he realized that God's actions weren't always understood but there was a reason. He had to be faithful regardless of his travails and he comforted her, but just stayed quiet. Soon, a nurse brought the body wrapped and placed in a wooden container used for such a time, left it with them and just patted Annie on the shoulder saying that she was so sorry for their loss.

As they took the body wrapped in a blanket and placed it in a casket provided by the mortuary, they headed home, forlorn and in disbelief, saying not a word the entire way. Grandparents John and Emma, notified by the Sheriff after having received a wire, were sitting on the porch with Shorty and Natasha standing nearby. None of them knew what to say but they wanted to stay so the young couple wouldn't be alone. Josh acknowledged them with the small casket in his arms. Annie just ran into the house and the bedroom, lying down and sobbing. Her husband went to her, told her he loved her, then returned placing the casket on the porch in the cool air.

Returning to the living room, he hugged them all and said, "This is really tough and Annie is having a hard time, but we've got to set up a funeral and do it soon. I told the hospital I wanted to bring my boy home so there was no time for any preparation. I don't want his body to decompose, I want to put him in the ground as we remember him."

What started as a joyous Christmas had turned very sober and the funeral had to be hastily arranged. It would be set up and held the next day. Josh noted the irony of a funeral on Christmas Eve, a day when we celebrate a wondrous birth, not a death. Then he just sat down and cried deeply, wanting to get the pain out of his system as fast as he could. He had work to do.

TWENTY

On a drab and overcast Christmas Eve afternoon, little
John Albert Eldridge was laid to rest in the small
Currituck Court House cemetery. As Josh looked
around, he was amazed at the outpouring of local people
who were there, all he knew and some he didn't. The
little casket was at the front in the middle of the gathered
mourners in a circle around the freshly dug grave. Pastor
Whitehurst and three of his most talented choir singers
were there to lead the service.

As the singers, two women and one man, finished
singing "Silent Night" chosen because of the day of the
burial, the Pastor talked about how very uncertain the
gift of life was and how we don't understand so often the
actions that take place and why God lets them happen.
He said, however, that the life of John Albert was very
valuable and there was a reason why his life was so
short. Then he closed by saying that John Albert was
very blessed, for being a young child he didn't have to
face temptation and evil in his life for he was with God
this day. God would never allow a little child to face
darkness, only light in heaven.

This time the choir sang Martin Luther's classic, "A
Mighty Fortress is Our God" before his final words
about the baby's parents. He told the gathering that they
had chosen a task for their life that was so important in a
rural, water divided area and that their service to the

Lord was not being punished. When they came to learn the answer, they would be with John Albert who was waiting for them.

Up the road at Mrs. Daniels' home, a reception was held. Annie was composed and thanked everyone for their support and Josh said they would grieve and then move on with life, but then they departed while the mourners stayed and celebrated the young boy's life.

When they got home, Annie and John changed from their Sunday best and sat by the fireplace while Josh stoked a fire. She sat down beside him and stroked his arm, smiling through her tears, deciding what she was going to say.

"You know, John," Annie began, "for a short time I felt sorry for myself and wondered why this happened to me. I thought about you in the war and all the families that lost young men and I felt ashamed of myself. Then listening to the Pastor, I know he was right. We were blessed with John Albert for a reason and he was taken from us for a reason as well. Could it be that he died so that little Rachel would have a special time with us when she needs a lot of attention? There must be a link there somewhere."

Josh held her close and told her all he knew is that God does things with a purpose and that he knew his purpose would eventually show itself clearly. They would mourn, then carry on. Its what life required.

"I know, Annie, that He wants us to do things to help those folks out on the Banks, too," he said. "More and more former soldiers and simple folk with little income are finding their way there and building homes out of scrap lumber and materials that have washed up from shipwrecks. They are a combination of scavenger, fisherman and farmer and they are supported by subsistence just like most of Currituck did during the war. We need to help them, too, and open their eyes to the future ahead. They need hope and we can help provide it."

Just then Emma and John Eldridge and Natasha and Shorty Weston came to the door, carrying enough food to feed an army. They had come directly from the reception.

"You two won't need any food until New Year's," Emma said. "Don't forget you are invited to Christmas dinner and Shorty and Natasha will be there, too. But if you want to be alone, we understand. Just do what you feel like doing."

Josh hugged his mom and said, "Thanks, Ma, we're going to be okay, but I think we just want to be alone and visit John Albert and talk to him tomorrow. Annie is going to put his gifts on his grave and tell him about them, then donate to someone needy."

Annie added something that let Josh know she was getting her old self back, saying, "Why don't the four of you plan to come over here for New Year's Eve? We're going to have ham with good luck and money (black-eyed peas and cabbage) and Josh has some fireworks that he got for the occasion to shoot over the sound. We'll be up to it by then. I'll need something like that."

All agreed and John's parents and the Weston's departed. The grieving couple sat on the sofa with a special bottle of brandy he had been holding for months. He poured, each took a glass and toasted together to the birthday they would celebrate the next day, the arrival of the baby Jesus.

That night they went to bed and made soft, sweet and passionate love for the first time in quite some time. It was needed by both of them. It brought them close as only intimacy can, eased their physical tension, reduced the pain and suffering and relaxed them as they just lay arm in arm, finally facing the finality of what had taken place. They knew healing would take time, but they could deal with it and face it a little easier each day that passed. For the first time in weeks, they fell into a deep and restful sleep that they needed.

In the morning, they exchanged their gifts that they forgot about the night before, had coffee and went to the cemetery with the wrapped gifts they had ready for the now deceased John Albert. Standing over the freshly covered gravesite with just a marker listing his name, Annie placed the packages and talked to her sweet little boy, describing each gift. Josh stood back with his eyes closed and prayed, thanking God for the time they had with their boy and asking for His grace in helping the two of them carry on. When they left, they carried the packages to the Currituck Court House donation box which was provided for gifts for needy children. It was held open late for donations up until New Year's Day. The deputy on duty looked sad, knowing where the gifts came from and marveling how the Eldridge's could leave them without tears. The time for tears was over and life must go on.

A week later, Josh and Annie were right in the middle of getting ready for the bonfire and fireworks down at the docks. Fresh apple cider was ready, many brought brandy and they gathered together to enjoy a relatively mild New Year's Eve with oysters roasting and chowder heating on a grate over the fire. The townsfolk gathered around nine and enjoyed the gathering and the fireworks were lit at ten. They were beautiful as they exploded and lit up the sky on a starry night, reflecting on a glassy Currituck Sound below.

At quarter 'til midnight, Josh had them gather around for an announcement. The townspeople were grateful for his support of this endeavor and they were also glad to see him in such good spirits after what the past week had wrought.

"Friends, in a few minutes we will welcome 1871 and cheer and toast a new year. We say goodbye to the old and welcome the future. Please get your cider or brandy and be ready for the countdown, then kiss the beautiful partner you brought and drink a toast after the clock strikes twelve. And I want to announce that Annie and I have special news. Yes, we lost our little boy John Albert and will always love him, never forget him and we plan on seeing him again one day. In about three weeks, however, we will welcome a beautiful little girl into our family, a child whose mother died tragically soon after giving birth. I buried her and Annie and I will raise her as our own, just like my ma and dad did for me. Her name, once adoption is complete, will be Rachel Salvation Eldridge. Her middle name was given by her mother for she said before her death that she had seen Jesus and she was saved. We're going to call her Sally."

The townspeople cheered, filled their glasses and at the stroke of midnight two men fired off a few shotgun blasts and Josh yelled "Happy New Year." A few additional fireworks lit the sky. Kisses and toasts were exchanged, they mingled for awhile and then the crowd slowly began to break up. Most were either farmers or fishermen and they had chores to do in the morning just like any day.

Josh and Shorty would spend New Year's Day on maintenance and then they would be off with a big delivery schedule. They had to reconfigure stowage arrangements on the barge to fit three new sailing dories on board along with his regular goods. Several more Edenton planters wanted the boats and one was going to Columbia. While there, Josh would meet with the Sheriff of Tyrrell County to receive all releases from

Sally's natural family and receive approval from the Sheriff for adoption as required by the local court.

The trip went as planned and Josh received all needed approvals and he spent some time with his soon to be adopted little girl. Miss Ruth, her temporary guardian, was so glad that Josh and Annie wanted the little girl. She hugged him and told him how sorry she was about John Albert. She lost a child as a young woman and knew the pain it brought. Ruth also had developed a fondness for the family and knew that she didn't need to act as a mother at her age. Still, she would miss the joys of having "Sally" in the house.

Before Josh departed, Ruth asked, "Do you think I could see her sometime, Josh? I would even be willing to keep her for you whenever you and the wife want some time alone."

Josh smiled and said, "Sure you can, Ruth, you have played an important part in her being so healthy with a smiling countenance. We'll take you up on your offer and we can either come and get you or bring Sally over to stay with you."

On the way home, Josh and Shorty stopped in Elizabeth City to give the paperwork to Sam Pratt for processing. Sam told him everything would be done within a month or so in Raleigh and then he could take the little one home.

"Be patient, Josh," Sam said. "The state works at its own pace and besides, you and Annie need some private time to completely have closure concerning your little boy. You can't bring him back but you can move on but only after you've come to grips with your grief."

The owners of the Miss Margaret stayed the night at the Seaman's House in Elizabeth City, took on Currituck bound shipments the next day and went home. That night the two partner couples and Josh's parents had dinner together at the Weston house, celebrating the coming arrival of Sally. Late in the dinner, John O'Brien joined them and offered a toast.

Looking gleeful and grateful, he said, "Wishing you and Annie a wonderful life with your new little girl. We know you'll always love little John Albert, but think of her as his sister as he looks down from heaven. Shorty asked me to add that you need to take some time off after what you've been through. We all agree. Take a week and you and Annie do something you want to do together. This January is kind of slow, so Shorty, Sam and I can handle whatever must be done and when you come back, you'll be raring to go. We want you to start 1871 with a bang, Josh."

Before another word could be said, Annie said, "We'll take it," as all laughed as it was a done deal.

Two days later, they were ferried to Norfolk by O'Brien on a supply run and then boarded the regular Chesapeake schooner run to Baltimore. This was the same route he used to sail from Carter's Creek, Virginia to Hampton Roads at the end of the war nearly six years earlier. He was taking Annie to see where he had come from at the end of the war. The plans were to stay a night or two at Carter's Creek, then sail north to Baltimore, where they would spend another night or two before returning to Norfolk. He knew he could show her from the water where Point Lookout was without the horrors of having to visit the site up close. They arrived at the Carter's Creek wharf around four and were given a lift over to the boarding house next to the bar and grill where he and Ed O'Reilly had quaffed a few from time to time.

He said, "Tomorrow, Annie, we'll rent a horse and buggy and you can see the beautiful countryside in this part of Virginia. I only hope I can find Ed O'Reilly, the teamster I told you about who lives here and helped me earn money for the rest of the trip home. We'll go by his house tomorrow and at least leave a note."

They were hungry and decided to have a light supper at the bar and grill, where the food was always good and plentiful. While eating, Josh was surprised when he saw O'Reilly and a pretty lady walk in with him. O'Reilly looked his way, didn't recognize him in the dim lighting and they were seated.

"Annie," Josh said with emotion, "the man who just walked in with a lady is O'Reilly. Let me go over and say hello and then I'll introduce you."

Josh walked over to the table and said, "Mr. O'Reilly? Remember me."

The wizened teamster looked up, didn't show any signs of recognition at first, then started to grin as he said, "Josh, well, I'll be. It's Josh. Son, I've thought of you often and from the looks of things, you've done well."

Ed O'Reilly introduced his wife, Penelope, and Josh told him about Annie, and turned and pointed her way. The older man invited them over and they ate together, the two fellows spinning yarns while the ladies got to know one another. Penelope had come to Carter's Creek shortly after Josh left, met Ed and the two married a year later. It was a good match as she was too mature and business-like for the young fellows and O'Reilly was so lonely. She could also be quite the charmer when she wished to be.

The two couples spent the following day together. It was chilly, but not freezing, so they wrapped up and went for a buggy ride and saw the countryside. Josh learned that Sam Montague had drowned a year earlier in a boating accident and that Point Lookout finally went out of business in early 1866. That last batch of prisoners caused quite a bad stir for the Union Army but it never resulted in any disciplinary action.

On the next morning as Ed and Penelope joined them at the dock to say goodbye, Ed surprised him when he said, "Josh, when the story broke about you and the Norfolk Navy Yard, we knew it wasn't true. Yes, I read about it in the Pilot, but I'm glad it turned out well. One of these days I'm coming down to see your Carolina shore all for myself."

Josh made sure they both had correct mail addresses, hugged his friend and he and Annie boarded the schooner for Baltimore. It was crystal clear and calm and as they passed the mouth of the Potomac, Josh pointed out Point Lookout, only about a mile and a half off the port bow. Annie looked, then turned away and shuddered. She didn't want to think about what her husband went through in those days not too long past. She did, however, enjoy their visit to Baltimore with the wonderful seafood and all the shops and then they returned to Norfolk. The trip was a wonderful idea for a change of pace and they enjoyed the time alone, but even Annie knew it was time to get Josh back to his tugboat and his mission of faith. He was itching to get going again.

The trip back was especially exciting because they returned to Norfolk on an Old Bay Line steamer, a much larger and plush hotel on the water for the overnight trip. It was used on the longer bay voyages calling on the large cities, delivering passengers refreshed and well fed. While it had been in operation since the 1840s, the war had adversely impacted it but it bounced back by 1869 as a combination of Yankee mechanical reliability and Southern grace. Annie loved it and Josh made record of it for future travel. Arriving a day later in Currituck,

Natasha was waiting for them on the dock with an envelope in her hand.

"Annie, Josh," she said excitedly. "This wire came for you yesterday from Raleigh."

Josh gave Annie the honors. Her fingers were shaking as she opened it and learned that Sally was now officially their child and they could bring her home once the enclosed official documents were recorded in the local court house. The next morning, January eleventh, the papers were recorded and with official copy in hand, Josh and Annie along with Shorty headed for Columbia with just a few goods stowed for that port and no barge. This was a special moment and they would immediately return to a family celebration for the occasion.

Miss Ruth was notified earlier and stood ready to prepare a meal whenever they arrived. She heard the "toot, toot" of the approaching tug and knew it was Josh, immediately springing into action. She made it simple and filling and fifteen minutes later she was ready. She was glad to see Josh and Shorty and welcomed Annie with open arms.

"No wonder this young man is so in love with you," she said with a twinkle. "Why, you are beautiful, Miss Annie."

They sat down to the meal and Ruth told them Sally's things were ready and she wanted to tell them a few things about her personality which would make the transition easier. Annie picked up the baby and immediately received a smile, but when the baby saw Josh, she reached for him and laughed.

When it was time to go, Josh watched as Ruth gently gave the child to Annie. The child looked at Ruth as if she would cry but hesitated, looked back at smiling Annie, returned the smile and settled right into her arms. Josh did see tears rolling down the old midwife's cheek.

"Don't worry, Ruth," he said. "I'll make sure you get to see her and we'll make sure that you have a way to the christening in a month." Then, they were off, back to Currituck Court House with a new baby and a new outlook on life.

True to his word, Ruth was provided transportation to the now budding church community in Currituck where Pastor Whitehurst from Moyock, with special words from the beaming new father and lay minister, christened the child Rachel Salvation Eldridge and then introduced her as Sally to the congregants.

Sally would never replace John Albert, but she would fill a big void and aching hearts with the laughter of a child again. It had to be an arrangement made in heaven.

TWENTY-ONE

1871 went well with little Sally growing like a weed and the tugboat business thriving, but the two principals were worried about getting into the same situation they faced earlier to the detriment of their marriages. Josh and Shorty called a group meeting before the end of the year with the immediate family members and the loyal John O'Brien and now fully qualified tug skipper, Sam Jarvis, Josh's young local friend. He turned the meeting over to Josh since he was better on his feet and they continued.

"We've had an excellent year and have made a lot of money," Josh said. "We've all put money away for lean times and are in a good position to weather whatever is bound to someday happen. And John, you and Sam have been wonderful additions to the team and we couldn't have done it without you and, I might add, your added equipment, the Lulu Belle. We think it is time to reward both of you by making you minority owners of the tugboat operation with ten percent ownership each plus your current salaries. While Shorty and I will handle the paperwork, you two will have full responsibility for tug operations and, of course, we will remain available for fill in as you need. I want you both to consider this for I think it will set each of you up for life and John, all of your boat expenses will be borne by the company, or you can sell it outright to the company. Afterall, you will be part owners."

"I have two things I want to be involved in. I want to add an area to operations to deal with ferrying hunters, fishermen and tourists to the inner and outer banks and devote more time to my ministry obligations. I also want to help my dad more with his boat building and he will remain a good customer for all waterborne shipments. Shorty wants to slow down a bit, but he'll still be the "go to" guy on major boating maintenance and operating issues and fixing any supply route problems."

Both men liked the idea. They loved what they were doing, loved the area and unbeknownst to the principals, both John and Sam had the eye of a couple of wonderful girls they were getting serious about. Shorty said he'd start making the arrangements to get the paperwork in order and then took questions.

Young Sam brought up the idea of his future marital status in a question when he asked, "So, Josh, if I were to get married to Sheila Harris, is there any possibility of buying the bungalow? John has indicated an interest in a house of his own just above the court house and he says Matthew can stay with him. I'd love to make the current residence a real home if that becomes the case."

"We can work it out, Sam," Shorty interjected, "and it would be a deal that only a part owner would be offered. You will be a major part in our operation, making money off of selling a house to you would not be in our best interest."

That settled, Josh would be spending the last month of 1871 on his ministry and assisting his father while planning a campaign for a hunting support business. Frank Meekins at the Norfolk waterfront located the perfect boat to ferry people, much better than pushing them with a barge. He found a small, older side paddle wheeler that was in good shape in Norfolk and was involved in a bankruptcy and could be purchased cheap. He suggested that Josh and Shorty come check it out and take it for a test. Arrangements were made and the wheels were set in motion for bank approval.

Josh envisioned a walk on passenger service from Currituck to Chickahawk (modern day Kitty Hawk) along with a small duck hunting guide service on both sides of the Currituck. The entire coastal plain of North Carolina was beginning to be noticed as a potential sportsman's paradise for fishing and hunting. Josh had some experience with his father from boyhood days and he also had found two youngish but well qualified guides to market for the endeavor. He saw it as a way to diversify in the event that business conditions change. After all, they were in the middle of a good after the war business run but he knew it wouldn't last forever.

So, he preached in a number of outlier locations including his first revival in Columbia, helped his dad and learned more about his business. While John O'Brien and Sam Jarvis handled the shipping operations end, he and Shorty maintained the administrative functions and worked as hard as ever, but he was home more.

A week before Christmas, one of those beautiful and unseasonably warm days that often happens in the Tidewater region, Josh and Shorty hopped the schooner to Norfolk and went to see Frank Meekins. He had the sidewheeler looking very fine indeed. It had plenty of deck space for passengers, was outfitted with a canvas top over the open deck and could easily fit twenty- five or thirty passengers on board and seated comfortably.

When Josh saw it, he came up with another purpose that it could fulfill. It was large enough that when docked in one of the remote locations on the sound, it could be the meeting point for a small revival or the center of attraction for one in a larger river port like Elizabeth City. He decided he would keep that idea to himself for now, not wanting to get his hopes up in case there were major problems with the vessel.

Shorty was busy checking the vessel in detail, from its structure to its steam power plant. Josh knew that he didn't like to be bothered by distractions when he was inspecting a vessel and he was a master at it. So, Josh and Frank went in the dock office for a cup of coffee while waiting.

Frank paid a compliment when he said, "You know, Josh, you have come a long way. I know that Shorty is the best trainer in the business, but still you have really become a top-notch seaman and captain in quick order.

You probably don't know this, but you are a bit of a legend on the docks already with the publicity you've gotten. The Pilot covered your trial, of course, and we all know that you two were innocent. Later, though, when the story broke about your saving that poor girl's life and your designation as the Tugboat Preacher, it was just natural that your reputation would follow."

"You are very kind, Mr. Meekins," he said, "but I don't want any fame, just a good life for my family and the love of the Lord. We have been very blessed."

Meekins was impressed and he told Josh that he, too, was a Methodist and then he asked a question.

"Would you ever be interested in giving a visiting sermon here at the Metropolitan Church about your salvation."

"Thanks, Mr. Meekins, but no thanks," he replied. "My place is with those isolated folks along the shores of the sound and sea in Carolina who need the word and what it means. That's where I belong."

Just then, Shorty came in with an excellent report. The sidewheeler was sound and had a good engine. Before he could say another word, Meekins spoke up.

He asked, "Want to try her out in the open waters? The owner has approved it as long as I go along. Let me close up shop and we're off."

The dock manager asked Shorty if he needed a refresher and was told no and sure enough, Shorty fired up the engine, let the diesel warm up and then slowly eased her out of the dock, then made a slow turn and they headed up the Elizabeth River toward Hampton Roads.

Josh was following every step he made and putting it to memory. Frank was impressed by the younger man's attention to detail as he told Shorty he could take her up the Chesapeake for a few miles and then bring her back.

The churning paddle made a swishing sound as it lifted and dropped volumes of water as it propelled toward the bay. As they turned to port heading northward, Frank asked Josh if he could handle it, inviting him to take the wheel to Shorty's nod of approval. Frank explained how the sidewheeler was much more maneuverable, that it was especially made for smaller, narrower rivers that the larger twin or rear wheelers can't handle.

"Even out here in the Chesapeake she handles well," Meekins commented, "as long as it's not too rough."

About ten minutes later, Josh brought her about smoothly and when approaching Fortress Monroe, he relinquished the wheel to Shorty who took her back to the dock. Once secured, the three men went into Meekins' office and talked business. A deal was reached and they stayed over that night to finalize the transaction with a Norfolk banker and to meet the seller. They would be returning to Currituck with the Miss Hattie where she would be named the Miss Caroline, for her new home state.

In mid-afternoon the next day, Annie, with Sally in her arms and Natasha came to the dock when they heard the unfamiliar toot of the Miss Caroline. They watched in awe as she slowed to almost a stop and Josh jumped onto the dock to secure the lines while Shorty kept her deftly parallel to the dock with just inches to spare. The on-duty dock hand said she could stay there for the night since the weather was good and there would be no large traffic until late the next day. They checked the cove where she would be kept when not in service and planned slight docking adjustments for the two tugs which they would accomplish in the morning, then bring her home.

That evening when they were sitting at the dinner table with Sally sound asleep in her basinet nearby, Annie surprised Josh when she said, "You know, Josh. That sidewheeler would be perfect for a small, at the dock revival in one of those small towns you visit. You should talk to Reverend Whitehurst and see what he thinks?"

John laughed and said, "Well, Honey, I was thinking of that while we were looking at it. Even if not, it could be a traveling advertisement for our mission. Oh, some might laugh, but so what? We were never told it would be easy, in fact, everything I've done that was worthwhile never was."

The following Sunday, Josh and Annie met with the minister after services and told him of their idea. Pastor Whitehurst thought it was wonderful and said he would push it up line to see if support could be provided.

Christmas was two days later and Josh planned a service at the Currituck town hall and he brought the sidewheeler up for all to see. As he arrived, someone in the waiting crowd suggested that they hold the service on board and the precedent was set. Even Shorty, not normally an active churchgoer was present and thought it was a great idea and Joshua knew he had the support he needed. He anxiously awaited word from the Methodist hierarchy but felt good about their approval.

With the coming of 1872, Josh was called back into tugboat skippering when John O'Brien got word of his father's death. Horatio O'Brien had been a legend on the waterfront in Norfolk until his retirement at the onset of the war and Shorty said he would represent the family since he knew him well. The service was joyous and the entire waterfront was strongly represented. A large model of a tugboat was used as a vase for flowers and showed the life of a man who lived his life doing what he loved while doing it well. He was the reason his son John became such a good skipper. Horatio was a master teacher.

The transportation business was busy and both Josh and young skipper Sam were running a tight schedule. His travels on the south side of the Albemarle also proved to him just how viable the sporting guide business was becoming, for guide notices were found in Plymouth, Columbia and East Lake. He even made his first stop in Mann's Harbor before returning with shipments outgoing.

When he returned, Josh checked on the sidewheeler and saw what a good job Shorty had done earlier on shoring up the Miss Caroline's permanent moorings. She would be as safe in her sheltered dock as she was back at the Norfolk pier. He then walked back to oversee the unloading of goods and placement on teamster wagons for ongoing shipment, then moved the tug back to the cove. Finished, he was now anxious to see his dear Annie and their new little girl.

Walking in to his cozy home, Josh could smell something good cooking. It was a pork roast with vegetables and corn bread. He lifted Annie off her feet with a bear hug and gave her a big kiss, then put her back on her feet. He looked down at little Sally nearby and she smiled at him. She truly had grabbed her daddy's heart.

"You got a note from Pastor Whitehurst, Josh," Annie said. "He got the okay on the sidewheeler ministry and wants to accompany you on a trip to Chickahawk Bay where they would like a revival. Apparently the Wanchese church needs support on the Banks and you are it. Aren't you pleased?"

"Indeed, I am," he responded. "I want to both grow business and the flock over there. Dad and I used to sail over to the Banks occasionally to go to the beach to fish and swim in the ocean. It's truly beautiful and mostly barren. There are, however, pockets of small communities that stick together. Most of the locals live by subsistence and don't have much. They scavenge and they fish and their life is tough, living in rough-hewn homes of scrap wood and material that are drafty and subject directly to ocean gales and storms. Many of them are war veterans like me who became disillusioned by what war did to them and they just want to be left alone. They do, however, need both physical and spiritual nourishment to survive."

Annie warned him that a revival over there could be touchy, for there are always some who are huge skeptics who like to create an issue. As she spoke, Josh thought of the Yankee guard on the Dismal Swamp a few years earlier and figured he could handle a rowdy crowd just like he handled that soldier, with calmness and firmness. This time, however, he had something else on his side. He had his faith. He would just have to play it as it goes using higher guidance.

The following week, a Wednesday, Pastor Whitehurst arrived with a buckboard full of supplies including some basic carpentry tools and items and foodstuffs. It was a donation from the church and would be a good way to break the ice.

Shorty surprised him when he jumped on board and with Josh, the Pastor and a seasoned deckhand and a load of supplies, they pulled out of the cove and headed southeast toward the Outer Banks. They had placed benches onboard which could be rearranged on arrival and the overhead cover was rolled up since the warmth of the sun would be warmer than the tarp. The water was nearly smooth, the sun was rising and it was chilly but not cold on this February day and their spirits were high.

The Pastor was amazed to watch Josh handle the sidewheeler while Shorty kept his eyes peeled continuously for any issues along the way. The trip to Chickahawk Bay (later named Kitty Hawk Bay) took about an hour and a half and they would be there before eleven, giving them time to unload the supplies. Two ladies from the Wanchese church would also be there to supervise the delivery and distribution to those in need.

As they passed the point at Chickahawk where the western shore turned sharply east, they followed the shoreline and entered the bay. Protected from the north by the natural geography of the shoreline and to the south by Big and Little Colington islands, the water was now smooth like a lake. Even in stormy weather, it was largely protected from the adjacent Albemarle, except from storm surges as a hurricane passed and the water which was pushed inland returns to the east rapidly with the wind change. The strong-willed folk who lived there largely built on the high ground in response and were used to replacing docks as needed.

Soon they saw the large dock and as Josh maneuvered to bring the Miss Caroline in, he cut back power and allowed it drift in to a stop right at the dock. Shorty threw the stern line to a man on the dock while the deck hand jumped over with the mainline. The vessel was secured in rapid order and as Josh looked up, he was surprised to see even at this early hour nearly twenty people on the dock waving to them. There were also boats all over the water, folks who could only get to the revival by boat from Colington Island.

The two skippers stepped on the dock, gave a hand to Pastor Whitehurst as he disembarked and he led the way over to the two Wanchese ladies who greeted him warmly. Josh remembered their faces but not names from a guest visit to Wanchese and they offered their hand.

The older lady, Nancy, got her instructions from Pastor Whitehurst, then turned and said, "Fred, you and Joe quit messing around and get over here and start carting this stuff into the storage building. Miss Wanda will tell you where to put things."

Recognizing her authoritative voice, Fred merely said, "Yes, ma'am," and got to work. The two ladies were in a hurry in order to not miss their ride back, so once done, they thanked the Currituck party and were gone. Once gone, Fred was very helpful, telling them he'd be there to listen and provide any assistance for what was needed. He also said his wife, Betsy, would be bringing a basket of food for them so they could eat before the revival started at two. They planned to spend two hours, then head home and arrive before dusk.

The crowd dissipated and the Reverend was worried that no one would stay, but old Fred relaxed his fears.

"Don't worry, Pastor," he said, "they just came down to see you come in but will be back. We don't get that many visitors except the mail boat and they were just curious. They will, however, be back to take whatever you will give them and I supposed a good dose of the Lord can help them all. You might have a few rabble-rousers in the crowd, but they're all talk. Just hold your ground and you'll earn their respect."

After a nice picnic lunch, Shorty put a temporary ramp from boat to dock for easier entry and stood by at the foot when Josh and Pastor Whitehurst took positions at the back of the wheelhouse facing the benches arranged on deck. Soon, locals began trickling down to the dock and came onboard, seating themselves.

The boat was filled to capacity as Reverend Whitehurst welcomed the crowd, telling them that those in need of food would be able to pick up some items from Fred on the dock when they were done. The crowd clapped in appreciation. To this point, all were receptive and very respectful. As Josh walked up and shook hands with the minister and began his message, he saw a surprise out of the corner of his eye. Down to the dock walked Fred's wife, Betsy, carrying a double barrel shot gun with the breach open. She walked over to Fred, told him to hold the gun and then walked onboard, interrupting Josh's opening remarks.

"Excuse me, Preacher," Miss Becky said, "but can we start the service with a hymn."

Josh was startled, but said yes and before he could say anything else, she broke into a solo with no accompaniment of the new hymn, "Hanson's Place," better known as "At the River." Written by Baptist Minister Robert Lowry, it was named for the church of the same name that he pastored in Brooklyn in 1864. It quickly gained a following around the eastern United States after the war.

To the amazement of Josh and his party, Becky sang it beautifully and some on the boat joined in. Not only could this tough Outer Banker woman cook, but she could sing and apparently shoot as well. When she finished, she merely said she was sorry and left the boat, grabbing her shotgun and taking up a position beside the storage building on the dock where she could listen and keep watch over Josh's flock.

Josh began delivering an inspiring sermon, explaining how the war changed him and motivated him to work hard for himself and for his God. There was a disturbance in the middle of his delivery when large sandy dirt clods began to descend from the incline on the small wooded hills on the shore.

Josh stopped speaking and heard the laughter from the darkness as a small group of young men began mocking him. Suddenly, Betsy's voiced boomed as he heard the familiar click of the shotgun breach being closed.

"Okay, Billy Gray," said Miss Betsy. "You and your hooligans better come on out here now."

There was silence, then came another volley of dirt clods as jeers and a few choice words from the audience erupted toward the troublemakers. Miss Betsy was fearful the crowd might rise up and go after those bad boys so she fired a blast into the water, then aimed the shotgun in the direction of the woods.

Fred went to Betsy and Josh ran up to her telling her to put the shotgun away as he then stood in the open, looking at the woods and spoke.

"Billy Gray, or whoever you are and your friends," he said with strength but not anger. "Come on down here and let's talk. I want to know what kind of a young man thinks he's being a man by throwing dirt at older ladies and gentlemen. Don't worry we're just going to talk; I won't hurt you."

There was silence except Josh could hear whispers and he knew the group was talking it over, so he added, "I'm not going to shame you, Son, you should be ashamed enough on your own. Let's figure this out."

Slowly, out came Billy and friends, each with hands opened to show they held no dirt clods. Josh figured none were older than sixteen, of course, not long before that was old enough to go to war.

He turned to the crowd on the boat and said, "Excuse me, folks, I'll be back in a few minutes. Billy and I are going to straighten this out."

The two walked over to a nearby clearing beyond the hearing range of the others. They talked for about five minutes with Josh placing his hand on the young man's shoulder. At the end, Billy bowed his head with Josh, then they shook hands. Billy sent his gang home and he came with Josh to the boat and took a seat on the rail. Josh returned to his place and continued his story until coming to the end which he changed. He asked Billy to come forward.

Josh closed by saying, "Billy here is just a little younger than I was when I went to war. I wasn't a bad kid, maybe just mischievous like Billy here. Billy was just looking to be noticed and we noticed him today, but not with yelling or a beating but constructive love. It works, folks, not just with Billy but with most people as well. Those who don't want to respond, well, just wish them well and move on. The Lord works that way as well."

The day was a hit and heading back to Currituck, Pastor Whitehurst told Josh he just had a way with people that opened them up.

"It's a gift, Son," the older preacher said, "and you are one of the few granted it with such power. Use it wisely and you will be of big help to the folks out here. You gained their respect here and the word will spread. Trust me, Son, it will spread."

When they tooted the "we're home" signal as they pulled back into the cove in late afternoon, Annie and Sally, Natasha and Josh's folks were there. They were anxious to hear how things went. They could tell from the smiling faces that it was successful.

Shorty spoke up saying, "You know, I was a bit skeptical at first, but Josh has a gift and he displayed it well, including the boy who wanted to throw dirt. I would have taken the kid down but Josh just talked him through it and he ended up joining in the revival. Josh won them over."

Pastor Whitehurst bid them all farewell saying that Josh passed his trial with flying colors and the rest gathered in Annie's kitchen for a light bite to eat and a nip. Josh was no teetotaler, he believed that strict moderation was okay and that since Jesus enjoyed a little wine now and then, it could be beneficial. He was determined to be a Bible preacher, but not so narrow minded that he'd run off all those who needed grace. And living in a land where bootlegging was common, it was probably a smart approach.

That night when he was lying in bed waiting for sleep beside Annie, he told her about the people he met and their simple, yet sincere lifestyle. She laughed when he told her about Miss Betsy and both her tough and artistic, sensitive sides. He knew that there were many more needing his help, both materially and spiritually, and he wanted to focus when he could on the Banks. Josh wanted to know more about them than just the walk over to the beach. He wanted to explore them from the north in Currituck and Bodie Island to Hatteras in the south. Whether he knew it or not, God was working on him and his plan, but he would have a few bumps in the road along the way. Now, side by side and arm in arm, he and his beloved Annie fell asleep.

TWENTY-TWO

The month of March 1872 was a tough one as the Carolina coast was hit with multiple bad nor'easters which put a crimp in both business and Josh's missionary zeal. While the protected cove where the partners' boats were docked weathered the storm with only minor damage to the docks, the main Currituck dock had significant structural damage. It was worse up the Albemarle where towns were flooded and the ports were closed excepting Elizabeth City.

Another problem cropped up as the weather cleared. John O'Brien's tug suffering from power problems. Shorty and John, the two best diesel mechanics around, put all their effort into repair while Josh and Sam handled supply deliveries of a smaller volume due to the supply line breakdown caused by weather. What they delivered was also difficult since they couldn't get to the docks in the damaged ports. Instead, they anchored in the sound and transferred supplies to smaller vessels that could go to shore. It was tedious and time-consuming and it meant that big ticket items had to be stored for delayed delivery.

Seeing the hardship of the people up and down the Albemarle and its tributaries, they quickly converted to a charitable operation with the help of area churches and good merchants in both Elizabeth City and Norfolk. When the Currituck dock was safe again, foodstuffs and survival items arrived for shipment and were supplemented by more supplies from Elizabeth City. With the weather now calm, part of the load from Currituck was taken to Elizabeth City by the Miss Margaret skippered by Sam Jarvis, where additional goods were added and carried to the hard-hit isolated Albemarle towns. The remainder was loaded on the sidewheeler Miss Caroline with Josh skippering her to Chickahawk, beginning to take recognition as Kitty Hawk. He was anxious to see the outcome of the storm in the sheltered cove.

On April 2, 1872, Josh and a small crew pulled up to the dock where the revival was held earlier and found things looking much as usual. Fred was working on a boat and Miss Betsy was bringing him a fresh pot of coffee to keep hot on his potbellied stove on the sheltered dock. When she saw Josh, she smiled and offered him a cup.

"Well, Preacher," she said, "it looks like you have quite a load of supplies. We're okay over here but the folks on the beach side were savaged."

She explained how the initial storm surge devastated the coastal side along the oceanfront but then pushed far west into the Albemarle before running back out as the wind changed.

"We only got about a foot and a half on this side of the bay because of the bend on the shoreline," she explained. "Further north along the Currituck shore it was bad and down in Nags Head it was devastating."

When Betsy left to get ponies and a wagon to bring to the dock to transport the delivery, old Fred, quiet while she was there, smiled and said, "Tell you what, Preacher. You have a friend in Jesus and a friend in my Betsy, too. She's spreading the word up and down these Banks and you'll be in big demand."

They enjoyed their coffee and Josh got to know this quiet but wise old fellow and he knew they would be friends. Very soon, Betsy returned with the ponies and wagon and four strapping boys including Billy Gray who told Josh good morning.

The unloading went smoothly and Josh and his crew had to do nothing, Miss Betsy got things organized and those boys were efficient and good. Josh whispered to Fred that Betsy and the Good Lord had put the fear of God in Billy and his crew. Fred said he would keep it to himself with a chuckle.

Loading done, Betsy told the boys where to take the wagon and that she would be there in an hour, then she told Josh to follow her. She led him up a reinforced path with oyster and clam shells packed into the sand to a small house in the woods, proclaiming it as Fred's Castle. There was a large stocky pony hitched to a buggy on the side.

"Take a short ride with me in the buggy and I'll show you something," she said and they hopped on board and off they went toward the east on a continuation of the trail. Josh was impressed by the strength of the pony and how effectively the shells worked to create a solid base on the soft sand.

"So, Miss Betsy, where did you get the ponies," Josh asked.

"Upper Currituck, Preacher," she said. "They are wild Spanish ponies that are found on a number of islands on the coast. Our best bet is they came ashore from Spanish shipwrecks. They have learned how to survive on salt grass and are amazing. Fred trained them. They are smart and with patience they become great work animals."

Josh was fascinated with their strength and determination as Miss Betsy continued driving through a pine forest on a series of sand dunes. Suddenly, Josh saw an opening ahead with a rise just beyond it. As the pony strained a bit to climb the last few feet, stopping at the summit. Looking down the slope of the dune was the mighty Atlantic, with a cool briny sea breeze lowering the temperature considerably. Looking down the dune, Josh could see where the shell road stopped, washed out with the watermarks on the lower base of the dunes noted by the cut out, indicating how far the water had risen from the shore.

As he scanned the land below, from the sea inward about the half mile or so to the dune and up and down the coast, there were various piles of rubble and people around fire barrels trying to keep warm. He noticed a tear in Betsy's eye as she looked directly at him.

"What you are looking at, Josh," she said, "are homeless beach dwellers and the remnants of their homes. Now I don't know what if any impact was felt down where the ritzy planters have summer homes, but I assume it is major. On the sound, above and below our little bay, it has to be just as bad as well.

"We got them the heating barrels and then set up a food kitchen in the village, but they are still suffering and there is no easy answer except self-help and the grace of God working through men like you, Josh. These and more are hurting and they can do very little on their own to fix it without supplies. It's not in huge numbers but it is a group or people suffering and having nowhere to go."

As they returned to her home and she headed to meet the boys, Josh knew how important it was that he brought what he did and he vowed to bring more, including building supplies. As he arrived back at the dock, his deckhands noticed the sad look on his face.

One of them, Timmy, an industrious lad asked, "Is everything okay, Skipper? You look like you just saw a ghost."

"Well, Jimmy," Josh replied, "I just walked through the woods and looked down on the beach and those poor people need everything we can give them. It's up to us to do it and we will."

On the way home, Josh changed his route to move north closer to the shore in order to get a better look. Near the area of what today is the Wright Memorial Bridge, piers were gone, trees were toppled in the water and he had to keep close watch on floating debris, including what looked to be pieces of a fishing boat and housing. He then headed to port to angle across the sound toward Currituck, still keeping an eye for debris in the late afternoon sun.

Pulling in to their private berthing cove, Josh realized how important it was when they prepared their own docks sheltered from the sound. While the worst was always to their south, he knew that they were in a position to weather all but a catastrophic storm with their slightly elevated cove and waterfront shielded dock. Shorty and John O'Brien were finally finishing up the engine repair and Josh spoke to them with a very serious expression on his face.

Josh began, "We need to put our heads together, guys. Is Jarvis back from his run? We've got to figure out what we can do for those folks over on the Banks. They are in big trouble. The oceanfront is ravaged and the cheap homes made from scavenged wood and materials are gone and the people are out in the elements. Come on in and let's see what we can do."

Josh walked in, hugged and kissed Annie and the baby with the others right behind him. He told her how dire things were for the subsistence beach dwellers. Annie quickly said she would notify Mrs. Daniels from the church women and call on Sheriff Doughty who loved boating to the Outer Banks.

"If we can get another big load of food and especially shelter materials they can survive," he said. "The food we delivered will keep them from starving but I'm worried about sickness. I'll send a wire to both Norfolk and Elizabeth City tonight. If we can get things together, we can load up all three boats. I can go in close on the low areas on the Banks' western shore and they can come out in anything that floats to retrieve. All else can go to Chickahawk where Miss Betsy will help determine what to send further south."

Just then Sam Jarvis walked in, holding a wire in his hand. It was handed to him by the Sheriff as he walked by. Delivered to Josh, Sam turned to return to the tug at the Currituck dock where the teamster wagon was waiting. Josh told him not to release them until he came to talk to them; he wanted them to carry the message for help back to Norfolk.

As he opened the wire message, a big smile broke out on his face as he said, "Well, what do you know. James Hewes, the wealthy planter from Edenton is sending a schooner full of food and supplies to us that will arrive late tomorrow afternoon at the dock. Colonel Winslow will lead the party and they will take things wherever we need them."

He looked up at the ceiling, then bowed his head in prayer of thanks as all joined in. He told them all to gather again tomorrow at the docks when the schooner arrived. The plan would create itself once they knew what they had to deliver. Then Josh went to the docks, wrote out a message and asked the teamster to take it back to Norfolk and tell them of the Outer Bankers' plight and what he intended to do.

Two days later with the schooner already docked, two wagons loaded from Elizabeth City and a large, loaded barge pushed by tug from Norfolk arrived at the dock. Emergency repairs had been made quickly to the dock, sufficient to enable them to use it. Josh, Shorty, Sam, John, Colonel Winslow and a large group of local volunteers loaded the sidewheeler, transferred supplies from the incoming barge to one of their own and got ready to sail. Josh and Shorty led the way in the sidewheeler, then came the schooner, followed by the two tugs skippered by O'Brien and Jarvis with their barges.

Two hours later they dropped anchor on a misty but still day at the mouth of Chickahawk Bay to start an orderly offloading in stages. First to dock was the sidewheeler, at the far end of the dock as its cargo would go elsewhere. With its low draft, it could go closer to non-dock shore locations where goods could be handed off to smaller local boats easily. He would depart to look for those places in need once all unloading was done.

As Josh tooted the folks on the pier and pulled in, he actually saw both Miss Betsy and Fred smile. As his crew secured the Miss Caroline, Josh signaled for John O'Brien to bring in his tug, the Lulu Belle. It was unloaded and then moved out to anchorage as Sam Jarvis came in with the Miss Margaret. He followed the same routine, then the schooner made her way to the dock. Despite concerns that the depth might not be sufficient, Josh was chancing it due to the drizzle. He wanted things delivered to those who needed them as quickly as possible.

As the skipper eased his way in, the schooner made it with room to spare and once unloaded all concern would be over. Once completed, Colonel Winslow told his captain to stand fast as he was going with Josh. The two Currituck tugs were released to John O'Brien and Sam Jarvis to return to home port as they had short runs and could likely complete them before dark.

Josh, Shorty, the Colonel and three deckhands pulled out on the Miss Caroline and headed over to Colington. It took more of a hit than the west side of the bay and John pulled into chest high water and stopped when he saw the bottom churn. He tooted his horn and waited. Within minutes three men came to the bank, pushed two rowboats into the water and rowed the short distance to the Miss Caroline.

"You folks need some emergency supplies," Josh asked. "I'll give you as much as I can in an assortment."

They eagerly nodded yes and the crew handed over boxes of non-perishables. Josh also asked about home damage and they said all was okay with their homes. One of them then told Josh what he already knew.

"Those poor people over the dunes are a different story, Skipper," he said. "I wish we had some things for them but we couldn't get it to them if we wanted to. There is still too much water trapped on normally dry land."

Josh informed him that the folks on the other side of the bay were working on that. They thanked him and Josh wished them good luck, then he pulled out, went west to the open sound and turned to port, headed for Old Nags Head.

Arriving there in about twenty minutes, they found the dock was demolished and the make-shift temporary one wouldn't hold the supplies. Josh tooted repeatedly and Shorty got the deck hands ready to get to work. The Miss Caroline was about thirty feet offshore and churning sand as two young men came to the water's edge.

"Can you help us, Captain," a tall lanky young man wearing fishing pants and shirtless yelled. "We're trying to shore up a few homes and we're running low on food. We caught enough water that we're okay with that."

Josh responded, "If you can get a couple of flat-bottomed rowboats out here, we'll give you what we've got."

Ten minutes later from behind a fallen tree in the water's edge, two large and quite wide rowboats with two men on each started heading for the port side of the sidewheeler. They took on food, a few tools, tarps and some two by fours. The houses on shore looked more tenuous than they were except for a few holes in the roof. The tarps would give them temporary assistance. Josh knew that these deliveries would just keep them alive, but foundational repairs would require a tug barge full of large timber. When Josh asked if they knew of any more places to the south where there were major survival issues, they both just pointed south.

The shirtless man said, "Most of the area to the south is open until the new lighthouse area that has only the keeper. He is surrounded by water but the mail boat has been able to get to him. We get our mail the same way we got your supplies. Other than that, no one has heard anything, or so we've heard from the rumor mill about Hatteras Island. Those folks always find a way to survive but they must need help."

As they departed, they crossed Roanoke Sound to Manteo, the larger island town that was of better elevation. Things looked pretty good but they were told at the dock supplies were short and except for a few lifesaving efforts on the beach they had nothing else to give.

While Shorty remained on board with Colonel Winslow at the unattended dock, Josh went to the central information point in the town, the General Store, to see what he could learn. Walking in, he noticed the nearly empty shelves, yet otherwise unimpacted facility and spoke with the man at the counter. He was engaged in a conversation with several customers upset that there were no supplies, including one, a wiry young man who seemingly had no concern for anyone but himself. Even the other men showed disdain for him.

The proprietor, a man named Louis, greeted Josh saying, "I see you came in on that sidewheeler, are you the Tugboat Preacher?"

John said, "Yes, and I just stopped by to see how you were doing. I know you are short on supplies but glad to see the town looks pretty normal and no one looks starving."

Before he could say anything else, the wiry guy piped in saying, "So, you came in here to tell us that you didn't bring anything? We have to wait two more days for the mail boat to bring anything to us. We don't need no Tugboat Preacher, we need more food."

The proprietor winked at Josh as if to say, put him in his place and the young skipper faced the antagonist, saying, "You should be ashamed of yourself. Those people over on the banks are starving and cold. Most of them have houses either in bad shape or unlivable and they just want to survive. You look like you've eaten, your homes are okay and you can make it until you get what you say you need. Those people might just die without our help. I will, however, follow up when I get back home to see that your supplies will come. I'll pray for you, Son. I think you need it."

The rest of the men at the counter clapped while the wiry fellow just slinked away, realizing how selfish he had been. The proprietor thanked Josh and said he should plan a revival in Manteo when things were better. He had a great gift. Once again Josh had turned what could have been a negative into a positive and smiled to himself as he returned to the dock.

They shoved off and headed back toward Chickahawk but as they cleared the small harbor, he peered in the distance over the starboard rail in the direction of Hatteras Island to the south. He could even make out on the now turned crystal clear afternoon the slight alteration on the horizon which was the new Bodie Island Light. He vowed to both visit it and return to that long and narrow island to its south in times to come. He was intrigued by what he saw at Hatteras Village on that one short visit and he knew there were people who needed spiritual support.,

Arriving back at the dock in Chickahawk, empty except for the schooner, he found Miss Betsy serving the crew a rich stew with cornbread. She told them to come and eat. They had worked hard and all supplies were now either received at their destination or on their way. Josh, Shorty the Colonel and their crew joined in for the meal, now famished when they smelled the wonderful aroma.

Josh took a spoonful and said, "This is delicious, Miss Betsy? What is it?"

She laughed and said, "It's an old family recipe, fish and turtle stew, Preacher. It has a few special ingredients that are my secret."

The men ate hearty but then had to leave fast, they wanted to make Currituck before dark. Miss Betsy even gave Josh and Shorty a kiss on the cheek, then thanked Colonel Winslow with much grace while Fred just stood back and smiled.

"That's a first," he said as she softly slapped his wrist and then the seafarers were off.

Arriving back in Currituck, the schooner would stay overnight and Josh and Shorty invited the Colonel and his skipper to stay with them. The Colonel accepted, the schooner captain said he'd stay with his ship and the day was over.

After sitting up talking with his guest and Shorty, Josh went to sleep thinking about his most recent experience. He knew that those Outer Bankers would need help for years and he vowed to be a big part of it. When he said goodbye to Colonel Winslow the next day, both men knew they would play a part in the coastal future. The seed was sown and had taken root. The future was becoming clearer. As he and Annie walked back to their home for a needed day of rest, she looked up at him and knew what was on his mind.

"You see those Outer Banks becoming a much bigger part of your life, don't you, Josh? I can sense it and I want to share it with you. I've only seen the ocean near Cape Henry outside of Norfolk. I can only imagine how beautiful it must be on those isolated islands. Those people need someone like you, Josh, with your courage, strength and faith and I think what has happened was pre-ordained by someone much bigger than us. If it's a calling that you think you feel, take it to the Lord, He'll show you the way."

"Thank you, Annie, you've read my mind and I want you to be a central point in whatever comes of it. I need you with me to be my best."

With Shorty home and off for the day as well, Josh and Annie walked home to spend some special time together. He silently thanked God for her love and His grace.

TWENTY-THREE

The late spring and early summer of 1872 was a hectic time for Josh. Business was booming, the calls for his ministry were growing, yet he and Annie made sure to keep some time for themselves together and for family. Little Sally was growing like a weed and developing quite a personality, immediately lighting up whenever her father returned home. She was now a toddler going through the "terrible twos" and Annie had her hands full, but when Josh was there Sally was definitely his little girl. Annie appreciated the relief and she already knew that Sally was definitely going to be a tomboy. As her ability to speak became clearer, she would tell everyone she was going to grow up to be just like her daddy.

As the fall came, Josh figured it was time to start getting serious about his plan to begin a hunting guide operation. For his work helping his dad at times, he was given three sailing dories at material cost. These boats would be devoted to hunting and fishing use for his sportsman's guide business. They would be guides to take sportsman customers to prime Mackey Island, only two miles northeast and to nearby Currituck Outer Banks' fish and game areas on any day weather was fitting. The beauty of the sailing dory was its speed and shallow draft, allowing quick movement across the sound. Then, in the marshy areas, the sail could be lowered, the running board raised and oars used to move around from place to place including those that were very shallow. If the business proved successful, use of the sidewheeler would allow larger groups to go longer distances. Chickahawk Bay was ever in his mind for fishing. Perhaps one day he could open a small office there and keep dories on site for use.

Josh pondered things in his mind for a while, then talked with Shorty and told him what he was thinking about. He knew Shorty earlier seemed supportive but doing and talking were two different things. He was pleasantly surprised by the almost instantaneous response.

Shorty just smiled and said, "Let's go for it, Josh, it's a great idea and John and Sam will be happy. They love the little extra money they make when they are covering all the tugboat runs and they can handle whatever comes in. We're still here for emergencies and I will keep my financial eyes open and my mechanical hands ready."

Josh laughed and was finally convinced it was time to go and talk with Tom Aydlett, the leader of the guide team he had in mind. Tom and the three who worked for him needed work and while it was too late for heavy work this year, by spring he could have it well under way.

As he drove the buckboard up above Sligo on a crisp later October day to the Aydlett house, he found Tom sitting on his porch carving a duck. He was a very astute man in his late twenties with about ten years of hunting and fishing guide experience under his belt. He was as good as any in the business and that's why he had several other hand-picked guides working with him. He was a winner and less seasoned guides always wanted to work with a winner. He was wrinkled beyond his years due to his outdoor line of work in the sun and wind but greeted Josh with his infectious smile.

"I was wondering when you'd get back with me, Josh," Tom said, "but I knew you would. We all know how busy you've been. I've been doing okay but some of my boys need more work. I think some of our planters have given the business to some Yanks and they don't know these waters like I do. Come on, let's grab a cup of coffee and go out to the shop. I think you might find it interesting."

A small standalone building behind his frame home contained a large work bench and tools and a number of excellent decoys that were realistic. Aydlett was an excellent decoy creator, having learned the art from his father and grandfather, both of whom were now deceased. Josh was impressed as he began to tell him what he had in mind.

He began, "I'll provide the boat and you will receive sixty percent of the take per paying customer. We'll also provide a picnic basket full of refreshments. I figure on no more than three customers per dory, later if it really gets going, we can ferry more customers over to the hunting grounds in the sidewheeler. We can tow a few dories with it and transfer hunters on site. I'm looking for top dollar hunters, Tom, you know, Yankee businessmen, Southern planters, those types. So, you'll make more by my brokerage and have less personal expense but we will need to establish a simple agreement to protect both of us."

They shook hands and Tom offered to take Josh on a hunting trip to try him out and they made arrangements for the following week, weather permitting. That was the major problem locally, setting up a schedule that the weather would allow. Rain was no problem, but high winds were and nor'easters were always unpredictable. Travelling hunters always needed to allow extra days for that very reason.

In the meantime, Shorty was looking at a recently vacated house a half mile to the south and was working on a lease of it for use as a guest house for hunters. It had at one time been a boarding house and would be perfect for a hunting lodge. It just needed some spit and polish and some work on the kitchen. With a few bucks for materials and some simple carpentry and paint which he and Josh could handle, it would be ready to use. If they could work out a good deal, it could be ready for the following spring when fishing would be the main attraction. If it paid off, they would likely want to buy it.

Shorty asked John Eldridge, Josh's dad, if he knew anything about the place. He said the owner was a man from out near Raleigh who used it when he came to the shore in the summer. He was deceased and a lawyer in

Elizabeth City was handling the estate but thus far had no takers on the house.

"Skipper," John said, "if I were you, I'd contact Sam Pratt. He'll get the information and find out what is needed and I'll just bet you can work out a great deal. By now they should be desperate."

The next day, Josh told Shorty about his meeting with Aydlett and that the two of them were invited on a duck hunting day. Shorty told him what he had learned about the empty house John Eldridge and that he sent a wire to Sam Pratt to look into it. The steps were in motion.

Three days later, Shorty got a response from Elizabeth City. The property owner was represented by John Donaldson in Raleigh who was indeed anxious to sell. He would consider a rental for up to a year but at that point he wanted it sold. He would apply the rent to purchase and wanted two months rent in advance. He was open to offers.

Shorty and Josh discussed it, asked for one week to respond in a wire to Sam and started getting ready for their hunting trip the next day. Josh got his and his dad's bird guns and asked Shorty if he ever bird hunted.

"Yes," Shorty laughed as he spoke. "I've been hunting east of Norfolk in Princess Anne County at marshland adjacent to the Back Bay. It was fun but I have no desire to clean ducks so, Josh, you better think of who will clean them for the rich fellows. They'll want them cleaned and they will want them to eat while here."

"Good point, Shorty," you see why we need your knowledge and skills on this team. You never forget any detail."

The next morning before first light, Tom rode up on his horse, put Cyrus in Josh's small, shaded paddock with feed and water and walked to the dock. At his side was Wilkinson, his trusty Chesapeake Bay retriever and a great bird dog. Tom received the dog from his cousin in Princess Anne County, a replacement for Sam Dog, his old companion who died and was sorely missed. Josh walked over and said hello, telling him he needed to get his bird gun and the picnic basket and then they'd be off.

Annie had been the early riser in the house, putting together the picnic basket for the hunters and Josh went back inside to tell her goodbye. He kissed her tenderly, complimented her on the basket and headed out the door. She stood on the front porch waving goodbye. She and Natasha were going to take Little Sally to visit the grandparents on Shorty's cart and would be back by early afternoon.

Josh and Tom walked to the dock where Shorty was getting ready to lower the dory into the water. Josh had rigged up a canvas cradle with three strong strands of industrial strength rope for raising and lowering the dory by hand pully. He had learned how to make it from Sam Montague, his now deceased Virginia friend from the

Northern Neck. Josh and Shorty lowered the boat slowly into the water. Then Josh stepped down carefully on the boat and checked to make sure that the slip knot release for the furled sails would release them when pulled and the lines to raise them were ready.

Tom climbed on board and Shorty lowered the guns, picnic basket and ammo pouch and followed. Now ready, they pushed off and caught the tide moving out without even having to lower an oar into the water. Then they hoisted the mainsail and jib and adjusted course to pick up the light breeze from the west. Slowly gathering speed, they headed northeast toward Mackey Island and the prime duck hunting marshland. Tom gave Wilkinson, named for the family name of his cousin, a biscuit and he settled in near the bow. He loved the water and was right at home.

As they were fully underway, Josh was curious about the bag that Tom wore over his shoulder. He had an ammo belt attached at the waist but the bag was a mystery.

"I've never seen a bag like that, Tom," Josh said. "What's it used for?"

"It's an emergency bag, Josh," he said. "I carry medical supplies that might be important in case of an accident."

He opened it for Josh and it contained strips of sheeting, heavy duty absorbent pads, a knife, extra fine fishing line and a sewing needle. Also included was a bottle of whiskey, a small container of black gunpowder and some home remedies for poison ivy and treatment of bug bites.

"Most of the things are due to accidents, but accidents still happen. "Tom added. "But when you are miles away from anyone and something serious happens, you need to be able to respond until you can get help. When I first started this work, a hunter gashed his leg on a jagged board and was bleeding profusely. Without being able to cut off the blood flow and keeping the wound sterile with alcohol, he might not have made it home."

Remembering the case of the young boy that bled to death from the attack by a rabid raccoon as a boy, Josh nodded in agreement. This man was the right one for the job.

By the time the sun was turning the darkness to gray then pink, the trio plus hunting dog were approaching the wet, grassy islands on the outskirts of Mackey Island. Tom told John to bring down and secure the sails and raise the centerboard. He would use an oar in the shallow water to negotiate his way to the shore. Josh then cleared the stern allowing Aydlett to take charge. Within ten minutes, the guide brought them through the thick grass to a small, sandy beach which was at the base of a trail going into the pines. He told them he would walk them to the duck blind and another close by ground location. The two spots would allow both hunters to shoot directly at the birds safely yet close to one another.

"They'll most likely be black ducks which are very prevalent, but others may be about. After you shoot at a flock and see birds drop, cease fire when the birds are past and I signal with one crow call to let you know that Wilkinson and I are going by boat to retrieve them. Keep your eye out and don't shoot again at anything until I give the all clear with two crow calls, back to back. With the cartridge ammo, you should have time for two shots, maybe three if they come in the numbers they sometimes do on a single pass."

Tom left and, in a few minutes, they heard the single call and waited. Suddenly out of the south came hundreds of birds, flying low like they were flying for their lives. As they flew over at close range like grasshoppers eying a grass field, each man let off two shells before they passed, Shorty from the blind and Josh from the ground location. They saw an undetermined number fall from the sky into the water beyond and almost as quickly heard the stop shooting call. They saw or heard nothing for about five minutes when the all clear was given.

Within two minutes another flock of ducks came out of nowhere and the two men again opened fire with time for two shots and more ducks dropped. It was like catching fish in a barrel and another ceasefire signal was given. Soon they saw Tom pushing the boat to the killing zone, where Wilkinson jumped overboard, returning with a duck held softly in his mouth numerous times until he was hoisted back into the boat. He yelled over telling them to get on the path and walk back to the beach and he'd pick them up.

Aydlett was grinning as they arrived, saying, "Not bad, gentlemen, you bagged ten ducks on eight volleys of bird shot and now you know sometimes it's just as good to find a hidden spot on the bank and you do just as well as in a blind. This is a great hunting area where the birds are thick and easy to bring down. I brought you here because this is what the rich boys like, quick and easy. We're going to move to another, excellent spot. to our north where the hunting picks up now that it's bright but dark along the banks. The thicket where we're headed helps to hide the blind. On the way, we'll pick up and move the decoys to a place where we'll also place some corn. "

In those days, with an unlimited supply of fowl and a short supply of hunters, there were no firm rules or limits. Within a generation or two that would all start to change when duck hunting would enter a commercial phase to feed a growing population.

Even though it was cool, Tom removed his jacket as the poling of the boat by oar worked up some heat. Josh knew why the man was so good at this. His experience and his strength from the years of doing it gave him immense upper body strength, making the poling look easy. Josh knew it wasn't.

On the way, Aydlett placed the decoys where he wanted them, added the corn, and then moved up the waterway about one hundred and fifty yards and put ashore where the large nearby trees gave the hunters cover. The added glare of the rising sun behind them made them nearly invisible to any passing birds. Aydlett knew the ducks would come to the grain out of habit and, seeing the decoys, they would figure it was safe. They were right next to the shoreline with a clear open view of the sky above the marsh. They climbed into the well camouflaged blind which they themselves didn't see until they were beside it. There were two windows in it so that both shooters could fire safely. Tom told them he would walk about fifty yards down the shoreline and they would soon understand why.

Within moments, they heard the call of a duck. It was Tom with his self-carved duck call and it sounded authentic. They could look out to the south and see the birds coming in for a landing in the marsh close to the decoys and they began to feed on the floating grain. After they were settled, Aydlett used the call to make it sound different, a sound that was frightening and the ducks took off. They headed directly within range of Josh and Shorty sitting in the blind. Suddenly widely spaced blasts were heard from each shotgun, firing into the air with so many birds that the blue sky was nearly obliterated. Hearing the cease fire sound, Wilkinson, sitting in the beached sailboat, was over the side and swimming in a moment, returning with a duck held softly in his mouth repeatedly until eleven birds were retrieved, bringing the total to twenty-one.

As he climbed back in the boat, he suggested they return to the small sandy beach and grab a bite to eat. He would also place the ducks under a large wet sheet out of the sun to keep them from spoiling. They pulled up to the beach and climbed out. Josh carried the picnic basket while Shorty helped Tom soak the large sheet and wrap the ducks, placing them under a tarp propped up with lumber to keep the air circulating.

"Gentleman, I figure it's nearing ten or eleven," Tom said. "I suggest we head back to Currituck soon for the ducks will not be found in good openings again until late afternoon and we can keep them fresh. This is how we usually hunt, from dawn to mid-morning. The fat cats don't like to work up a sweat. Is this enough for you?"

"You're the boss, Tom," said Shorty, "besides we aren't wizards at duck cleaning and this is plenty. You can have some if you want as well."

"Don't worry, fellows, I'll clean them once we get back to fresh water," Tom said. "You may just have a few feathers to pull when I'm done but the blood will be drained and the innards will be removed. That's the critical part."

Shorty said he had gotten water over the tops of his boots and wanted to set them in the sun while they ate. Then in his bare feet he walked across the sand to the edge of the woods to relieve himself. As he stepped over a small fallen branch, he hollered in pain and yelled "snake." He fell back and the other men saw it attached to his ankle. Tom responded instantly and ran over with his gun and loaded a cartridge. As the snake let go and tried to slither away, Tom fired the round at short range, leaving only the muscular reactions left of the creature's life. It was an adult Eastern diamondback, the deadliest snake in the area.

Meanwhile, Josh knelt with Shorty and told him to remain calm. He pulled him over to a tree and propped him up against it to elevate his heart while Tom grabbed his emergency bag. He pulled out several strips of cloth and made a tourniquet, tying it just below the knee after winding it tight over a stick and told Shorty to hold it steady. He then pulled out the bottle of whiskey and told Josh to give Shorty a big gulp and, telling Shorty it would hurt, poured the alcohol directly on the wound. Then he poured alcohol on knife and then cut a small X over the sites of the fang marks and let some blood flow. He was not a proponent of trying to suck out the venom as his dad said it was useless. He did, however coat the bite area with black gunpowder, which acted as a drawing agent. The combination of actions left Shorty in pain, but he was stoic, merely grimacing.

"We've got to get him back to Currituck as soon as we can," Tom told Josh. "That was a big rattler with lots of venom. There's a lady, part Indian, named Miss Clara near my home who might be able to help when we get there. Ask my wife, Nancy to help you find her."

They quickly loaded the boat. Then they carried Shorty like a chair and stretched him out with his head propped with a jacket on the raised side of the boat while Tom gave him another big shot of whiskey. He was conscious but in a lot of pain but was remaining still.

Fortunately, the wind had changed and there was a steady ten knot breeze from the east which made the return trip fast and straight. Once they poled out of the marsh, dropped the running board and hoisted sails, they made it to the Currituck docks within thirty minutes. Josh was sailing, Tom was staying with Shorty and just trying to keep him calm. As they pulled in, Josh hollered for help.

It was John O'Brien who heard the calls. Fortunately, he had no calls this day and was doing some maintenance. He ran over, helped the others get Shorty out of the boat and, again chair style, they carried him to his home. Natasha, who had just arrived with Annie after visiting Emma and John Eldridge, turned pale when she saw him, but held the door as they brought him in and put him on the sofa.

Josh," Tom said, "go to my house and ask my wife to find Miss Clara. She's the lady I mentioned and the one person who might be able to help. I've seen her do so before and tell her it's for a rattlesnake bite and bring her here."

Josh was off, Annie remained to sooth and comfort Natasha, telling her to let Tom do what he was doing.

John O'Brien stood by for anything that Aydlett needed. There was nothing more to do until Josh returned with the medicine lady.

Josh met Aydlett's wife for the first time when he rode up on the buckboard. She was a very shy but pretty woman, running to the door thinking that her Tom was in trouble.

She excitedly asked, "Did something happen to Tom, Mr. Eldridge? Where is he?"

"I didn't mean to scare you, Mrs. Aydlett," Josh replied. "No, Tom is fine but my partner was bitten by a rattlesnake and Tom is with him. He asked me to get your help finding Miss Clara."

Nancy Aydlett went to get her wrap and climbed aboard the buckboard. She directed Josh to Miss Clara's house, a small bungalow with a white picket fence, less than a mile away near the sound.

Nancy Aydlett talked with Miss Clara who went to her pantry, retrieved two containers and some wrappings and came back with her coat on. She spoke to her grown daughter and told her where she was going.

Josh dropped Tom's wife at her place, thanked her and said he'd send her husband home as soon as he could. Then he and Miss Clara carried on a lively conversation on the way.

"You know, young man," she said. "When the two of you pulled up, I thought Tom was in trouble. His hunting takes him into places where rattlers and moccasins are always around, even on cool days if the sun is warm. I don't know what Nancy would do without him. She's a great wife and housekeeper but she's so shy I don't know how she could handle it."

Josh tried to stay noncommittal but did say that Tom was very good at what he did and he knew where to go and where not to. Then the conversation turned to Josh's pastoral life as Clara was a believer, she just didn't like the politics of organized religion. She knew, however, of his good deeds.

"I'm not a big fan either, Miss Clara," Josh responded, "and it's why I like to go out to the people in outlying places where they need me. There is, though, something about the resources that an organized church can provide in disasters which can't be done very easily when they hit."

As they drove in, John and Tom were on the porch, taking a break and clearing their head. The ladies were obviously inside sitting and watching over Shorty.

Tom walked up and said, "Sorry we had to call for you Miss Clara, but this one is bad. It was a big rattler."

She asked, "How's he doing now? Is he awake?"

Tom said he was and that he was in a lot of pain. She asked Josh if someone could take her to water where she could mix up a poultice. They walked inside, Josh introduced her to Natasha and with tears in her eyes, Natasha led her to the kitchen and showed her the pump on the back porch. Clara asked Natasha to stay and help, trying to keep her away from the suffering on the sofa in the main room.

Natasha retrieved a pail of water, poured some in a large pot and put it on the stove to heat. In the meantime, Clara took the containers of the solid, butter like substances, waiting for the pot to heat. When warm enough, she added measured amounts of both containers in an empty bowl, sprinkled powder out of small vial in her apron into the mixture and added water, mixing it by hand and adding as needed until it had a paste-like consistency. She asked Natasha to accompany her to the patient.

"Shorty," she said to her agonizing husband, "this is Miss Clara and she is here to help. She has a poultice that will help draw out the poison."

Shorty nodded as if to say that they could do anything to help. He was being very strong and controlled but the contortions on his face gave it all away. Clara saw that the bleeding from the cross cuts had stopped and that Tom had wisely loosened the tourniquet but not totally. The foot area near the ankle where the knife cuts were made at the sight of the strike, was swollen and developing a dark color indicating the tissue could die. Overall, though, that was good news since it was not yet spreading up the leg but limiting itself to the point of bite and below. She was also glad to see Tom had used black gunpowder.

Clara leaned over Shorty and told him that she was going to apply a poultice to fight the poison. She told him of the good news that would be to his benefit. She also said it might hurt when the poultice started to work.

"You just stay still and try and relax if you can," she said. "The more you relax, the more likely we can stop the poison."

Clara was handed the mixture and mixed it in her hands, then placed it in a small mound packed directly on the wound. A thick towel was placed under his lower leg and another on top over the poultice, the top one was damp and warm and she told Natasha to change that every hour and the poultice every two, also warm. She made enough for two days.

"Captain, do you feel anything different," she asked Shorty. "You should soon feel a warming then burning sensation but that's what we want. It means it's working."

Shorted nodded and told her yes softly and she told him she was going to get him something to ease his pain. She made a pot of sassafras tea, then added several powders and honey, stirred it and took it to him.

"Drink this slowly and it will help with pain," Clara said. "I'll bring you more every few hours."

Shorty seemed more relaxed quite soon and he just needed to rest and let the process take its course. Clara nodded for all except Tom to come into the kitchen for an update. Tom would keep an eye on Shorty and she wanted to be open and candid with Shorty's wife and closest friends.

"I'm not going to put sugar on it," she said. "Natasha, your husband received a bad bite from a rattlesnake that could kill him. There is, however, good news. The bite being on his lower extremity means we got him before it spread too far and Tom did a good job of slowing the process. If we can stop the spread of the poison and limit or reduce the discoloration, that means the tissue is still alive.

"The poultice contains gunpowder and a number of old Indian herbs. The gunpowder draws out the poison and the herbs promote healing. I've used it successfully many times but sometimes it fails but I know of nothing that works better. The tea I gave him also contains herbs that fight pain and ease stress. I'll stay here for as long as it takes to know how things are headed, but I'll tell you, this could take four or five days to find out. Just keep me with plenty of towels and things I ask for and pray, just pray."

Natasha went over and hugged her and they all gathered around in prayer. Ultimately, what would happen depended on God and the work of this unpretentious part

English and part Indian woman who was given the task of doing his work.

John O'Brien and Sam Jarvis told Shorty they'd take care of business, they both shook hands with Josh and headed back to work. Tom, with his Indian friend well in charge went to see if the ducks were salvageable. Natasha went out on the porch, not wanting Shorty to see or hear her cry.

Annie and Josh went for a walk, stopped by the dock and prayed. They thanked God for his blessings that He had provided and asked for Him to spare Shorty and ease his pain while comforting Natasha. Lastly, they asked for His guiding hand to direct the work of that good woman, Miss Clara.

After completing the prayer, Annie and Josh talked about things and came to the one conclusion that both now recognized in their strong faith. It was all up to God. They ultimately had to leave the life of Shorty, the welfare of his wife and the future of their friendship and business relationship in God's hands.

Walking back to maintain their vigil at Shorty's side, Josh knew that it had been quite a day, a day that started off well and suddenly took a terrible turn. It was just another page from a day of life and just another reason why he needed someone much more powerful and wise than himself. He would just have to take his future, day by day, with his wonderful wife at his side and His God in charge. That was the only way.

EPILOGUE

Two days later, things were relatively the same as they were on the day of the snakebite. Shorty was calm from the herbal tea, but the poison was still in his system and the odds in a time with no anti-venom meant that things were as likely to get worse as they were better. It was still a critical life and death matter.

After a non-stop vigil since the men returned from the hunt, Clara finally relented and allowed Annie to take over, following the instructions for care that must be followed thoroughly. She was glad to see that at least his breathing was steadier and the black coloration of the skin had not progressed much.

Josh, John and Sam joined together on the porch to discuss business while Annie stayed close to Natasha's side. Josh told his able men that work had to go on, but the future might be different.

"Honestly, fellows," he said, "things might change but we will survive that change. It will be hard for me if Shorty doesn't recover since he got me started, but we made a commitment to you fellows and I made a commitment to myself that I would succeed, so we will."

Both of the working part owners went back to work and Josh went to join Annie who now had Natasha at her side next to Shorty.

He addressed them solemnly, saying, "Ladies, we're being tested by God and He's using Shorty to test us. We're in uncharted territory, but I want both of you to know that we will survive. Natasha, I especially want you to know that if, God forbid, Shorty doesn't make it, feel secure at least in knowing that what is Shorty's is yours and I'll always honor the commitment we shared. That's a promise you can count on."

The future was very uncertain and the odds weren't very good, but Josh knew that these two women and their other partners needed reassurance. Josh would pray for a miraculous recovery for Shorty as he, at least for now without the guidance of his good friend, partner and mentor, was facing a big challenge. He had successfully navigated the long road back to the home of his birth, but now it was his task to chart the long road forward for the next major phase of life and he knew it would involve those mysterious Outer Banks and the challenges they would provide. Only time will tell what course he would be required to fulfill in the challenge of the rest of his life.

There was one other thing on the horizon that would be of major impact as well, but neither Josh or any of the Outer and Inner Bankers knew anything of it yet. In the following year, 1873, the United States would enter a six-year Great Depression that would impact them all. The long road forward would test Josh severely in the days and years to come.

ACKNOWLEDGMENTS

Any historical fiction takes review of history to make sure the background is accurate. Accordingly, the sources cite helped in that review. They also supported much of the family history which I have gathered from my maternal family archives of the Outer Banks and Currituck County, North Carolina. While the local events of the story and characters are fictional, they are set within that background and history to make the story real and alive to the reader.

History.com: The Algonquins
History.com: Battle of Plymouth, 1864
The Treatment or Prisoners: Prison Life at Point
    Lookout, by the Rev. J.B. Traywick, Southern
    Historical Society Press, June 1891
Currituck County Confederate Soldiers, North Carolina
    Troops (1861-65) Volume 4, pages 533-542
Address by Charles T. Loehr, Past Commander, Pickett
    Camp Confederate Veterans, Richmond (VA)
    Times, October 11, 1890
The Battle of Roanoke Island, National Park Service
Siege of Petersburg, The American Battlefield Trust
North Carolina Shipwrecks, blogspot.com/federal-
    transport-Pocahontas
The History of Currituck, Barbara Snowden, Aug 1995,
    The Currituck Times
The Chicamacomico Races, Drew Pullen, Oct 10, 2011,
    Emerging Civil War

ABOUT THE AUTHOR: JAMES DICK

Author James Dick follows his true story about summer as a boy, "Summers at Old Nags Head," with another story about the same general area, this time a historical fiction, "The Long Road Back." It is the first volume of three in his "Coastal Carolina Series" about an ex-Confederate soldier and prisoner of war returning home after the war to live and forget. This first book in the series tells the story of his travel home and getting started in a productive life on the water. It covers the years 1865-1872.

James Dick knows the area for his stories well, the son of an Outer Banker and a man who spent every summer of his life until high school graduation on those beautiful barrier islands. His maternal lineage includes the longest serving lighthouse keeper at Bodie Island Light and a former Confederate soldier who was also a prisoner of war, returning home to live on the beach. The latter relation gave James the idea for writing the book, but the lead character is not modeled after him. Both men were his great-grandfather.

He also has written a fun book about horses, "Confessions of a Horse Husband," the story of learning to care for and love horses under the tutelage of his wife, an experienced equestrian teacher and rider. All of his books are on Amazon Prime and Kindle Unlimited.

James and his wife, Charyl, live in rural North Florida with their horses, dogs and barn cats.

Made in the USA
Coppell, TX
11 February 2020

15734221R00213